BOHEMIA LIGHT

by

Lucy Lakestone

VELVET PETAL PRESS

Florida

Published by Velvet Petal Press, Florida

Learn more about the author at LucyLakestone.com

Cover design by Sky Diary Productions

Original photo by Renzo79, iStock

Print ISBN: 978-1-943134-00-7

Kindle ISBN: 978-1-943134-02-1

First edition

PART 1

I felt naked without my camera.

I always felt naked without my camera, even if part of me wanted that weight lifted from my shoulders.

I wanted to feel lighter tonight, at this flashy New Year's Eve party in Bohemia Beach. I wanted to forget I was losing the photography job I loved. Of course, in my little silver purse, the one sitting on the pile of jackets and bags in the guest bedroom, I still carried the press pass with the only identity I'd known since college: Calista Goode, Staff Photographer.

It was good for one more week.

There was only one cure for the future: another glass of champagne. I headed for the bar.

A jazz trio on standup bass, drums and guitar delivered a peppy version of "It Had To Be You." The band played by the shimmering lights of the funky stick tree Alex and Sloane had put up for Christmas, a glowing masterpiece of white branches, silver balls, crystal snowflakes, seashells and red ribbon. Giddy waves of happy people danced and talked, ebbed and flowed around me. Happy couples.

I felt off, unprotected, as I slid through the crowd, even though I'd worn a slim, sleeveless dupioni silk dress that I knew enhanced my modest curves and matched my ice-blue eyes. My blond hair was twisted up and pinned but still sprouted rebellious strands. I wore low black heels, though on the job, I was the sneaker type.

But tonight, I wanted to forget about the job, forget a lot of things. Like losing yet another boyfriend, not all that long ago. Losing my date for tonight, a friend from the camera store, because he'd reunited with his ex-girlfriend. Maybe losing my mind.

I could go with that. The champagne might help. At the bar, I picked up a bubbling flute and took a sip. One thing was for sure: Alex knew how to choose a good champagne. My cousin Sloane, glowing in her super-high heels and little black dress, looked so happy with him. It had taken me a while to realize just how good he was for her, but I could see it in her face, in the way he deferred to her. And maybe it helped that Alex had just told me the Bohemia School of Art and Design was looking for a photographer to teach portrait techniques. That was a part-time gig I'd be happy to take if I could get it.

Maybe I was overdue for a change. I'd been here nearly all of my life, except for my four-year escape to the University of Florida. I felt a familiar spark inside me, the rebellious ember that always glowed when the night was darkest. The next few months would be challenging, but I was up for a challenge. Wasn't I?

"Cali, how you doing?" my brother asked as I walked up to him. Damien, a multimedia artist a few years older than me, looked vaguely Goth tonight as always, with his black eye makeup and longish black hair sticking almost straight up and then falling over like a wave. But his tux showed that he was something more than Goth. His black bow tie had little red and white skulls on it, and one of his tattoos crept just above his collar line. His date was a dreamboat from Miami, a slender, handsome guy named Javier with a gentle Spanish accent. I had no idea where they'd found each other; maybe Art Basel. But I had no doubt Javier was just passing through. Damien wasn't known for long-term relationships or for being nice to anyone, though he'd been unusually kind to me since I was laid off.

I shot them a smile. "You know what? I'm starting to feel pretty good. The champagne's great." So great, it was starting to go to my head a little. "Is that Ron Raker over there?"

"Yeah," Damien said, sipping a clear cocktail in a rocks glass garnished with a slice of lime. He had a thing for gin. "He must be between surfing tournaments."

Ron Raker was a local celebrity and an international surfing champion, and somehow, he and his entourage had found their way into Alex's party.

"I don't think I've ever seen him in person," I said. "He was here for a charity event a couple of years ago, but one of my colleagues shot it for the *Bugle*."

"He's clearly slumming," Damien said dismissively.

I laughed. "I'd hardly call Alex's condo slumming." It was huge, on the eighth and top floor, overlooking the Atlantic Ocean. And this party had all the trimmings: The band was divine. A swank bartender mixed high-end cocktails. A spinning mirror ball warred playfully with shifting colored lights. And caterers trotted back and forth with delicious morsels from the kitchen.

"Bohemia Beach is slumming for him," Damien replied. "He almost never comes to Florida anymore. Shouldn't he be in Hawaii?"

"What a waste that would be," Javier purred in his silky voice, looking across the room at Raker, scanning him appreciatively.

He had a point. Raker, with his shaggy blond haircut, was beautiful in the way surfers were beautiful, his body sculpted, lean and tan, with impossibly broad shoulders barely contained by a loud Hawaiian shirt. He towered over his friends; he must have been at least six-foot-four. Women flitted around him, like hummingbirds drawn to the red flowers on his shirt, and he occasionally caught one's glance or touched one's shoulder, smiling at them, keeping them in his orbit. He attracted my attention the way a firecracker does, with a thrilling snap, but I instinctively mistrusted that much charisma. My eyes wandered, drawn to another one of the guys in his group.

Raker's friend seemed more intriguing. His aloha shirt was more muted, black, printed with white sketches of palm fronds and islands. His sable hair was streaked with a narrow swath of white-blond that flopped over his forehead. He had pronounced cheekbones, dark eyebrows and eyes that glittered like chocolate diamonds. His mouth was defined by an elegant upper lip, an elongated, swooping "M." He seemed less giddy than the others, as if he had more on his mind; he assumed an ironic expression as he listened to Raker's monologue.

As if he felt my gaze, the dark-haired guy turned toward me and smiled.

I smiled back and took a long sip of champagne, watching him from over my glass.

I've been accused of being a serial monogamist. I've had a lot of boyfriends, all one at a time, and all for sadly short intervals maxing out at about a year. On a night when I was seeing my entire life transform, on New Year's Eve, I was willing to entertain the idea of an even shorter-term relationship.

"Calista, Calista," Damien said, shaking his head.

"What?" I glanced at him.

"Not another one."

"You're one to talk."

"Oh, really?" Javier gleamed with mischief.

"She has excellent taste," Damien said, "at least in looks."

"Ay, she does," Javier said. "Let me know if he doesn't swing your way, blondie."

Damien glared at his date and took a gulp of his drink.

"Tonight, looks are all I care about," I said. "I've had it with being serious. I'm going to have some fun. Besides, New Year's sucks when you don't have anyone to kiss at midnight. And if I don't work fast, this will be the first midnight in" — I tilted my head to think — "ten years that I won't."

"What happened ten years ago?" Javier asked.

"I was fourteen. I had braces. Don't ask."

"Geek," Damien murmured over his glass.

"Emo," I said into my champagne.

"Shut the fuck up," he said, but he suppressed a smile.

"Ten minutes to midnight!" someone called.

The silver-haired bartender aimed a remote and awakened the huge television on its credenza. He muted it and tuned to one of those scenes of freezing, drunken New York pandemonium that the rest of the country watched with dazed indifference over chips and dip.

The jazz trio swung into "I Could Write a Book," and the

minuscule dance floor got even more crowded. I looked around. Alex and Sloane had disappeared, and Damien and Javier drifted into a dark corner where they could enjoy some privacy behind a potted palm. And the surfer boys? Where were they?

Damn. Vanished.

I pushed through the dancing couples, went back to the bar and got a refill, feeling tipsy now but unaccountably happy. Champagne did that to me. That, and a perverse feeling of hope. I wasn't going to let the bastards get me down.

I scanned the room, the lights, the people, the colors. This was a splendid scene. It would have made a nice picture. I bit my lip, feeling naked again, and saw a few people heading out the balcony doors. I quaffed my champagne, set down the glass and followed, ambling to the railing and its view of the beach.

The night was breathtaking, cool and breezy, or at least cool for a native Floridian like me. Still, it was balmy for December 31. My skin awakened to the refreshing sensation of the wind caressing my shoulders, my arms, and I breathed deeply of the sea air. The moon, somewhere to the west of us, would be glinting off the lagoon and bathing Bohemia, sister city to Bohemia Beach, in cool blue light.

Though it was behind me, the moon still cast its glow on the ocean to the east. The waves glimmered in the soft night, and the happy chatter and murmurs from the couples and clusters of people strung along the long balcony were muted by the roar of the surf. Far below, a handful of revelers circled a bonfire a few feet from the water, and their laughter drifted up to me like sparkling moths.

I'd grown up here, but still, I was rarely afforded a view

like this. I'd hung out on the public beaches like the other kids. I'd been raised in a house at ground level. I'd lived life at ground level. This was flying.

"I can't believe Ron grew up on those little waves," said a deep voice in my ear.

I made a half turn and saw him, the guy who'd caught my attention earlier. He looked taller out of the shadow of his surfer celebrity buddy, a couple of inches taller than I was, even in my heels. And he had one of those delicious surfer bodies, too — slender, muscular, but on a more accessible scale than Ron Raker. I smiled.

"That's why he's so good," I told him. "You learn to make the most of these waves. And then you have mad skills you can take anywhere."

His face lit up with a grin. "You a surfer?"

"Never," I said, suppressing a shudder at the thought of going under, even under one of those shallow Bohemia Beach waves.

"I'm Wyatt." He held out his hand, just as the shouts came from inside: "Ten! Nine! Eight — "

I grasped his hand, feeling a jolt of electricity between us, and he hung on, his eyes twinkling, as the countdown roared and the tittering on the balcony grew louder.

"I'm Cali," I said, almost drowned out by the noise, transfixed by his golden-brown gaze, his smooth grip.

"Three. Two. One!" echoed through the open door. "Happy New Year!" they shouted, and the party on the beach shot off a barrage of fireworks.

Wyatt drew me to him in slow motion and leaned close, and then, just when I thought this New Year's Eve would go by kissless, he touched his lips to mine.

His feather-light kiss felt like a hello, a hello and a goodbye, but maybe there was something in my response that encouraged him. The hello became a sweet conversation. I tasted champagne on his tongue as he held on to my arrested handshake as if the wind might sweep me away.

Ahhh. Champagne. Fireworks. The beach. And a stranger's kiss, a first kiss, the best kind. A kiss with a man I'd never see again.

Wyatt's kiss was like a perfect piece of chocolate, dark and sweet, increasing in intensity as I closed my eyes and met his mouth with tipsy eagerness. His tongue entwined with mine as I opened to him, taking him in, hearing the joyous noise around me as "Happy New Year" passed from voice to voice and more fireworks crackled. He let go of my hand and slipped his arms around me; I hung on to his neck, drunk and dazed. This was so easy. No strings. No expectations. Just a gorgeous boy, my body warming fast with his hands on my back, fire flashing in the skies of Bohemia Beach. He consumed me; I lost myself in his heat, running my hands through that floppy hair, and one of his hands strayed lower, crushing me into him, every hard angle. I moaned into his mouth. And then, in one dizzy, drowning wave of desire, it was over.

When we came up for air, the balcony was almost empty. The party had moved inside. I heard a bellowing voice yelling: "Wyatt! Next party, buddy!"

Wyatt's dramatic eyebrows came together in a look of frustration. "Damn Raker," he muttered. He reached up and touched my cheek, his eyes luminous with something like longing. "Happy New Year, Cali."

He looked at me for one more heart-stopping moment. And then, to my sudden and surprising regret, he walked into the condo and out of my life.

"YOU'RE TELLING me you were actually at a party with Ron Raker and you got no photos of him?" Bart Ruderman, my balding, paunchy photo editor, sat on the edge of the desk in front of mine with his arms crossed and shook his head. "He's a fucking celebrity, Cali. You know we want photos of fucking celebrities."

"Yeah, not news, for Christ's sake," I responded in a similar tone, trying to focus on the restaurant photo I was cropping on the computer screen in front of me, and not Bart. "At least we haven't graduated to celebrities fucking."

"Maybe with the next corporate directive," my colleague Jordan said drily from the desk next to mine, a smile cracking his handsome ebony face. A couple of years older than me, he was the other photographer losing his *Bohemia Bugle* job this week. "Wall Street will love that shit."

I saw Bart trying not to laugh. He mastered himself, and his expression grew stern again. "Explain yourself, Goode."

"I was at a party. My cousin's boyfriend's party. And I — " I didn't want to admit it, but I saw Bart meant business, so I confessed. "I didn't have my camera."

"What?" Jordan exclaimed, turning to me, almost spilling his coffee — coffee in a paper cup from the tiny cafeteria, because the newspaper had stopped buying us coffee, too.

They both knew I had committed an unpardonable sin. I had broken the rule every photojournalist knew: *Always have your camera.*

"Unbelievable," Bart said. "You had your phone, didn't you?"

"Oh, in my purse. In another room. I was drunk. I was at a

party, you dimwits. What the hell were you doing New Year's Eve?"

"Sleeping, thank God," Jordan said without hesitation. "It was the first night the baby gave Ruby and me any peace."

"Congratulations," I said, wondering what Jordan was going to do next. His wife was a lawyer, and he was talking to some of the aerospace firms in Cape Canaveral, but with the baby and all, I knew he was worried.

"I was downtown at the street party *working,*" Bart said. "Maybe I should have assigned you instead."

"I worked New Year's Day. I moved over the weekend. And I had vacation to burn before I get *fired* this week," I pointed out, not a little miffed. "Unless you want to fire me now for not getting photos of your stupid celebrity surfer."

Bart looked chastened.

"You know I don't want you to go," he said. "Either of you. I never thought the paper would be that politically incorrect."

Jordan chuckled, but I felt Bart's pity and hated it. He'd fought like hell to keep us, but numbers were numbers, and my number was up.

"It's OK," I said. "I'm sorry, Bart."

"Raker *is* kind of a big deal," Jordan mused.

"Well, it's too late now." I thought not of Ron Raker but his friend Wyatt, about that moment on the balcony. About the disposable stranger's kiss that seemed more than enough at first, and not nearly enough in retrospect. About how I would never get a do-over on that first kiss.

"Actually," Bart said, a wily look in his eyes as he picked up a piece of paper from his desk, "you may have one more chance."

For a second, I thought he knew about Wyatt, too, and then I realized he was talking about Raker.

"Don't tell me I have to play paparazzo," I moaned.

"Worse," Bart said. "It's your final assignment. He's going to be at some art-museum shindig Thursday night."

I sat up, interested. "The regional show opening?"

"You know about it?" Bart perused the paper. "The release says it'll have dozens of artists, a band, patrons, yadda yadda yadda. And an auction. They're going to auction off a date with Ron Raker."

"Seriously?" I couldn't believe it.

"Actually, they say it's a surf lesson and dinner, but I thought you would be more interested if it was a date, given your recent dry spell," Bart teased. That was Bart. Always borderline inappropriate.

Jordan laughed as I crossed my arms.

"I'm just fine, and I have no interest in Ron Raker," I said. "And especially not in surf lessons." However, if a certain other surfer was there . . . "Besides, I was going to go to that anyway."

"With your camera?" Jordan asked.

"Looks like I'll have to," I joked with mock exasperation.

Bart chuckled. "Don't tell me you had a hot date."

Not yet, I thought.

"My brother has a piece in the show," I said. "So does my cousin. And I have some friends who will be there, and maybe some future students. I'll be teaching a class at the art school starting next week." One of the photography teachers had dropped out after getting a plum assignment for a travel magazine, and Alex, a heavy donor, had hooked me up. I'd faxed my resume and had the phone interview this morning, and I got an offer within the hour.

"That sounds great," Jordan said, but I could hear a hint of anxiety in his response.

"It's just part-time," I said. "I'm setting up a little photo studio in the arts district. I'm jumping into the portrait and wedding business."

"Brides. They're all sharks," Bart muttered. "Be careful."

Sharks. They didn't scare me as much as the ocean. I shivered.

"Cali?" Jordan elbowed me.

"Fine," I said, focusing on Bart. "I'll shoot your surfer and the Bohemia glitterati."

"That's a small group," Bart sniffed, sitting at his desk to get back to his long list of daily phone calls. He picked up the receiver of the old beige phone and punched in some numbers. "Hi. Yes. This is Bart Ruderman, calling from the *Bugle*. I need to get a photographer over there to shoot some photos of the new potatoes you have at the market. Who can help me schedule that? . . . What? It's a trend story on colorful vegetables. Features is doing it. . . . I don't know. I hear you have purple potatoes. . . . You have to clear it with corporate? Really? It's just a photo of potatoes. Nobody's going to be naked or anything. . . . Yes, I'll hold . . . "

Jordan and I exchanged a glance.

"I may not know what I'm doing next," Jordan said, "but I won't miss that bullshit at all."

BOHEMIA'S GLITTERATI might be drawn from a relatively small pool, but they knew how to sparkle when it counted. The regional show at the Bohemia Art Museum featured competitively selected artists from throughout the Southeast, and it was a major fundraiser. So the gala opening drew not just the artists, who were guaranteed invitations, but the museum's wealthy ticket-buying patrons and any celebrities the board could round up to contribute to the auction.

I got there right when it started, wearing what I hoped were chic, black flaring pants that were skirt-like enough to get by but comfortable enough to let me work, along with a scoop-neck, silvery tank that, with dangly rhinestone earrings, gave me a bit of sparkle. I also wore a fuzzy black shrug and silver sneakers, nothing more exotic than what some of the artists were wearing. My press pass hung around my neck, and my blond hair was tamed in a twist.

With its big flash and diffuser, my Nikon got a workout as I shot people arriving for the event. This wasn't a limousine kind of thing, but there was a hired spotlight roving the cloudy sky, and a red carpet gave me an excuse to stop people outside the museum and get shots of them beaming in their finery.

When Alex and Sloane arrived, I breathed a little sigh of relief. It was always easier approaching someone I knew.

"Cali!" Sloane said, giving me a hug. She looked lovely in a short, green velvet dress that complemented the red high-lights in her dark brown hair. Around her shoulders was a soft, shimmering black wrap that was perfect for the cool evening. Alex, his dark-gold hair and gray eyes set off hand-somely by his black suit, gave me a nod. A swirl of green in his silk tie echoed the color of Sloane's dress.

"Ready for your big night?" I asked my cousin as I motioned them together and snapped a couple of photos.

"A little nervous, actually," Sloane said when I was done.

Alex smiled. "She's still worried people won't like her piece."

"I saw it in there. It's so cool," I said. I meant it. It was a kind of fountain, a compact ceramic scene that depicted the depths of the ocean, happily oblivious sea life and a tentacled monster arising from its heart, sinister and threatening. I could always identify with the idea of sea monsters.

"Thanks," Sloane said shyly, and I saw a look come over Alex's face: pride and, I was embarrassed to notice, desire. He kissed her neck. I looked away.

"See you in there," I said brightly, moving on to the next couple, wondering what it felt like to have someone love you like that. I'd had a lot of boyfriends, but I'd never had *that*.

Several posh patrons later, a new cluster of guests arrived, about eight artists donned in what you might call funky formal, led by my brother, Damien.

"Holy shit," I said, admittedly unprofessionally, when I saw what he was wearing. It was a suit made entirely of a fabric in a loud geometric pattern that looked as if it came from a mid-century couch, with red and gray and black diamonds on a white background. "You look like a reject from the Norwegian curling team."

"Thank you," he said, and I noticed Javier was with him, dressed much more fashionably if effeminately in a burgundy velvet jacket and ruffled white shirt over black tuxedo pants. Burgundy stripes ran up the sides of the legs. Boys who were prettier than I was annoyed me.

"Hey, blondie," Javier said smoothly, and I smiled and nodded before turning back to my brother.

"Where did you get that suit?" I asked Damien as I waved the group together and shot off a few photos.

"I had Penelope make it. Pen!" A tall, stunning young woman with flaming waves of pink and yellow hair, pale green eyes and a cut-to-there pinup-style dress in sea-foam green stepped forward and smiled. "She's a fabric artist."

"Hi, I'm Cali." I shook her hand.

"I hear we'll be seeing you around," Penelope said, her voice curiously lilting, as if she were reading a line in a play.

"Oh, yeah. I'm opening a photo studio near the art school."

"Excellent," she said. "Maybe we can work together." She flashed a coy smile and moved off with the crowd into the museum.

This was going to be an interesting year, I thought.

The arrivals thinned. I was about to head inside when I saw a massive black vehicle lit beneath by pink neon pulling up to the front of the museum. Its booming stereo shook the sidewalk. So much for this not being a limo kind of thing. It was one of those SUV limousines, almost the size of a school bus and a lot less maneuverable. It groaned to a stop at the curb.

The driver scurried around to open the back door, and Ron Raker stepped out.

Despite the insanely large car, he still looked huge, a towering mountain of manhood. Remembering Bart's orders, I snapped photos of him as he headed toward the entrance, but between shots, I scanned his entourage.

There were four guys. Wait, a fifth. The last out of the limo, saying a few words to the driver, was Wyatt.

I let out a slow breath and took him in. He dressed simply, in a slim gray suit, white shirt and narrow silver and black tie, and he looked completely delicious.

Shit. Raker and his guys were moving past me.

"Ron? Mr. Raker?" I called out, and the mountain stopped walking, his friends almost plowing into the back of him as he turned to look at me.

"Ron is fine," he said, giving me a slow, broad grin.

He wore a black jacket over a tropical shirt — a pattern of

black and white waves and surfers with turquoise surfboards — along with black jeans. No tie. His blond hair looked tousled, as if he'd just come ashore. Had to keep up the image, I guessed.

"What can I do for you, sweetheart?" he asked.

Oh, great, *sweetheart,* I thought, but I gave him my pro smile. "Would you all mind posing for a photo here?"

"Wyatt, hurry up!" Raker bellowed, never taking his eyes off me, and Wyatt waved away the limo and trotted up the red carpet. He got into the cluster as if he was used to the pose and smiled, but he did a double-take when he saw who his photographer was. His golden-brown eyes narrowed.

I tried to ignore the sparks I felt alighting on my skin and held the camera up to my eye. "OK — three, two, one!" I shot off three frames. "A couple more!" Four more, just for insurance and blinkers. "Thanks, guys."

"Any time, sweetheart," Raker said, watching me over his shoulder as the group moved inside. All except Wyatt, who looked kind of pissed.

"Cali."

I took a photo of him standing there, flustered. I couldn't resist. Plus I felt a little safer behind the lens.

Reluctantly, I lowered the camera. "Wyatt."

"Sorry about Ron."

"What? Oh, that's nothing. At least he didn't make The Joke."

"What joke?"

"The one everybody says about them breaking my camera."

Wyatt shook his head, taking a few steps closer. "He would never say that. He thinks he's God's gift to photographers."

"I suppose he is rather picturesque," I said offhandedly, and Wyatt narrowed his eyes again. "But not my type," I hastened to add.

The corner of his mouth turned up. He reached out and touched my press badge where it hung dangerously close to my breasts, and I swallowed nervously.

"Calista Goode," he mused. "You're a photographer."

"Is it that obvious?"

He laughed. "I do a little shooting myself. Getting into it more, actually."

"Really." Probably another surfer with a wide-angle video camera stuck on his board.

"Yeah," Wyatt said. "Maybe I can get some pointers sometime."

"Anytime," I said with a smile, then kicked myself for being so pliant.

His smile grew wider. "I might take you up on that."

Sure, I thought, remembering he spent his time traveling the world with a platoon of surfers.

"I guess I'd better head in," I said. "Before the auction starts and all."

"Oh, yeah. Gotta see Ron sold off," he said drily.

"So how long have you been friends with him?" I asked as we walked toward the doors.

"Friends? About five years. Though now, I'm not so much a friend as a walking calendar. Transportation coordinator. Et cetera."

"Seriously? That's a job?" The doors slid open, and we passed into the entry hall and then a massive exhibition space awash in bright lights and the sounds of a band.

"It didn't start as a job, but it's kind of become one," Wyatt said. "Not for much longer."

"I thought you were a surfer."

"That, too."

"Interesting," I said, but I was more interested in the subtle, clean scent of him, the way the fabric of his suit delineated his lean, muscled body, and how the lights brought out the white-blond streak in his floppy hair.

He turned to me, as if sensing my scrutiny. And he returned the favor, subtly scanning me, his eyes barely moving from mine. "It's nice to see you again."

"Yeah," I agreed, abruptly feeling a tiny bit embarrassed by the tonsil-swallowing kiss we'd so heartily exchanged on New Year's Eve. "I've got to work now, but maybe I'll see you later?"

"I'm counting on it," Wyatt said, watching me with an intensity that made my skin flush hot as I smiled weakly and walked away.

Get a grip, I told myself. *Time to work. Not to drool over an unavailable surfer boy.*

I headed toward the band, since I recognized them: my friend Ez singing and playing the piano and the four Emeralds backing her up with drums, guitar, bass and banjo. Ez must have noticed me shooting. In the middle of a chorus, she looked up from behind her long, dark, slanted bangs, the defining feature of her short, mod haircut, and gave me the kind of emotive expression photographers die for. After I'd gotten a few shots, she turned to me and winked, never missing a note. We needed to get together and talk soon. Maybe with Sloane and whoever else we could round up for a girls' night. I needed a break from my freaking major life changes.

I moved through the three main rooms that featured art from the exhibition, taking pictures of guests and artists. The show was organized loosely by media, though the sculptural pieces tended to have featured spots in the middle of each room. Sloane's piece, on a pedestal, gleamed under a spotlight, its gurgling water barely heard above the chatter and music, its sea monster gleaming. Nearby was a cluster of more traditional ceramic pieces, and I saw Gary Gorski, one of the school's best known ceramic artists, hanging out near a beautiful vase he'd contributed, his long, curly locks flopping around as he talked animatedly to a well-dressed older couple drinking champagne and munching on canapés.

Damien's tall piece had its own corner. Constructed of metal, wood, light bulbs, papier-mâché and video screens, it showed three dronelike figures with morose faces standing on one another's shoulders — a man, a woman and a child; the child had a skeleton of a bird on her head. Each held a working screen outlined in lights. The top and bottom screens flashed bright, cartoonish advertising images interspersed with clips of war and suffering. The large middle screen, I realized, replicated my own shape as I moved, creating a figure made of black dots against a background of shifting grays. I leaned closer, finally spotting a tiny camera embedded in one figure's eye. Whatever computer he'd used was well disguised by the sculpture.

"Clever!" I exclaimed, and in response to the noise, a burst of red, like the explosion of blood from a gunshot, spattered my screen image and slowly faded away. "Holy crap!" I responded and was instantly greeted by another bloody visual. All the while, the sculpture emitted happy but creepy music that reminded me of a circus. It was pretty damn dark. Sometimes I worried about my brother.

When I got back to the main room, I browsed through the silent auction items, lined up on long tables. They ranged from movie nights to art to airline tickets, most already bid to amounts well out of my range. A vase made by art school potter-in-residence Montrose King had already reached seven hundred dollars, and the artist himself kept swinging by to check out the bid sheet, rubbing his silver and black goatee, looking more and more annoyed. I quietly got photos of him looking at his vase, and I shot a few images of sparkling ladies jotting down their offers. The only item up for live auction was the surfing lesson and evening with Ron Raker.

The music paused, and I looked toward the band to see the museum director, a striking woman with long brown hair, a floor-length beaded dress and serious glasses, stand in front of the microphone.

"Ladies and gentlemen, as you may know, I'm Cora Melo, and I'm the director of the Bohemia Art Museum. Thank you for coming, and I'd like to welcome you to the annual Juried Regional Art Exhibition!"

Hearty applause greeted her, the crowd's enthusiasm no doubt helped along by the wine everyone was holding. A few of the artist types chimed in, shouting "BAM! BAM!" as they punned on the museum's name.

Cora looked amused as she continued. "We have the work of more than fifty exceptional artists on display here tonight, and thanks to the generosity of our community, we also have a number of wonderful items up for auction. You have just thirty minutes left to get your bids in on those, so make sure you check them out. But we have one very special item — or should I say celebrity — who has put himself up for auction tonight." The crowd tittered, and I tried hard not to roll my eyes. "Ron Raker, Bohemia Beach's own surfing champion, has offered to give a surfing lesson to the highest bidder, as well as an evening on the town. And remember, you can buy this wonderful day for someone else — the surfer in your life — if you don't feel up to catching some curl." She sounded really awkward saying that, and she couldn't quell a girlish flutter as she called upon her famous victim. "Ron, come on up here!"

I worked my way in front of the applauding crowd, doing the rude journalist thing so I could get photos as Ron strode up and politely embraced Cora, gave her a chaste kiss on the cheek and waved at everyone else with that come-hither grin. *He knows how to work it,* I thought, shooting off several photos. Then he winked at me. *Holy shit.*

I felt someone close at my elbow and turned. It was Wyatt, looking unhappy. Or maybe resigned.

"You're not going to bid, are you?" he whispered in my ear as the crowd applauded.

I laughed amid the noise. "I'm about to be between jobs, so no. Not that I would anyway," I added when Wyatt gave me that narrow-eyed look again.

"Then I hope you'll forgive me," he said, taking a few steps away as Cora started the bidding.

My forehead crinkled in puzzlement, but I focused on photographing the bidders as they shot up their hands, pushing the price quickly to fifty, a hundred, two hundred, three hundred dollars. Above five hundred, with bids going up at twenty-five dollar increments, the bidding started to slow.

"Come on, ladies and gentlemen — this is for art!" Cora called out, and Ron grinned, shrugged out of his jacket, threw it over the piano (to Ez's look of disdain) and did a slow spin for the audience, his arms in the air. He was greeted with drunken "Woohoos!" and a new round of bidding, but above eight hundred dollars, the bidding slowed again. It looked as if the date — er, lesson — would go to an elegant woman with a piled-high silver coiffure, and I wondered if she had a grandchild who might get a dream surfing day. And then, out of the corner of my eye, I glimpsed another hand go up. I looked over to see who the new bidder was.

Wyatt.

Wyatt? Wyatt wanted a date with Ron Raker? No, of course not. They hung out. He'd essentially admitted to being an employee of Ron Raker. Then what was he doing?

Cora didn't seem to care. She glowed as the bidding topped twelve hundred dollars, and at twelve hundred and fifty, the elegant woman shook her head, dropping out. Wyatt, his face impassive, kept his hand in the air as Cora at last pointed to him.

"Going once — going twice — and the surfing lesson goes to the young man in the gray suit for one thousand two hundred and fifty dollars! Your name, sir?"

"Wyatt Brooks."

"Mr. Brooks, You may make your reckoning with the auction volunteers," the museum director said, pointing to a couple of docents at the auction table amid a roar of shouts and applause.

Wyatt nodded, and then he looked at me. He walked back to me, leaned in. With him so close, his breath on my neck, all I could think about was our kiss. My mind rebelled and shut down, wanting to ditch this party, wanting him.

He whispered in my ear: "Congratulations. You just won a date with Ron Raker."

I turned to look at him, my mouth open in shock. And he shrugged, his face a mask, and walked away.

I looked up at Raker, and the big surfer grinned at me. At me?

And all I could think about was his sexy friend who'd just screwed me over.

WYATT CAUGHT me at the door. The party was still in full swing, but I had to get out of there and file my photos. And I just wanted to get out of there.

"Cali," he called.

"I'm just going to give it away," I said, pushing through the doors. It was misting now and a little bit cold.

"Don't," he said, following me. The doors clanged shut behind him.

"You couldn't pay me enough to get in the water, no matter who was giving the surf lesson, and I don't want a date with your boy." Though I wouldn't have minded a date with Wyatt, if he hadn't pulled that little trick.

"He's not my boy."

"You come with him in the limo, you arrange his rides and, apparently, his dates, and you're not his boy?"

"He liked you. I did it as a favor. I don't want to piss him off. Not yet, anyway."

"What do you mean, not yet?" I looked up to where the spotlights were shooting their dramatic roving beams through the mist and stuffed my camera in my bag so it wouldn't get wet.

Wyatt glowered, but not at me. "I'm quitting the job, and it's going to tick him off. I want to let him down easy. He's been a good friend. I can't burn that bridge."

"And I fit into this how?"

"He took a shine to you, OK? It's just a date. You can skip the surf lesson. Just go out to dinner with him. He'll be relieved. He hates surfing in the cold."

I ran a hand over my pinned-up hair, feeling fine droplets settling into the wavy strands. His eyes followed my motion, and his look softened.

"Why me?" I asked.

"You're pretty," Wyatt said, snagging my gaze, and I sensed he wasn't as indifferent to me as this deal implied. He paused. "And he likes to be seen with someone who looks good in pictures."

"I usually *take* the pictures."

"It will be painless. I'll make sure of it."

"So *you* want me to go out to dinner with him?" I asked, knowing I sounded sulky.

"No," he said flatly. "But if you would do me this favor, it will make my life easier, and if I can do a favor for you — just name it. Besides, this doesn't have to be like a real date."

"What if I want it to be?" I asked, feeling contrary, testing him.

Wyatt's jaw froze in a hard line for a moment. Then: "Do you?"

"Of course not. This is freaking me out."

He looked relieved. "I'll be around. He's weird that way. He takes his merry band with him everywhere he goes. The guys get drunk in the bar while he shows off for the cameras."

I rolled my eyes. "You're making this sound better and better."

"Listen." He stepped up to me, grasped my elbow. "I wish it hadn't been you. I would've — " He paused.

"Yes?"

Wyatt leaned in closer, speaking softly. "I would have asked you myself."

He didn't pull away. He just stood there, his mouth to my ear, breathing, and my body started having that same crazy reaction that only he seemed to create, a wave of heat that washed over my skin and roared into my core. I turned my head slightly toward him, wanting to say something, anything, but he didn't let me.

He leaned down and sealed my lips with his, his kiss more needful this time. His hand slid to my waist, pulling me close, and I made a sound of, I don't know, desire, anguish, frustration, as my mouth opened under his, taking his tongue, completely betraying my angry brain.

He stepped back abruptly, ruffled, breathing hard. "I probably shouldn't have done that."

Oh, hell. Now he was taking it back?

"I'll go on your date. With *him*," I snapped.

And I walked off into the night, with the ghost of my body still standing back there, wanting to feel Wyatt's tongue in my mouth again, his hand on my waist.

And wanting to slap him, too.

So this was my last day in newspapers: a half day, since I'd worked last night covering the art show. There were a lot of "lasts." Last cup of mediocre coffee from the cafeteria. Last mileage report. Last look out the glassed-in hallway into the tropical jungle where I'd seen so many birds and lizards, rainbows and downpours, vines and palms.

I cleaned out my desk. I signed papers in human resources. I ate a coconut cream cupcake, one of a few dozen

Bart and the metro editor had teamed up to buy, since the executives down the hall were pretending this wasn't a heart-breaking day of farewell for a third of the staff.

Just a few months before, my most recent boyfriend, anticipating the layoff, had moved to New Jersey for a job. The idea of me going had never even come up. Like all the guys before him, it just wasn't meant to be. Maybe I'd always known that, but it had been nice having him around.

The other photographers chatted quietly in a corner of the photo lab as I finished emptying my desk. Standing by what used to be my computer, I dropped the last few bits of me in my box: a framed photo of Damien and me as kids, eating ice cream on the boardwalk in matching Batman T-shirts; a pica pole — an obsolete metal ruler from the days when pages were laid out by hand; and a Bohemia Beach snow globe that featured an alligator under a beach umbrella. It had been too weird not to buy.

Joan, my now-ex-roommate and, like me, future ex-employee of the *Bugle,* poked her head in the door. At thirty, she was giving up reporting and taking a PR job at a theme park complex in Orlando. She nodded to Bart, Jordan and the other two photographers who were staying as she walked over to my desk.

"Here's to the next chapter," she said, tossing her short, light-brown hair, toasting me with a chocolate cupcake, her dark eyes melancholy.

"I hope it's a page-turner," I said, taking the last bite of mine. "You all set for tomorrow?"

She crumpled her cupcake paper and nodded. "Moving truck, fiancé and manly cohorts are all lined up."

"I'll help."

"You will not," Joan said. "Aren't you still unpacking at your new place?"

"Sort of." The truth was, I'd barely unpacked a thing at my new apartment, a one-bedroom above my soon-to-be photo studio in the charming (real estate code for "small") old brick building I'd rented in the Bohemia arts district. And I still had to whip the studio into shape. I'd signed a lease for a year. At this point, with my savings and a small business loan, I could cover the rent for about eight months. But I had to start my adventure somewhere.

"And you have that date on Saturday," Joan said, wiggling her eyebrows at me.

"What?" Bart asked from across the room. "Date?"

Damn. He had some kind of radar for tease-worthy subjects.

"It's not a date," I said. "It's an obligation."

"Yeah," Joan said, "with *Ron Raker.*"

"What? Have you been holding out on us?" Bart exclaimed as he and the other guys perked up and gathered around me. "Is that why you didn't get pictures of him New Year's Eve?"

"Hell, no. I got roped into it. One of his buddies bid on Mr. Dream Date at the art show opening."

"And somehow, you are going?" Bart said. "Do I sense a conspiracy at work?"

"Definitely," I said. "I didn't want it, but his friend talked me into it."

"His cute friend," Joan said with authority, though she'd never met Wyatt, only heard about him from me.

"Oh-ho, the plot thickens. Tell me all about it," Bart said as the other guys looked on.

I scowled. "Why? You going to take photos?"

"Absolutely!" Bart said. Jordan laughed, and the two other photogs who were still employed grinned and echoed him.

"No way. I'm not telling you vultures anything," I said, though I was trying hard not to smile.

"You're going to miss us," Bart said.

"I already do." I felt my eyes moisten.

They all got quiet, and we exchanged a round of hugs. Joan and Jordan promised to stay in touch with everyone. And in the middle of our last goodbyes, the phone on my desk rang.

I stared at it as the crowd dissipated, all except for Bart, his face creased with woe.

"You going to get that?" he asked, staring at the old phone as it made that jarring, endangered, analog sound of a bell rattling within an almond-plastic case.

"Oh, all right," I said, sitting down for my last phone call in newspapers.

"*Bugle.* Calista Goode."

"Thank God," came the crisp male voice on the other end. "You're a hard woman to reach, three calls and about six transfers later."

"And how may I help you?" I asked, ignoring the complaint. It wasn't unusual. *The Bugle* didn't have many people left who answered phones.

"It's about tomorrow night," he said, and then I realized to whom the voice belonged.

"Wyatt. I wondered when I'd be hearing from you."

"Given I only knew that you worked for the newspaper, I suppose it's lucky I got you at all."

"Especially since I'm about to walk out of here forever."

"How's that?" He sounded confused.

"Laid off. I told you. Sort of." I supposed he couldn't be

expected to decipher my remarks at the art show opening. "So what's the deal?"

"You're sure you don't want to do the surfing lesson?"

"Completely," I said, imagining how many people would kill to have a lesson with Ron Raker.

"OK, then. You're going to meet Ron at Trifles at the Boardwalk at 8 p.m. I'm going to pick you up."

"Why isn't *he* going to pick me up?" I knew I sounded cranky, especially since getting a lift from Ron Raker was about the last thing I wanted.

"Because he's an asshole," Wyatt said matter-of-factly, and I barked out a laugh. He laughed, too. "At least sometimes."

"I could just drive."

"No, he insisted," Wyatt said. "He wants nothing standing between you and a good drunk."

"Goodness, you're frank. Not much of a wingman, are you?"

"Not anymore," Wyatt said with a sigh. "You only have to put up with drinks and dinner. You don't even have to drink."

"I think I'll *need* to drink," I said wryly. *"Just* drinks and dinner?"

"I wouldn't stop you if you threw a drink in his face and walked out *before* dinner," he said. "The earlier the better."

I laughed from the belly, then, and tried to avoid Bart's curious gaze. "So when will I see you? About 7:30?"

"Sure." Wyatt paused. "Unless you want to get a drink with me first."

My annoyance with him had eased with each of his take-downs of Ron, and my traitorous heart leapt at his offer. Why not? It's not as if I had someone. Wyatt could be my someone, my Mr. Right Now.

"OK," I said. "I'd like that."

"Then I'll see you at 6:30. Oh, wait. Where am I going? And what's your cell?"

"You mean I could have hung up on you and avoided this date altogether?" I teased. I gave him my new address and my phone number. "So I guess I'll see you Saturday."

"I was dreading it," Wyatt said. "But now that I get to see you first — I can't wait. See you then."

"See you then," I echoed softly, feeling a thrill at his undisguised interest. I gingerly replaced the phone in its cradle, wondering what I was getting myself into.

I took one more last look around my space, thoughts of the strange date replaced by desolation at leaving the job I'd learned to love. I picked up my camera bag and box, said more goodbyes on the way out of the building, and headed to my little SUV in the parking lot. An osprey circled overhead, its sharp cry echoing the pang I felt in my heart.

I wasn't used to being alone. Whenever I'd been boyfriendless, admittedly a rare condition, I'd at least had my job, my friends. I'd always been surrounded by people.

I put the box in the back of my car amid the tangle of tripods and other gear and looked up as the osprey cried again. It had something in its talons — a fish, fresh from the nearby lagoon. It settled on the uppermost branch of a dying oak tree and called out one more time. Months away from breeding season, it was beautiful and sure, strong in its solitude.

Not at all terrified.

~

MY BUILDING WAS NESTLED amid the galleries and a few encroaching bars in the Bohemia arts district. I had brown paper covering the glass windows facing the street until I could get the retail space in order.

The small front room would work as a gallery and reception area. The main studio was in the center of the building, behind closed doors, and it was still a riot of boxes, camera gear and random furniture. Behind it was an office, a storage room and stairs that led up to my apartment, which almost as chaotic as the studio below. There was a precarious outdoor staircase, too, but I preferred the indoor entrance. A tiny back parking lot completed my kingdom.

I spent most of Saturday imposing order on the apartment, but only the kitchen and the bedroom became remotely livable. The spacious living room, with tall windows facing the street, was filled with boxes and furniture.

Still, I could look around and see that this could be one groovy pad when I was done. Dark wooden floors were attractively worn and polished to a deep patina. Similar details declared this a historic building, including the pretty crown molding where the cream-colored walls met the tin ceiling. The latter was a weathered light blue, a painted antique sky above my head. There was even a non-functioning fireplace that came with a bracket that would hold nice, fat candles. I loved it.

Thanks to my efforts, I could actually look through my clothes — now organized in a small walk-in closet and a couple of dressers — and find something to wear for my dueling dates tonight. First, I'd have drinks with Wyatt. And then I would endure Ron Raker.

I mean, I wasn't entirely immune to Ron Raker. He was a celebrity, yes. But more to the point, he was a large hunk of manly man, and while his clearly enormous ego made me grit my teeth, he had a certain sex appeal. It might be fun to hear what he had to say, to see what it was like to be with him, to *be* him. He might not be famous if he walked into a supermarket in Minnesota, but in the world's surf spots, and especially in Bohemia and Bohemia Beach, he was a god. He was a few years older than I was, and I'd heard about him my whole life. So at the very least, I had to admit I was curious.

I was also, against my better instincts, flattered that he'd chosen me for his little dating scheme. Even though I knew someone had to win the date, and he'd just been trying to control the outcome, I couldn't help but think of it another way: He'd paid twelve hundred and fifty dollars for a date with *me.*

Put that way, I sounded like a high-class hooker, and this was *not* going to be that kind of date.

I favored blue colors that set off my blond hair and light blue eyes, and I was happy to find a pretty sweater that might fit the bill. It was chilly tonight, around fifty degrees, and it was rare a Florida girl got to pull out a sweater. This one, in soft merino wool, angora and alpaca, was knitted in light blues and blue-greens, in shallow, variegated stripes. The neckline was wide and thick, standing up a bit, and it would show off the matching necklace and earrings of blue, turquoise and clear glass beads and crystals I planned to wear.

I paired it with a light blue denim skirt that came just above the knee; under it, I wore sensible cotton bikini panties in light blue. But I matched the bra, because I hated the idea of not matching. I was one of those people. No one would see them but me, but I would know.

I had the perfect funky shoes for the outfit: wedge heels with tie-dyed denim uppers that laced up like boots and had a buckle, too. They showed my toes, pink polish and all, and were tall enough to suggest I made an effort, but comfortable enough to keep me happy.

I checked myself out in the mirror over my low dresser, piled up my hair with the help of a long clip, and applied light eye makeup and pink frosty lipstick. I picked up my roomy denim purse, the one I'd bought for one reason: It could hold a camera. But did I want to bring a camera? I wasn't shooting for the paper anymore. I was shooting for myself.

That was enough reason for me. I'd bring it. There was nothing worse than seeing the perfect photo and not having my camera with me.

A few minutes later, I locked the front door behind me, stood on the sidewalk and looked around, shivering a bit in the chill. There was a stiff breeze tonight, with winking stars above and increasing traffic as the Bohemia nightlife started to pick up. My old apartment had been in an ugly, modern complex well away from downtown; this was a completely different vibe — streetlights, road noise, distant music, voices, life. Maybe I wasn't so alone after all.

I heard rather than saw the car pull up to the curb to my left, and I turned to see if it was Wyatt. It was a big, boxy, silver SUV with expensive lines, not your average rental car. Reflections from the street lights prevented me from seeing through the windshield, but in a moment, with the car still running, Wyatt stepped out.

He walked toward me, grinning, *God,* melting me with that beautiful smile. He wore a black jacket over a white shirt with a skinny black tie and dark-blue jeans that hugged his firm behind as if they were good friends. I snapped my gaze up so he wouldn't catch me looking, but his eyes twinkled as if he had.

I lowered my eyes toward the sidewalk and saw he wore leather sandals. You can take a boy out of the surf, but you can't take the surf out of the boy.

"Cali," he said, leaning toward me, kissing me lightly on the cheek, his lips lingering half a second longer than they should have. His breath warmed my face as he spoke softly in my ear. "You look great."

"Hi." I smiled as he pulled back. "You smell good." *D'oh. What made me say that?*

"Never underestimate the power of hotel soap," he joked.

"It's working for you," I said, trying to recover my cool. I felt shy all of a sudden. We were actually going on a date. A date before my date. This was crazy.

"Where should we go for a drink?" he asked, looking around. The wind ruffled his thick hair, setting the blond streak askew.

I nodded toward the east. "There's a little bar I like that overlooks the harbor. We can go beachside later, since that's where we're meeting your boy."

He grimaced. "Don't remind me. Should we drive? I'm not really familiar with the area yet."

"It's several blocks, so that might be best," I said, moving toward the vehicle with him. "What kind of car is that?"

"Mercedes G-Class," Wyatt said, not altogether enthusiastic. "Local dealer loaned it to Ron while he's in town, so we're all using it."

"You don't like it?" It sure was a pretty car.

"I love it. I'm just constantly baffled at the perks of celebrity," he said, opening the passenger door, offering his hand as I made the big step up to my seat. He closed the door behind me, went around and climbed in. "Which way?"

"Straight ahead." I directed him as we moved slowly

through the pedestrian traffic and lights toward the harbor. We found a parking space in a small lot across the street from the bar I had in mind.

Plumeria Bar was named for the frangipanis that grew among the palm trees around the small, stucco building. This time of year, the bar's namesake plants looked like stick trees. Still, plumeria flowers were painted in an attractive mural all around the heavy wooden front door.

Inside, the look was dark and rich, with red walls above polished wooden wainscoting. Large, sensual photographs of flowers hung on the walls. Red-glass sconces mounted on narrow wooden panels provided up-lighting. Small tables and a cozy area with couches and comfy chairs filled the space around the horseshoe-shaped bar, dimly lit by low-hanging pendant lights with red glass shades.

Behind the bar, windows looked out onto the small Bohemia harbor, where lights sparkled on the water and boats bobbed shoulder-to-shoulder against the docks. You could sit out there and drink, but on a crisp night like this, it was nice to be inside the comforting interior. It was warm and dark and sexy — kind of like my date.

Wyatt had a hand on my back as he guided me to the bar. I liked the pressure of it, the warmth it transmitted, and I was sorry to lose his touch as we each took a stool.

The bartender, a young guy I didn't know, wandered over. "What can I get you?"

"Old-Fashioned, please," I said.

"Do you have any local beers on tap?" Wyatt asked, eventually agreeing to a Bohemia Brewing Red Ale.

"Not a cocktail guy?" I asked as the bartender moved away.

"Not when I'm driving," Wyatt said. "Later, one of the

other guys takes over driving duties, and I'll be able to have whatever I want. And there's always the cab option. But for now, I have to get you safely to your destination."

"That's too bad," I said wryly, unable to look away from his caramel eyes, luminous in this light.

"You like living dangerously?" Wyatt asked as a corner of his mouth turned up.

"No. I mean, I want to be safe. It's just too bad the — other date is looming over our heads." *Oh, nicely handled, Calista.*

"Then let's not think about it." Wyatt smiled as our drinks arrived. He lifted his beer. "To Date No. 1. And living dangerously."

I clinked my rocks glass to his pilsner and took a sip, letting the whiskey calm my nerves. It was a good thing I wasn't driving. I hadn't eaten anything since late morning, and I had a feeling this drink was going to go right to my head. Either the drink or Wyatt. Just the sight of him was enough to make me lose any sense of judgment.

He was sitting so close to me, our knees were touching, and he leaned in even closer.

"I haven't stopped thinking about you since New Year's Eve," he whispered.

"I thought you'd be long gone by now," I deflected him. Maybe I was looking for an excuse for my excessively friendly behavior on the condo balcony. "Aren't you one of those surfers who travels a lot?"

"I've been known to chase the big waves. And Ron has a tournament in New Zealand next week," he said vaguely, taking a sip of his beer before turning back to me.

He had a bit of foam on his upper lip, and I instinctively reached up to brush it off with a finger. This part of him felt warm and soft, and I got a little tangled in the sensation. He grasped my wrist and sucked the foam off my finger, shooting heat through my body. Then he turned my wrist toward him and kissed it once, twice. He didn't let go of my hand, just brought it down to his knee, holding it there.

"Cali," he said, as I foundered in a flood of arousal.

"Yes?" I took a sip of my drink, feeling something akin to panic, only more enthralling. The whiskey was sweet on my tongue, but all I could think about was the taste of Wyatt, his tongue in my mouth, the champagne on New Year's Eve.

"I'm thinking about our next date." His voice was low and intense, those brown eyes glittering.

I laughed nervously. "I thought we were still in the middle of this one."

"Later tonight," he said. "After you've ditched Ron."

"That's presumptuous."

"Is it?" he asked, and he leaned in and kissed me, drinking me in as if I were the last glass of water in the desert.

Damn his kisses. They consumed me, wrapping me in a thorny thicket of roses that drew hot blood, and I responded, closing my eyes, taking his tongue in my mouth, sucking on it, opening further to him. A moment later I was left breathless, bereft, as he pulled away. I opened my eyes and sighed deeply. He looked somewhat less than composed.

"Maybe we should just enjoy this date," I said.

"Oh, I am." Wyatt took another sip of beer as if nothing had happened. Except that he still grasped my hand, even more firmly now, and my glance took in a bulge in his jeans that showed he was anything but uninterested.

I looked up at his long nose, those striking cheekbones. "Maybe I should know a little bit more about you."

Or maybe I shouldn't. He'd be back on the road in a few days. Why know more?

"Maybe you should," he responded, a dimple betraying a hint of amusement. "I'd expect a journalist to ask questions. But this is off the record."

"I told you. I'm not a journalist anymore," I said, a little sadly. "Friday was my last day. Though I'm still a photographer."

"And still carrying your camera." He nodded at my bag, hanging off the back of the barstool. The shape of the camera protruded vaguely from the fabric, but it was surprising that anyone but a photographer would notice.

"A good photographer always carries her camera," I said.

"What are you going to do next?"

"Portraits. Events. Weddings. Whatever comes my way. I'm hitting all outlets." I took another sip of my drink. It was starting to go to my head. His grip on my hand had loosened, and now he carelessly caressed my fingers, making me giddy. "Oh, and I'm going to teach a portrait class at the art school starting next week."

He nodded. "I've heard a lot of good things about the Bohemia School of Art and Design. Is that the one?"

"Yes. It has a really good reputation. I'm excited to be teaching there."

"You're more than qualified."

"How do you know?" I asked, puzzled.

"I Googled you. I found your photos on the newspaper's website. And I found your site, too. You have a sharp eye for light and color."

"Huh," I said. He'd been scoping me. "Thanks."

"I wouldn't say it if I didn't think you were talented." He smiled. And then he got distracted by the clock on the wall. "Oh, hell. Better drink up. Almost time to go."

"What?" I followed his eyes. It was 7:25. "Damn."

"Thank you," he said.

"For what?"

"For saying 'Damn.' I feel the same way." He waved down the bartender for the bill and paid it.

"I should've treated you," I said. "I brought you here."

"Your date night is all-expenses-included," he said, and then he got a sly look in his eye. "Even the first date."

"So Ron will pay for the second?"

"Or one of us will. And he'll pay us back. Though I think the restaurant has agreed to pick up the tab for the publicity. They called the *Bugle*."

"Oh, shit," I said.

He laughed. "Don't worry. Tonight's *third* date is on me. And the *Bugle* doesn't know anything about that."

The heat in his eyes could have melted a glacier.

"We'll have to see about that," I said, trying to be flippant, but as he took my hand, helped me down from the barstool and led me outside, I felt a low fire flicker in my belly.

A fire fueled by whiskey. And Wyatt.

WYATT CRANKED up the stereo as I directed him toward the causeway that would take us over the lagoon and to the beach.

"I know it's a cliché," he said as surf guitar ripped through the speakers, "but I really do like surf music. Most of the guys listen to a lot harder stuff, but there's something about this that makes me nostalgic."

"For what?" I had more or less gained my composure, separated as we were by the gearshift and center console.

"Oh, I don't know. What surf used to be. The pure, wild feeling of being on a wave. Old-time California."

"Is that where you grew up?"

"Yeah. Though I'm not exactly nostalgic about that." His tone was dark.

"Why not?"

"Is this where I turn for the causeway?" he asked, ignoring my question. I got him going in the right direction, and he notched up the volume as another tune came on.

"Dick Dale," he said. "Still the best."

It wasn't easy to talk over the music, so I didn't try. The car seemed to glide into the sky as we soared over the artificial hill of the bridge, over the dark water, toward the strip of lights that marked the barrier island and, on its eastern edge, the beach.

The Bohemia Beach boardwalk was nothing like the northern boardwalks I'd heard so much about. It was a great observation gallery for watching swimmers and surfers, at least during the day, but it was short — perhaps the length of a couple of football fields. And there were no arcades, no amusement park rides, no businesses adjoining it, except one.

At its terminus was a large 1920s building that had in turn housed a beach resort, a dance hall and a private club before becoming the restaurant and bar complex it was today: Trifles on the Boardwalk. It was a silly name for a place that had become the go-to spot for everyone from traditional diners to beach revelers, depending on which restaurant or bar one chose to patronize. It was popular for special events, too, with a ballroom that overlooked the ocean. I hoped to see a lot more of it as a wedding photographer.

We parked in the lot that ran along the boardwalk. On the

other side of the lot, near Highway A1A, was a cluster of less glamorous tourist traps — beach emporiums, fast food and pizza places, surf and kite shops. They would have all killed for the beachfront property Trifles had. But in this corner of Bohemia Beach, Trifles remained king.

As we got out of the big Mercedes and started walking, I could hear music mingling with the sound of the ocean — a cover band playing "Margaritaville."

"I like that song," Wyatt said.

"Good, because if you spend any time in Florida, you're going to hear a lot of it." I was pretty sure it was a law that every bar with live music had to feature at least one rendition of "Margaritaville" a night.

"Don't be bitter," he teased. "You sound like you lost your shaker of salt."

"Oh, stop." I rolled my eyes, but I was amused. And confused. I noticed he didn't take my hand. Maybe he was worried about his buddy catching him in the act. I don't know why I missed his touch so much.

The facade of the Mediterranean revival building was lit up with magenta spotlights. There were multiple doors, depending on which venue you were visiting. We were headed for The Mix, widely considered the party bar, not far from the ballroom and a snack cafe that opened up for beachgoers during the day. Upstairs was a more elegant piano bar and the main restaurant.

Wyatt held the door for me, touching my back one more time as he escorted me, and we were in The Mix.

Inside, the band was ten times louder. It had moved on to "What I Like About You," and a cluster of mostly women, dressed far too lightly for January, were bouncing up and down on the dance floor to our right in front of the stage. To the left, the nightspot was divided by plush booths and screens and plants, so you could never really take in the whole space at once. It was large, however, and it was packed. It wouldn't be easy to have a conversation here; it was all too loud and chaotic, the kind of place where people shouted over their drinks and went home with a sore throat.

"Where'd he say to meet?" I shouted in Wyatt's direction.

"What?"

I repeated the question in his ear.

"He said the bar."

I nodded and beckoned for him to follow. And then I heard a great roar go up somewhere in front of us.

"He's here already," Wyatt said as we put a little distance between us and the band and got to where the noise wasn't so overwhelming.

"How can you be sure?"

"I'm sure." He looked unhappy again. I wondered when he planned to tell Ron he was leaving. Maybe he was one of those people who always talked about making a change and never did.

We came around the corner and got our first full view of the long bar. It had a brushed aluminum facade and a thick glass top lit from beneath by changing colored lights. But the modern decor was not really what drew anyone's eye. It was Ron Raker standing in the center of a circle of hooting patrons with two buxom blondes, their hair much more yellow than mine, more like Ron's, but long and curling halfway down their backs. Twins, I think, and really pretty. Way out of my league. Each was wearing a corset top and a miniskirt. Each had a shot glass stuffed between her boobs and a lime wedge in her mouth. Ron had a salt shaker in his hand. First he licked one pale throat and sprinkled salt on it, then licked the other and did the same. The women giggled and the crowd howled. His buddies up front were the loudest, screaming: "Do it! Do it!"

Ron leaned in and licked the salt off the first woman's neck, then dove between her breasts, taking his time pushing his nose into the crevasse there, and clutched the shot glass with his mouth. He knocked his head back and swallowed the liquor — it had to be tequila — and tossed the glass to a bartender. He touched the first girl's mouth with his and plucked the lime from her lips. He sucked it, dropped it into his hand and kissed her hard to the intensifying screams of the crowd.

Then he turned to twin No. 2 and did the same, only this time, he finished with a long lick over the slopes of her cleavage. I thought the crowd would lose its mind. And then I noticed Bart shooting photos discreetly from the end of the bar. Those pics were bound to get some hits on the *Bugle* website.

I wondered if I was supposed to find this scene titillating. Then again, I wasn't a guy, and I wasn't nearly drunk enough. I was never much of a spring breaker type, and that's how I viewed these antics, even though it wasn't spring break. It all seemed like some anthropological case study, a YouTube video waiting to happen.

I shook my head. I'd lapsed into spectator mode. It was something I did; I withdrew from the reality of the scene right in front of me and viewed it as if it were a photograph, something I wasn't really a part of. A few seconds passed before it dawned on me that I was watching my alleged date for the evening licking some bimbo's boobs. I supposed I should be pissed off, but I really wasn't. Ron wasn't the guy who turned me on. I turned and looked at

Wyatt, who was observing me with a mix of horror and remorse.

"Want to leave?" he barked into my ear.

"I don't think — "

I didn't have time to finish my sentence.

"Wyatt! You've brought my date! Calista, isn't it?" Ron Raker's voice boomed over the music and the dying shouts as the revelers turned to other diversions.

"Y — yes," I said, looking up into his wild grin.

"Want to do a body shot?" he asked, as if that was the first thing he asked any woman at the start of a date.

"Probably not just yet." I think my irony was drowned out by the ambient noise.

"OK. Let me buy you a drink, and then we'll go up to dinner. Unless you want to go to dinner now?"

"A drink is good," I said, feeling pulled along by the tidal wave that was Ron Raker's personality. The big surfer put a hand on my shoulder and guided me toward the bar, away from Wyatt, and I took one glance back to see him fading into the crowd.

Ron's touch on my shoulder did nothing for me. It just felt heavy. But what felt even heavier were the stares as other women noted me, his new companion, with curiosity and envy. The twins leaned against the bar, and Ron nodded at them. "See you later, girls," he said with a grin, and I got the feeling "later" wasn't a generalization as one of them winked and they, too, vanished into the throng.

I turned and saw Bart at the other end of the bar and gave him a pleading look. He smiled, took a couple of photos of me and Ron, looked at his watch in an exaggerated gesture, shook his head and headed for the door.

I shot my ex-boss a grateful smile as he started to move past us, just as Ron reached out and touched his shoulder.

"Want to get a shot of us? This is the girl who won me at the auction," Ron told Bart with a wink. So he'd known Bart was there all along.

"Fantastic!" Bart said, and I could tell he was enjoying every second of this. "Why don't you put an arm around her and smile?"

Ron clutched me tightly against his Giant Redwood of a body and grinned. I managed a weak smile as the flash went off two, three times.

I blinked away the afterimage and gave Bart a look that promised revenge. He shot me a wave and made a beeline for the door.

Ron, his arm still around me, spoke into my ear.

"What'll it be?" he asked.

"Old-Fashioned." I was grateful when Ron eased his hold and ordered my drink and another shot of tequila. At least he was consistent.

"So what are you into?" he asked. "You surf?"

"No," I declared, then softened my tone. "I'm a photographer."

"But that's a job, right? I mean, what are you *into?*" He knocked back his shot and tapped on the bar. The female bartender who was hovering nearby, apparently assigned to cater to his every whim, poured him two more. Just in case, I assumed.

"I'm really into photography. It's not just a job for me." But then I wondered. I'd shot little more than photos for work in the past few years. Now my world had opened up. My mind was going to have to open with it as I adapted the way I thought with the lens.

"That's cool," he said. "Wyatt shoots some bitchin' surf shots. He's really talented. Maybe he can give you some pointers sometime."

I looked sharply at Ron, but he was giving the eye to a cute brunette. She was hanging on the arm of an oblivious guy while she turned all her attention to the celebrity surfer.

"I always like to learn," I said, not even sure a response was required. Ron was like some kind of multitasking flirt savant, constantly looking around him, winking and nodding at interested females. I wondered if he was telepathically transmitting his phone number to them.

I was halfway through my drink when he suggested we go upstairs to the dining room, so I took it with me, looking around as we walked through the crowd to the lobby and the wide, curving wooden staircase. Wyatt was nowhere to be seen, and in a few minutes, with the help of an obsequious manager, we were seated in a quiet booth, with gentle piano music playing from the speakers. There was no safety in numbers here. I was trapped with Ron Raker.

Alone with him in this small space, I felt his physicality more strongly. I could see the muscles ripple through the hip, button-up black shirt he was wearing, with a red, embroidered tiki pattern running vertically through the front panels. His black slacks also left little to the imagination. This man had toned his body to its finest form, the better to tame the giant waves he rode, and it showed in his every movement. He started telling a story about the rough waves he'd conquered in a tournament I'd never heard of, and my mind drifted, admiring him the way I might admire a statue, only this one breathed and spoke and laughed.

I did my best to make conversation over a couple of steaks, never once understanding why he'd chosen me as his date. Maybe it didn't matter. After all, he'd seen me for all of thirty seconds before the auction.

Despite his celebrity shine, with servers stumbling over each other to bring him the best wine and morsels from the chef, and the owner coming by to get his photo taken with Ron (I had to take it, of course, with the owner's crappy phone camera), I didn't bask in his reflected glory. I felt myself observing him, reminding myself that we grew up in the same place. It was hard to imagine, looking at him now.

I got him to talk about Bohemia High a little — he'd graduated a year before I entered high school — and we found out we had a few teachers in common. That led to a more comfortable conversation, and by the time we'd split a caramel-slathered slice of apple pie, I was actually enjoying myself.

"Thank you," I said as we left the dining room and headed back downstairs.

"I should be thanking you," said Ron, who seemed more laid-back than when we'd gone up. "That's the first normal conversation I've had in a long time."

"Really?" I asked, but then, as we got into the wide downstairs lobby that connected all of Trifles' venues, and people turned and stared at him, I realized how hard it was for him to just *be* without the world worshiping him.

"Yeah, really. Nice way to spend my last night in town," he said as we paused just outside the entrance to The Mix, where people were entering and exiting through the constantly swinging double doors. "You should think about coming over to the hotel later. It'll be a good party."

And just like that, he leaned in like a toppling tree and planted a big kiss on my mouth. It felt like a hammer being

applied to my lips, and to my relief, it was over almost as soon
as it began.

"Ready to go back in?" He grinned as he caught the
swinging door and held it open.

When he did, I saw Wyatt just inside, watching us.

I BARELY HAD time to take in Wyatt's stony expression before
Ron's entourage burst through the outside doors.

"Hey, Ron, how was your date?" one of the surfers asked.

"Who cares?" another chimed in. "The twins say they're
going to get naked on the beach! Come on!"

"Isn't it a little cold for that?" I asked as Ron grabbed my
hand and dragged me along with the crowd.

"That's what happens when you play truth or dare,"
another surfer said, eagerly pushing forward with the others
and out the lobby door that led to the beach. It looked as if
the bar had disgorged half its patrons, everyone eager for a
show. It probably didn't hurt that Ron Raker stood tall among
the moving pack, a blond beacon of fame among the obscure.
I was swept along with the fray and onto the sand, Ron still
holding me by the hand, laughing at something his buddies
said.

There was a lot of laughter, drunken laughter, as a giddy,
volatile mood bubbled up through the revelers. I looked
around for Wyatt, but I couldn't see him anywhere. I really
didn't like where this was going.

We reached the water's edge in the near-darkness. I tried
to tug away from Ron, but he seemed to have forgotten I was
there. His hand remained clasped around mine like a vise as
he looked out to the surf.

"Woohoo!" he shouted. "Go, girls!"

One of the twins he'd licked salt off earlier — the human margaritas — was splashing into the water in the altogether. Even in the dim light, I could see her bikini tan lines and frigidly erect nipples. The other twin loosened her corset and, in a strip-tease move, tossed it to the sand on top of her skirt and ran in after the other girl. Within seconds, they were waist-deep and bitching about the cold water. Their simpering didn't deter the guys.

"I'll keep you warm!" one of the surfers shouted, dashing into the waves, and soon half the party crowd was jumping in the water, most still in their clothes.

"You next," I said in Ron's ear, hoping he'd let go and just plain go away.

He turned toward me, finally noticing me again, and answered me with a wide grin.

"I think it's *your* turn," he said, "especially after you refused my surfing lesson."

There were whoops around me as Ron stripped the purse from my shoulder and swiftly scooped me up, then shouts of "Throw her in! Throw her in!"

"No!" I screamed, slammed by a wave of terror. "No! Put me down! Let me go!"

A sense of unreality seized me. My heart thudded in my chest. I felt dizzy. In the span of a few horrifying microseconds, Ron laughed, taking a step toward the water. The half-wet crowd hollered. The freezing naked girls yelled, "Me next!"

I started beating on Ron's rocky chest and shoulders, still screaming "No!" The black ocean roared in my ears, ready to suck me in, drag me under. Blind fear motivated me now as I struggled. I tasted the salt in my mouth. I dimly heard Ron saying, "Relax!" as I writhed and screamed even louder: "No! No! Let me go! *Let me go!*"

I was almost sobbing when I felt another set of arms grabbing me and pulling me from Ron's grasp.

"I've got her," Wyatt said, carrying me easily as I instinctively clutched at him, burrowing in the fortress of his embrace. "Go play with the twins."

"Fine," said Ron, taken aback and obviously relieved to be rid of a screaming crazy woman. "But they've got to come to me. I'm not going in that cold water."

The joyful crowd, its spirits slightly dampened by the chill, gathered around him, the dry ones laughing, the wet ones dragging themselves from the waves. I heard Ron promise them all a round of drinks as Wyatt carried me, trembling, back toward the lights of Trifles. My body calmed as he held me; I felt warm in his strong arms, protected.

And then, as if waking from a dream, I recovered my senses.

Mortified by what had happened, by my reaction, I twisted out of Wyatt's grip and half-fell to my feet.

"Take it easy," he said, grabbing my elbow, steadying me. "Are you OK?"

I tried to school my breathing. "Fine."

"Here." He handed me my purse, which had been slung over his shoulder.

"Thanks." I tried to make light of the situation. "Not every guy will carry a girl's purse for her."

"Only the indisputably masculine ones," he said drily. "Why don't you come with me?"

"No. I'm going home."

"Just for a minute. You need to calm down."

"I do not!" I snapped, and then I felt bad for it. He was being so nice. "Sorry."

"It's OK. I'm sorry for asking you to go on such a shitty date."

"It wasn't bad, up until the last five minutes."

The corner of Wyatt's mouth twitched, but he still looked serious.

"You kissed him," he said.

I searched his eyes and couldn't believe what I saw. He was actually *jealous*. And now that I felt more myself, I was pissed off.

"Maybe you had obstructed-view seats, but he kissed *me,*" I said, glancing back toward the crowd and Ron, who had an arm around each twin — clothed again, fortunately, if you could call what they were wearing clothes. "And then he tried to drown me in the ocean."

"Come with me, Cali."

"I want to go home."

"Come with me."

He held me fast with his gaze, sincere, persuasive. His tone, his face were so compelling, I finally nodded and took his proffered hand.

I let him guide me back into the building and down a hallway, away from the bar and the crowds. He found another door, a double door, and pulled it open, drawing me inside. It clicked shut behind us, and we were in near darkness.

The space was large; I felt air moving around us. It took a moment for my eyes to adjust, and then I realized we were in the ballroom. Large windows on one side of the room looked out on the ocean. Around us, the floor was empty. Tables and chairs were stacked against one wall. Muted noise leaked through the walls and doors from elsewhere in the building, and a door with a small, round window glimmered dimly; it must lead to the banquet kitchen. With its high ceilings, the room felt hollow and strange.

Wyatt faced me and pushed a strand of hair away from my face.

"What happened back there?" he asked.

"Ask Ron."

"I'm asking you. Are you OK?"

"I'm fine," I said, though my senses were keyed up, honed by adrenaline. By fear. Wyatt didn't need to know that.

"You seemed pretty shaken up."

"I just — never mind. Don't worry about it."

He frowned. "I'm worried about you anyway."

"No need. Though I have to thank you for keeping me out of the water. Winter and all," I said lightly.

Wyatt was silent for a few moments, and then he took a deep breath. "That's not the only reason I grabbed you."

"What do you mean?"

"I couldn't stand watching you with him."

A spark of heat, like a freshly lit fuse on a stick of dynamite, sizzled through me.

"I always stand by and watch him with women," Wyatt said. "He's stolen women right out from under me, practically."

"You were watching us at dinner?"

"I walked through a couple of times, just to check on you," he said. "You didn't seem to notice. That made me even crazier."

The spark flared, the fuse shorter, a befuddling attraction on top of my fading panic.

I turned and wandered toward the windows, and he

followed. It wasn't quite as dark here, thanks to a subtle glow from the lights lining the railing of the vacant deck outside. Beyond was the darkness of the now-empty beach and the sea.

"You're sweet," I said, turning to him, "but he actually was OK, at least until he answered the siren call of the twin bimbos."

Wyatt granted me a brief smile and moved a step closer, so close I could feel his body heat in the chilly space. For a few seconds, I thought he was just going to watch me. His silence made me nervous.

"I wasn't just worried about you," he finally said, his voice low and electrifying. "I *wanted* you. I've let him take other women from me. But I didn't want him to have you."

The fuse in my body grew dangerously short, shooting out embers. No one had ever said anything like this to me before, and in my nervous state, it was intoxicating. Maybe I was still reeling from my rescue, but Wyatt seemed strong and strange and enchanted in the scant light, like a visitor from another realm, a handsome prince who had just swept into my world and would be gone just as fast.

As I studied his face, seeing the hunger there, the focus in his eyes, I heard the waves, the waves he lived on, the waves I grew up with, the natural rhythm that somehow lived in our genes, luring us into a trance that only the ocean could generate. From this safe place, the sound wasn't scary; it was seductive.

His eyes bored into mine. I admired the curve of his lip and remembered touching it earlier, the way he kissed me afterward. I scanned his taut body in that crisp shirt, under the well-cut jacket, inside the clinging jeans. I inhaled the scent of him, heard him breathing. Yearning built inside me, and I knew I wanted him, too, in a way I'd never wanted anyone before.

He took another step toward me.

Boom.

And then he was wrapped around me, his mouth devouring mine, and I was kissing him back. I let my purse slip to the floor so I could feel him against me without obstacles, the length of his body pressing into mine.

He reached under my sweater, ran his hands over my back and pulled the soft knit over my head. My skin prickled at the cold air leaking from the windows as the winter wind laid siege to the building.

He reached into my hair, pulled out the clip and dropped it so my mane spilled around my shoulders. He ran his hands through it as he kissed my neck, slowing his pace. He reached behind me again, unclasping the bra in one deft movement, letting it fall to the floor. He kissed his way down my naked chest, slowly, mouthing the slopes of my breasts, sucking on my hardening nipples. He licked and teased one peak until I didn't think I could stand it anymore, and then the other, pulling at the tip with his teeth, making me groan as the pain transmuted into pleasure.

"God, you're gorgeous," he said, cupping my breasts, squeezing them until I tilted my head back and felt the window behind me. He'd pushed me to the glass, and I was unconscious of anything except his body, his hands. I reached up and pushed off his jacket, pulled off his tie. A mischievous smile crossed his lips, and he kicked off his sandals and reached down and unbuttoned his jeans, watching me intently.

His every movement mesmerized me. The wetness grew

between my legs as he drew down his jeans and briefs to reveal the length of his cock, veined and hard.

"Do you want me, Cali?" he whispered into my ear, kissing my neck, my mouth, pressing up against me. I could feel his erection through my skirt and made an unintelligible sound under his mouth, all my reason in tatters. At least he'd asked.

"Yes — yes, damn it," I gasped.

Wyatt clutched the back of my thighs and ran his hands up under my skirt, feeling the panties there. He slowly pulled them down and off over my wedge heels, planting kisses down my legs on the way. I almost lost it. Then he stood before me again, slipping his hands under the skirt, over my hips, my behind. He moved one hand to my triangle as he looked down at me, one clever finger swirling around my clitoris, penetrating my folds. I grasped his waist, wanting his cock but transfixed by his magical finger as it hooked inside me, finding my sweet spot, coaxing waves of pleasure from my center until I was whimpering into his shoulder, into the shirt he still had on. And then the last remnants of rational thought shattered in ecstasy.

He withdrew his finger after my shuddering orgasm. I opened my eyes to see him ripping open a foil square, rolling on the condom.

"Turn around," he commanded.

It wasn't a request. It was an order born of desire. And at that moment, awash in emotion, I would have obeyed any command to have him.

I turned and faced the ocean, feeling exposed, deliriously turned on. He pushed against me, and my breasts flattened against the glass, my nipples cold and hard. He pushed up my short denim skirt and pulled my hips back a little. I could feel him teasing me as he rubbed his cockhead in my wetness.

"Please," I whispered as he teased my pussy.

"Tell me what you want," he hissed.

"Please — I want you inside me," I begged.

He gently pressed a hand against my back. I bent over and braced myself against the window. He felt hard against me. His tip grazed my crack, and then he thrust his thick shaft into my slick slit.

My knees would have buckled with the power of it if he hadn't held me up, his chest pressed against my back, the hard buttons digging into my skin, his hands grasping my hips as he pounded into me. I pressed my palms against the glass and held on, trying to balance in my heels, pushing back against him as he fucked me. For it was a fuck, an urgent, primal thing, and I wanted it with a primitive imperative.

"Cali," he growled into my shoulder as his rhythm built, as he made me moan. And then he adjusted positions slightly, pushed more deeply into me, holding, filling me, and he spasmed with a groan. His detonation triggered a new wave of agonizing pleasure in my core. I was lost, lost in the sensation of him, of his length driving inside me. I felt myself slipping to the floor, to my knees, still clenching him, and he knelt against me, thrusting slowly now, extending my plea- sure until he gently withdrew and kissed my back. He turned me around and embraced me, consuming my mouth, kissing me as we knelt on the rough carpet of the Trifles ballroom, my breasts crushed against him, the waves filling my ears.

It was a few minutes before we came to our senses. He helped me up, and we got dressed in silence, sneaking looks at one another; he found a trash can where he could dispose of the condom. I tried not to imagine someone seeing it there, evidence of our forbidden tryst. I'd never had this kind of sex before, practically public sex, and with someone I barely knew. I couldn't think about it. I wouldn't. I'd lost my mind, is all, and Wyatt would be heading to New Zealand or wherever, and I would get on with my life.

But as I straightened my clothes and put the clip back in my hair and looked up at him shrugging on his jacket, I already felt the pang of loss.

Ridiculous, I told myself. *It's your hormones talking.*

"I should go," I said abruptly.

"The guys will want to keep partying at the hotel," Wyatt said softly as he knotted his tie. "I could get out of it. You could come with me. To the hotel, I mean, not the party."

"No."

"Come with me, Cali."

"No," I said, unreasonably, considering what we'd just done. I picked up my purse.

"Why not?"

"Because this is crazy," I said, as if stating the obvious. "This whole night has been crazy."

"It's perfect," Wyatt said.

I moved toward the exit, and he reached out and grabbed my arm. "Don't go like this."

I stopped, hung my head, then turned and faced him. "What do you want?"

"You," he said. "Hey, have you used that camera yet tonight?"

"What?"

"The camera in your bag. Take my picture. And I'll take your picture. And you can email it to me so I'll have it."

"Why?" I whispered, feeling the schism of goodbye.

"Because that's what you do," he said, sliding the purse off my shoulder and pulling out the camera. "Here, by the window. There's a little light. Just enough, maybe. You first." He gestured toward the window, and rather than resist him, I moved toward it, leaned against it. "Stay very still," he said as he messed with the dials, and I knew he was setting it to a slow shutter speed and a high ISO for the low light. So he did know how to use a camera.

He snapped the photo as I looked at him, not smiling, and I reached out for the camera. He stood where I had, and I duplicated the photo, framing it so, I hoped, his subtle reflection would show up in the glass. Wordlessly, I put the camera back in my purse, slung the bag over my shoulder.

"How are you going to get home?" Wyatt asked. "Let me drive you."

"You've been drinking."

"I'll call you a cab. I'll go with you."

"No," I said, wanting more than anything to go with him into the night, hating myself for wanting him so much, hating myself for resisting.

"I'll get my own cab," I said, a traitor to my own desire. "The date's over."

I left him standing there, still and alone in the dark.

I awoke sore and only mildly regretful the next morning in my nice queen-size bed, under my mod, gray and black comforter with the huge polka dots. The silver-colored metal headboard had crossed bars at its center, simple and clean, traditional meets industrial. I liked that kind of thing, in the way I liked shooting rustic barns and decaying factories. Of course, I'd decorated it with white fairy lights, because I liked anything that sparkled, too.

I lazed in bed, watching the sun dancing on the sheets through the narrow gaps in the Venetian blinds. I heard church bells in the distance and thought of Wyatt.

I closed my eyes, remembering him moving against me, inside me. I shouldn't be thinking of him. I shouldn't. He was probably already on a plane. But I remembered how he filled me, and I reached down under the blankets, pulled up my thin cotton nightgown and touched myself.

I never slept in my underwear. My fingers met flesh that was already moist, and I slid one finger into my slit, remembering how he'd touched me there. I pushed my finger in the way he did, reaching up and inside and rubbing that place, imagining him finger-fucking me, his cock getting harder and harder, him wanting me so much. "Yes, Wyatt," I whispered to his ghost as I felt his fingers inside me, two now, and I moved to my clit, rubbing, wanting more.

I rolled to one of the nightstands, pulled out the vibrator, turned it on, touched it to my nub. I cried out with the intensity of the contact, aroused as I was, and imagined him fucking me. Imagined him watching me fuck myself.

"I'll do anything for you, Wyatt," I moaned as the fantasy took over. He was watching me and I was coming, drowning in my own wet surge of pleasure as I performed for him, came for him.

"*Oh, God.*" It was like an explosion of stars behind my eyes as I bucked upward, touching the vibrator to my pleasure point until my shuddering stopped. I collapsed downward again, turned it off, set it aside and breathed hard, my body utterly relaxed, but my mind still anxious somehow. There was something about him that made me want to do things, wicked things. And I felt that sense of loss again.

I rolled over, lethargic, longing for closure, and went back to sleep.

A couple of hours later, I awoke, feeling more myself. I showered, dressed in jeans and a sweatshirt, and faced my mess.

I walked through the mountains of boxes in the living room to the kitchen to make myself a cup of tea and toast. I had to exert control over my space today; I wanted the studio ready for the electricians and sign painter before I taught my first class at school in the morning.

Downstairs, I found the boom box with the iPod dock and cranked up my favorite dance music. I got to work, bouncing around the room, excavating the ultra-modern blue-green couch and the two white, molded fiberglass chairs that would sit in the center of the space.

I hung framed samples of my work . . .

. . . a diver in mid-leap, a ray of light from a high window in the indoor swimming arena silhouetting her gleaming body.

. . . a bride and groom kissing as they leaned against a creamy 1950 Cadillac on a golden afternoon, the couple dreamy, the bouquet dripping with white pieris and popping with blue cornflowers and pink roses, the car all shiny curves.

. . . two boys and a girl from a nearby ranch, freckled siblings in overalls, sitting on a low stone wall, holding chickens.

That one had been for a newspaper story about raising poultry. I didn't even have to ask the kids to pose, though it took almost an hour to get that shot as they got more comfortable with me and the camera, enough to show me their fluffy birds and grin.

I relived my most satisfying shoots as I put out eight more photos, a wide variety of portraits and scenes, all with a special quality — emotion. Light. Light not just from without, but from within. That's what I strived to capture.

As I sorted through my best images, I realized how few of them had come from the past year. There'd been something stale in my work as my relationship with my boyfriend grew more tepid, as my relationship with my job grew more frustrating. I needed to send my soul on an expedition to seek out that light. I wanted my clients to see it. More urgently, I needed to find it again for myself.

I ordered pizza for dinner. As I waited, I surveyed the room. I was excited. The boxes were gone, and it looked open and inviting. A white, curved desk sat in one corner, a place to put my brochures and portfolio. Once I had the gallery lighting in place, this would make a great reception area.

I texted Sloane to confirm that she could hang out with the workers who would be there in the morning while I taught class, and then, exhausted, I gave myself the night off.

I took the pizza upstairs, cleared boxes off the comfy black couch and coffee table, and turned on the TV. I drank Pepsi and ate the pizza — pepperoni and mushroom, a classic — as I flipped through channels: detective shows, family dramas, comedy, supernatural mysteries, football playoffs. I skipped through the sports channels, then stopped and went back when a big blue wave caught my eye.

The show recapped a big-wave competition at Mavericks last year. The surfers zipped across impossibly huge waves off Half Moon Bay in California, sliding down a mountain of water as it collapsed behind them. Countless boats and watercraft floated in the foreground, safe from the pounding monsters spawned by the Pacific. I found myself searching for someone I knew — Ron Raker. Or Wyatt. Finally I saw them in a sequence of shots from surfboard-mounted cameras.

Raker was controlled, powerful, at first perilously close to the lip, then shadowed by the beautiful wave as it curled overhead and he glided through it. It was obvious he'd found the sweet spot as he shot out of it safely, as naturally as breathing.

Wyatt looked tense as he surfed, coiled like a spring. He made it look anything but easy, but it seemed like he had a good ride, at least before the curl crashed over him. I sucked in an anxious breath as the whitewater battered him, dragged him down.

The scene cut to a close-up of him on a boat, shivering slightly even in his wetsuit. His hair, lanky and damp, almost covered one eye.

"That was the worst beating of my life," he told the interviewer who asked about his wipeout. Wyatt was favoring one arm, bandaged where he'd been slashed by the fin of his own board.

"You going back out there?" the interviewer asked.

Wyatt looked at him as if he was crazy. "Always," he said.

Wyatt didn't make the finals. Ron did, but I switched the channel in the middle of the interview with him. I didn't want to think about the surfers anymore, but I couldn't push them out of my mind, especially Wyatt. That single-minded guy on TV didn't seem like the Wyatt I'd met.

Ignoring the old movie flickering on the screen, I grabbed my purse off the hearth and retrieved my camera. I turned it on and flipped through the last couple of photos. The shot Wyatt took of me was moody, grainy, the weak light catching a glimmer in my eye, a glow on my cheek. I looked as if, I thought with irony, I'd just been fucked.

I couldn't resist moving forward to the photo of Wyatt, the length of his sinewy, neatly clothed body reflected in the tall glass window as he leaned against it, arms crossed, looking at me intently. I felt a rush of heat just from that image, that echo of him.

Emotion and light.

Oh, hell. I had it bad.

Wipeout, dude, I scolded myself. *Get over it.*

I GOT up early to go over the syllabus I'd been working on over the past week. Sessions at the art school weren't as long as college classes, and no grades were given. Still, I wanted to give the students their money's worth. Then I got ready, dressing in khakis and a light blue blouse over a white tank top. It was dressy enough, at least until I confirmed what I suspected, that teachers wore jeans as often as the students did. I pinned up my hair and put on a pair of new, sky-blue high-tops. I had every confidence in my choice of sneakers.

I tucked my laptop into a backpack that would also hold a camera and a few lenses, enough to get me through my first day, and took it downstairs to await my visitors. I expected the sign painter at 8:30, and there she was, at 8:15, hanging outside the door next to a big, rolling toolbox and drinking coffee out of a paper cup.

"Hey," I greeted her. "You should have called me. I would've let you in."

"I haven't been here long," she replied cheerfully. "Just enjoying the day. I'm Thea."

She was tall, taller than I was, and what my mother might have called big-boned. Her long red hair was woven into a French braid with enough escaped strands to give her a halo in the morning light, and she looked comfortable in jeans, sneakers and a paint-stained white T-shirt. Her eyes were a darker blue than my own, striking against her pale, lightly freckled skin. She reached out her free hand, and I shook it.

"Calista," I said. "You're one of those morning people, aren't you?"

"Afraid so." She smiled and rolled her box inside. "So where do you want it?"

"Let me show you." The space was gloomy, the brown paper still on the windows. I began to tear it off, and she helped. In a few minutes, the room was filled with morning light, and the old wooden floor and white walls shone.

"This is nice," Thea said, looking around.

"Thanks. I'm working on it." I pointed toward the second of the four big windows. "I'd like it there. 'Calista Goode Photography,' like we talked about, in all caps, not too big."

"And you wanted a nice, open, san-serif font, right? This one?" She pulled a printout from her box and held it out for me to see.

"Exactly. That's beautiful. Very modern. That's what I want."

"I was thinking of using silver for the lettering with a thin, light-blue outline. I noticed you have a lot of blue on your website. It's a good branding thing to carry through."

"Sounds great. I love that you think about that!" I said.

"I love that you want a sign *painted,* not a decal. It feels more permanent, more like art that way. Though we do decals, too." Thea started arranging her tools and brushes on the floor by the window. "The sign painting is something I do mostly because my dad owns Bohemia's last old-school sign-painting business, but I'm also an artist and a graphic designer. So I tend to think about overall impressions, not just getting the lines straight."

"Did you grow up here?" I'd never seen her around before.

"I lived with my mom growing up. Not here. I just moved here a few months ago, actually."

"Cool," I said. "We'll have to hang out sometime."

"You might want to wait to see if I misspell your name or something," Thea joked, and I laughed.

The front door pushed open again, and two guys in work clothes came in: the electricians, also toting toolboxes.

"You got a ladder?" asked the leader, a guy in his forties who seemed twice as awake as his colleague. "Ours got run over on I-95."

I told them where to find mine and went over what I'd requested on the phone: track lighting in the front room and a ton of extra outlets and overhead lighting in the studio. They seemed knowledgeable enough. One headed to the back to start work, and the other went to their vehicle for the lights I'd ordered, passing Sloane in the doorway.

"My, you're busy," my cousin said as she came in with a big purse and her own cup of coffee. She looked cute in a short burgundy dress, tights and flats, her red-highlighted brown hair hanging loose — but then again, she always looked cute. And these days, happy, now that she was with Alex.

"Thank you so much for doing this," I said, giving her a hug. "You sure I'm not keeping you from anything?"

"I have classes on Tuesdays and Wednesdays this session,

so I'm good," Sloane said. "I'll get my hands into some clay this afternoon, once you get back. Are you nervous?"

"A little," I confessed. "But I've got this."

"Of course you do," Sloane said. "And how'd your date with Ron Raker go?"

"Oh, shit, you heard about that, too?"

"Ron Raker?" Thea called from where she was sitting on the floor, going through her paints. "You had a date with Ron Raker?"

"I — won it, I guess you could say. It wasn't awful."

"A ringing endorsement," Sloane said. "And what about his friend?"

I almost regretted mentioning my interest in Wyatt to Sloane. I'd done so before Saturday night had made my entanglement with him so — personal.

"What does it matter?" I answered brightly. "It's not like I'll ever see him again."

The other women nodded knowingly, and I felt my cheeks turn pink.

I picked up my bag. "I'll see you this afternoon," I said, just as there was a loud crash from the back.

"It was just the ladder!" a voice called from the studio.

I grimaced. "Call me if the walls start falling down."

"Just as long as they don't break my window," Thea said with a smile.

"Leave it to me," Sloane said, a twinkle in her blue-green eyes. "Go get 'em."

MY CLASS HAD twelve people it, though there was room for fifteen. That's how many computers were in the room. While

I would lead them through advanced digital darkroom work, I planned to have them spend a lot more time in the field, as well as in the school's photo studios.

Maybe half of the students were in their twenties, the rest older. I had them tell me why they'd signed up for the class. Some were just looking for ways to stretch their talents, but several wanted to hang up a shingle as a professional photographer. The sheer numbers of photographers in the digital age almost made me want to go into landscaping or something. But at least they seemed enthusiastic.

I turned off the lights and went through a leisurely computer slide show of what I considered exemplary portrait photography, from the flashy popular stuff of Annie Leibovitz to the evocative black-and-whites of Eve Arnold, just to get their minds working. Then I turned up the lights and went over the lesson plan briefly.

"Take a few minutes now and find a partner," I told the class. "You'll be taking photos of each other and will help each other out on shoots as needed, though of course we'll have you taking photos of other people, too."

When they'd found their partners — many just connected with the person sitting next to them — I continued with an overview of the final project. I turned out the lights and moved to my next sequence of examples.

"Though your assignments will vary throughout the session, your work will culminate in a series of portraits of one person." The door to the lab opened, letting in a sliver of light and one more student, who sat in the darkness in the back.

"I see we have a latecomer," I said. "You haven't missed much, but pick up a syllabus before you leave. And since you're the odd number and don't have a partner, you'll have to put up with me." The students chuckled. "As I was saying, you'll be building up to a final project: a series of portraits of one person. I want you to find creative ways to express your subject's personality. Of course, that means you'll need a willing subject, especially if you want to get them naked," I joked, to nervous laughter. "Just kidding. While nudity isn't forbidden, I'll be just as happy to see your subjects in clothes. Though I will suggest, for one assignment, that you do a portrait of a nude, even if he or she is tastefully covered." There were more titters.

"One really cool thing to look forward to," I continued, "is that we'll have an exhibit in the school at the end of the session to show off your best work from the next several weeks." A murmur of excitement filled the room. "So make sure your subjects know that, too. We don't want any surprises. You're going to give them releases to sign, just to be sure.

"More than anything, I want you to tap your creativity. Take risks. You don't get a grade here. I check a box that says you passed so you can get a certificate if you're doing the full sequence, but this isn't like high school."

"Thank God," one of the guys in front said, to laughter.

"Not with nude photos, that's for sure," added a woman in her forties with short reddish hair and a wise grin.

"Any questions?" I asked, amused.

"Can we take portraits of someone related to us?" came a soft voice from the front, a young woman who'd said she was still figuring out her career while she worked as a waitress and a library clerk.

"You may, but not for every assignment. In some cases, you'll photograph your partner. But I want you all to go through what I had to go through as a newspaper photographer: meeting a stranger, bonding with them quickly, learning enough about them to capture their essence. You'll be hearing more about that in a future class. Anyone else?"

Silence.

"That's OK. You have my email on the syllabus, and I'll see you Wednesday morning. Before then, I want you to put together ten of your favorite photos of people on a flash drive. That's photos you took, just to be clear, in JPEG format. I realize you may not have attempted portraits before, but you may be surprised at just what you've captured. We're going to talk about what makes a portrait good. OK? And make sure you bring your camera and any lenses you might think you'll need to every class, because you're not always going to be sitting in the dark and looking at slides. Got it?" There was another rumble as they gathered their stuff together. "See you next time!" I said, and they started getting up and filing out of the room, its darkness relieved only slightly by the open door.

The girl who'd asked about taking photos of her family came up to me. Millie had a short, dark bob and a cute, round face — a wholesome Betty Boop.

"I really only have one lens," she said to me. "A fifty millimeter. Will that work?"

"If you had only one for portraits, that's not a bad one to start with," I said. "The school also has a few you might be able to sign out for particular assignments. Why don't we take it on a case-by-case basis?"

"OK," she said. "I was worried this would be really technical."

"Do you know your way around an F-stop and shutter?"

"Yes, I got that in the basic photography class."

"Then we'll have no problems. Remember, Millie, I don't grade you — I just pass you. So have some fun, OK?"

I could see her smile in the dimness.

"OK," she said, sounding relieved as she hoisted her bag and headed out the door.

I started to relax. I'd made it through my first class. But there was still someone sitting in the back.

"Did you need something?" I asked, moving toward the door. I turned on the lights.

And there, in the back row, was Wyatt.

WHAT? The? *Fuck?*

I tried to shut down the chaos that had erupted in my brain, in my hormones. He was so out of context.

"Hi, Cali," he said, not moving. He looked good, but didn't he always? He wore loose khakis, the big leather sandals and a dark blue hoodie with a white T-shirt peeking through at the neckline. His hair was sticking up, that blond streak impertinent in the dark, thick mop. I damned his unruly hair as my fingers remembered the luxuriant feel of it.

"You are *not* in my class," I said. It was part statement, part question.

"I just enrolled today." I heard the caution in his voice, as if he didn't want to upset me.

"You — because — why aren't you in New Zealand?" I finally asked, flabbergasted, as I sat like a stone on one of the desks in the front row and stared at him.

"I was never going to New Zealand. I told you I was going to quit being Ron's right-hand man."

"You didn't give me the impression you were doing it so soon," I said, my tone cold. "And that you'd end up here."

I don't know why I was mad. Or maybe I did. I'd done a lot of things that I might not have, if I'd known I'd be seeing him again. And in my class, for God's sake.

But a little part of me was dancing, elbowing me in the ribs, saying: *Hey, girl! Jump on that!*

I told her to shut up.

"I was definitely not going to New Zealand," he repeated. "I was definitely going to quit. I'd been considering the school for a while. And once I got to see this place — to spend a little time here — " His voice faltered, and his intense gaze flickered. "I decided to go for it. I'm a photographer, as you might have figured out, but I need to refine some of my skills to do it full time. I want to specialize in surfing and also surfer portraits. Do photography as a business."

"You and half the class," I said, in full sarcastic mode now. "Why didn't you go back to California?"

"I'll never live there again," Wyatt said. His sharp tone took me by surprise. "I want to be honest with you, Cali."

"You can start anytime."

He frowned, and I knew I'd hit a nerve. "I probably would have signed up for the school anyway. And this class. But the fact that I met you — I am sure that it influenced me. You *are* one of the reasons I'm here."

That was nice to hear. But his declaration also incited that panic he seemed to generate in me.

"And did it cross your mind that this might be just the teeniest bit awkward?" I asked, pointing out the elephant in the room. *Awkward, as in me bent over a desk . . .*

"It did," he nodded, looking down, relieving me for a

moment from his penetrating stare, distracting me from my wayward fantasy. "But we can keep it professional."

"Can we?" I asked, and I knew I was asking myself, too.

"Or," he said, looking up again, the chocolate-diamond sparkle back in his eyes, "we could not worry about it so much. You did point out that this isn't high school."

"You mean, just go 'Hot for Teacher' and date?" I asked sarcastically.

He smiled. "Yes, sure. Date. We could get to know each other."

As if he didn't already know parts of me extremely well.

"What you are suggesting would not exactly be encouraged by my bosses," I said.

"You don't have to grade me. You said it yourself. We're both adults. And you could ignore me in class, keep your distance. I could hire you as my — private tutor."

I could tell he was barely suppressing a grin. I didn't find the idea all that funny.

"And then you'd be back on the road," I said, "to New Zealand or Hawaii or South Africa or wherever the next big wave is."

"If I got a gig to shoot a tournament or something, of course I'd go. I already have some clients who've promised me work. I've decided not to surf competitively anymore, but I might still travel for good surf, too. I've been nomadic for years. I'm always moving. That's who I am."

"So why would I invest my precious time in you?"

Now he let the grin shine through. "Because you want to."

I closed my eyes to think. He was tempting me with hot chemical attraction, wrapped up in so-called dates. Or photography lessons. We could get to know each other, he said. But what was the point? He'd be gone, probably right when I thought I couldn't live without him.

If I did want to see how our connection played out — and it would play out, he'd all but guaranteed — his logic wasn't entirely off. It would take a lot to fail this class. I was going to pass anyone who put in a reasonable amount of effort. Nobody had to sleep with the teacher, or bring her an apple, to get by. This wasn't high school. This wasn't even college; the Bohemia School of Art and Design didn't award degrees, only select certificates. And a teacher in, shall we say, a special relationship with any student might be pushing the boundaries, but as long as it didn't spill over into class . . .

Oh, hell, what am I thinking? This is impossible.

I looked up, my anguish interrupted by Wyatt's movement. He was up and walking around the row of desks. On the way past the door, he pushed it shut and flipped off the lights. Only the square of the projector's image on the screen — a mirror of my laptop, with its luscious background photo, a macro of a dark red hibiscus — cast a dim glow over us. And then he was next to me, holding my hand, touching my face, running his fingers over my cheeks, his thumb across my bottom lip. My breathing sped up with my heartbeat. He looked into my eyes.

"I'll back out if you want me to," Wyatt whispered. "But Cali—" he lifted my chin — "don't say no."

And then his mouth was on mine, a thrilling shock of heat as he consumed me. His tongue moved lazily between my lips, claiming me the way he had before, but now with more history, more promise. *I'm here,* the kiss seemed to say, *and I'm not going anywhere.*

But his kiss was a liar. I knew what it was really saying: *I'm not going anywhere yet.* Because he would go, and soon. And instead of a one-night stand, I'd be spending real time with him, opening myself to something really dangerous: a broken heart.

My body didn't give a damn. I opened to the kiss even as I kept my fists clenched at my sides, letting him speak to me through his mouth, first sweet, then strong, powerful, undeniable.

Finally, I lifted a hand and pressed against his chest, pushing him away.

"Yes," I said hoarsely. "Yes. Stay in my class. But we can't do this again."

"Don't say that."

"Not in school, I mean," I said weakly, and I could see him smile in the faintly red light.

"You'll be my tutor?"

"I suppose that's one word for it," I said, and he laughed. "But, seriously, I barely know you, Wyatt. Let's get to know each other, and I'll teach you what I know about photography. And we'll see how it goes."

"That sounds reasonable," Wyatt said, brushing a strand of hair from my face. "But around you, I lose all sense of reason."

I nodded, looking into his eyes, knowing he did the same thing to me. That's why I couldn't let him get under my skin, because when he decided to leave, my mind would go, too.

Was I a horrible, unethical person or a grown-up for even entertaining the idea of being with him? He was my age. This wasn't grade school. And since we'd agreed to keep whatever this was out of class, I decided I could live with it. I recognized that we'd set a boundary, even if it was a thin, delicate, gray one.

Ethical questions aside, I worried I might be setting

myself up for the biggest misery of my life. I knew I was high on him, and I needed to come down, sober up. But when I looked into his eyes, it was like taking a shot of tequila. *Wyatt was back. Oh, God.*

"OK, teacher," he asked slyly, "when's my first lesson?"

I ENTERED my gallery-in-progress with only a dim memory of the walk from the school. I'd spent another hour surveying the facilities there so I'd know exactly what was available to my class. Besides, hiding in the school's photo studio was a great way to avoid Wyatt.

My eyes refocused on my space. It was brighter, for one thing. New track lighting cast the photos on the walls in pleasing swaths of light that brought out their color and detail.

"Hi, Cali. How'd it go?" asked Thea, who was packing up her paints. "And how do you like your sign?"

"Oh, hi. Um, let me take another look." The truth was, I'd been so distracted, I'd walked right past it. A sign announcing my first photo studio, and I'd ignored it because I was thinking of Wyatt. *Ridiculous.*

I stepped back outside and wondered how I could have missed it. The sleek silver lettering on the window, with its thin blue outlines, shone softly in the midday light: CALISTA GOODE PHOTOGRAPHY. I was legit. Or I would be, once I had my first customer.

I reentered with a grin. "That looks fabulous. Sorry I didn't really take it in, earlier. I have a lot on my mind."

"I was worried there for a second," Thea said, returning my smile. "It's never good if someone can't see your sign."

"I was in blond mode," I joked. "Are the workers still here? Where's Sloane?"

"Studio," Thea said, nodding her head toward the back.

"OK, thanks. You take cards, right?"

"Sure," Thea said, pulling her iPad Mini from her box. She plugged a tiny device into it. I handed her my credit card, and she typed in the amount and swiped the Visa through the gadget. Then she held the tablet out for me to sign, along with a stylus.

"Pretty slick," I said. "I ordered one of those, too."

"Pretty soon we'll just pay by flashing our retinas at each other."

I laughed. I liked her dry sense of humor. "I'm thinking of getting some friends together at the end of the week. You interested in joining us?"

"That would be great," Thea said as she grabbed the handle of her box and smoothed the wiry red hairs escaping from her braid. "I don't know many folks in town, and I think I'm getting on my dad's nerves."

"You're staying with him?"

"Just till I get my own place. Maybe you can give me some advice."

"I'm kind of an expert on moving right now," I said.

"I figured. See you soon!"

As soon as she was gone, I hauled my bag through the closed double doors that led to the studio and stopped short.

The room had miraculously cleaned itself. No, not miraculously; Sloane was breaking down the boxes she'd unpacked, and my gear was laid out, perfectly organized. Meanwhile, the electricians were packing up their own stuff, and above my main photography space, a new array of LED light panels promised fun shooting ahead. My rolls of back-drop papers were already set up against the back wall.

"Cali!" Sloane said, looking flushed as she set a folded box down on the pile. "I didn't set up everything because there were way too many pieces. It's like some kind of horrible jigsaw puzzle."

"I know. The worst thing about photography is all the gear. You didn't have to do this." I walked over and gave her a long hug.

"Is something wrong?" she asked quietly when I released her.

I shook my head, glancing over at the two electricians. One of them was trying to catch my eye. He had a bill in his hand.

I settled it, bade them farewell and came back to where Sloane was now sitting in one of the two big, mid-century-style black leather chairs I'd bought for the space. I also had a weathered, antique wing chair with Queen Anne legs, uphol-stered in a rich, red damask fabric, a thrift store find I thought might look really nice in certain portraits.

I plopped down in the black chair catty-corner to Sloane's and leaned my head against the low, soft back.

"What is it?" Sloane asked. "Did something go wrong in class?"

"I think the class is going to be awesome," I said, looking up at her. "It's just that I have an unexpected student. My favorite surfer boy."

"No kidding." Her eyes widened. "Wyatt, right? I thought he was heading to another hemisphere."

"So did I."

"But this is good, right? I mean, you really like him."

Sloane smiled, kicking off her flats and tucking her legs underneath her, looking cozy in her burgundy tights.

"I really lust after him. And I have a — I guess you'd call it a good feeling about him. But I don't know if I really *like* him."

"Now that's an interesting thought," Sloane said. "Can't it be both?"

"We haven't really had the time to find out. At least not about the liking part."

She pursed her lips. "How much did you, uh, find out about him before you thought he left town?"

"Oh, I think you could say we shared intimate knowledge."

"Really?" Sloane grinned. "Why didn't you mention this before?"

"Maybe I was embarrassed at my complete lack of self-control."

"It's not like you're the only one who's ever lost control," she said, and I thought back to a conversation I'd had with her when she started seeing Alex.

"But I've never lost control like *that*," I answered. *And it freaked me out,* I wanted to add. "With every guy I've dated, it's been conventional. We go out a few times. We see how it goes. If it's pleasant, we keep going. He becomes my boyfriend, with all the rights that entails." I saw Sloane trying not to laugh. "And then, at some point, he usually breaks it off."

"Why him and not you?"

"They always just do. Just when I'm feeling really relaxed and comfortable."

"Maybe it's not supposed to be that comfortable," Sloane said.

"I thought that was the ideal."

"I used to think so, too," she said. "Now I think it should be comfortable but it also should be challenging. I think he should want the best for you and challenge you to be your best."

"Laziness has worked for me so far."

She chuckled. "Except for all the breakups."

"Maybe we're not meant to be with one person forever."

Sloane shrugged, but her coy smile told me she didn't agree. "I'm moving in with Alex."

"You what?"

"I'm over there all the time anyway. By the end of the month, I'll be living in the condo."

"What about your apartment? I mean, the carriage house?"

"I'm going to use it as a pottery studio."

"Cool," I said, but my head was spinning at the news. "I think you're way more advanced than I am at this relationship thing."

"Hardly," Sloane said. "I just got really lucky."

"I believe in making my own luck. If only I knew how."

"So what's the plan with Wyatt?" she asked.

"We keep our distance in class, and we get to know each other outside of class. And I've agreed to teach him what he doesn't know about photography. Though I'm beginning to suspect he knows more than he lets on."

"Hot for teacher," Sloane joked.

I groaned at the same words I'd used earlier. "It's not like that."

"Sure it isn't." She laughed. "So when do you see him again?"

I grimaced. "Tonight."

"You don't sound too happy about it."

"He's going to leave town sooner rather than later," I said. "I don't want to get invested."

"I'm not terribly experienced in these things," Sloane said, "but I suggest you just ride the wave and see where it takes you. Maybe it's about the ride and not about where you wash up on the beach."

"Oh, shut up," I said good-naturedly, but I felt a little better about seeing Wyatt, about what might happen between us. "Now I'm taking you to lunch because you're so awesome."

She beamed. "I can live with that. Can we go to Picasso's? I'm dying for a BLT."

THE NEW BELL on the front door jingled at 6 p.m. Or maybe I should say the old bell — it was the Victorian type that attached to the door and rang pleasantly whenever someone entered. I'd found it in a drawer of an old wooden desk the previous tenants had abandoned, in the office in the back of the building. I had a feeling the desk had weathered several tenants, given its scars and heft. No one had moved it in a long time.

I'd worked most of the afternoon, and even the office was somewhat organized. I rewarded myself with three Oreos and a glass of milk, in my still-messy apartment. And then I got ready for my first photo lesson with Wyatt.

I took a shower to wash away the dust of unpacking and dressed casually, in jeans and a black, boat-neck knit shirt with three-quarter sleeves. I added light blue socks, black leather flats and my camera charm earrings and twisted my hair up in a big clip. I was the opposite of flashy, and I was ready for a non-date. I felt I needed to put up a few barriers, even if they consisted of sensible clothes. Maybe it was too late to be sensible, but I wanted to try, to undo my impulsive behavior and find my footing.

Though I did put on a bit of lip gloss. Because I could not be a hundred percent sensible, knowing Wyatt was coming over.

I was in the studio fiddling with lights when the door jingled.

I walked out through the double doors and met him in my lobby, the gallery space, which now looked modern and clean and even better with Wyatt in it. He carried a black camera bag and wore jeans and a black sweater, one thin enough to show off his nicely sculpted form beneath it. We could have been twins, in our jeans and black shirts, and I think we realized it at the same time, looking at ourselves and each other with bashful smiles.

"You look good, Cali," Wyatt said.

"Nice color scheme," I said, gesturing to encompass his outfit.

"Great minds and all that. Hey, are you holding me prisoner?"

I finished locking the front door. "Just keeping out the riff-raff. The studio is closed, except for you."

"I think you may find you've let the riff-raff in." He grinned.

I quirked my mouth at him, determined not to respond to his flirting but charmed by it anyway. He had an appealing confidence I couldn't deny.

"Oh, wait a sec," he said, reaching into his pocket and pulling out a slip of paper. He handed it to me. A check.

"What's this for?"

"These are lessons. I'm serious about learning, and I want to make it worth your while."

"We never talked about price — "

"It was on your website. You'd put lessons on your price list. I multiplied it by the number of weeks the school session lasts — assuming a couple of lessons a week — though of course I wouldn't say no to more." His eyes twinkled.

"I — thank you." I didn't know what else to say. This fee would cover a month's rent, though I found it hard to delight in getting the work when I knew there was more going on between us than just photography.

I dropped the check into a drawer of the lobby desk and gave him what I hoped was a unruffled smile. "Why don't you come on back, and we'll get started."

I walked ahead of him and pushed open the double doors that led to the back. They fell shut behind him, and he looked around appreciatively. I'd finished the work Sloane had started, and my studio looked not just functional, but open and inviting. The black backdrop was in place, and the LED lights were on, casting a pool of light in the shooting area centered in the back of the room. The only two windows had long since been blocked by boards and painted over, creating the perfect indoor photography space, where I could completely control the lighting. I loved natural light, but playing with artificial light was almost like painting to me. I could brush a subject with the perfect amount of glow and shadow. And Wyatt would be an incredible model. Shadows would worship the devastating angles of his face, the sparkle in his eyes.

"Cali?"

He'd set down his bag and was looking at me curiously, a smile playing around his lips.

"Right," I said, trying to pretend I wasn't completely distracted by that winsome face. "We're going to work on lighting tonight. I figure you have the sunlight thing down, since you shoot surfers. Right?"

"For the most part. It's a matter of me thinking less about the action and more about the composition. But I definitely want to learn about artificial light. I expect to do more portraits for the magazines and websites I'm getting work from."

I drank in his words. He spoke my language. He was a *photographer,* like me. We could be so great together. I needed him the way a flower needs a bee. But he would be buzzing away almost as fast.

Best to get to business.

I showed him my gear. I started with the LED light panels on stands and hanging from the ceiling that provided static light. Then I pointed out the slaves, the strobes that would fire when triggered by the device on my camera, which I'd set up on a tripod. I talked about umbrellas, soft boxes and reflectors. And he followed me around, nodding, close to me, reaching up to touch the same switches I was, practically breathing down my neck. He smelled good, not quite hotel soap this time, I thought, but something enticing and fresh. I thought it was his hair. I wanted to touch it.

Oh, yeah. Hair. "A backlight can define a subject's hair, giving him, or her, that nice glow and separating him from the background," I said, showing Wyatt the now-dark spotlight I'd set up behind the Queen Anne wing chair in the middle of the shooting space. "You can also light a subject completely from behind, perhaps filling with reflectors; the backlighting can bring out body shape, which is nice when you're shooting nudes."

"Is that so?" His dark eyebrows slanted with interest.

"Not that we'd be doing that," I added awkwardly.

"You said in class that we'd be expected to attempt a nude," he said. "And you *are* my lab partner." He was grinning again.

"I didn't mean people should shoot their lab partners nude! And especially not when you're my student."

I imagined his body haloed by the lights and snapped the photo in my mind anyway.

"If you say so," he said. "But I suppose I should shoot something, right?"

"Let's try the halo light and the front lighting with the soft boxes. We'll skip the strobes for now," I said. "It's a little tricky getting the backlight in the right place. You can sit in the chair."

"Oh, I don't think so." Wyatt moved toward his camera bag and pulled out his DSLR. He removed mine from the tripod and clicked in his own. "It's my lesson, and I want to do the shooting."

PART 2

I stood there next to the spotlight and realized I'd lost control of the situation. Mentally, I shrugged. It only made sense to have him do the shooting. I flipped on the spotlight and sat in the chair, looking him over as he checked the settings. He stood in front of me, lit by the glow of the spot and the side lights, impossibly attractive. I was in trouble. I knew it. And deep inside, I wanted to be in trouble. That pulse was still there between us, just as it had been when I first met him on the balcony on New Year's Eve.

Ride the wave, Cali.

"I suggest manual focus so you don't accidentally get the background," I said. "And make sure the spotlight looks good. You just want a glow, not the light itself."

"Got it." He was already striding toward the backdrop. He shifted the height and angle of the spotlight. I could feel its faint warmth behind me; it was one of the last old-school hot lights I had. Or maybe it wasn't the light I felt.

Wyatt brushed past me on the way back to the camera, and my arm tingled with the contact. *Tease.*

Fine. Two could play that game.

"Where do you want me?" I asked, my tone softer, more suggestive.

His eyebrows shot up, and then he schooled his expression. "Just chill in the chair and let me get a couple to see how the lighting looks. And then I'll tell you where I want you."

I'll tell you where I want you. The subtle change in his inflection told me much. A flash of our moment in the ballroom came back to me, the feel of my breasts against the glass, of him taking me in the semidarkness. I hoped the burn in my cheeks wasn't too obvious under the LEDs.

He snapped a couple of photos and pressed the button to review them, looking at them quizzically. "I'm not sure I have this right."

I bounded up from the chair and moved to look over his shoulder. The lighting was a little off-balance, with too much in the front. I suggested a faster shutter speed and reducing the intensity of the light panels. He made the adjustments, then pointed at the chair with humorous authority.

I smiled, my first real smile. We were playing. And it was fun.

I sat in the chair again, only this time I kicked off my shoes and crossed one leg over another.

Wyatt snapped another photo and looked closely at the preview.

"Better?" I asked.

"Yes, but something's not quite right." He walked toward me, and I thought he was going to adjust the spotlight again. Instead, he pulled the clip out of my hair, much as he'd done that night at Trifles. He tossed it aside. My breath sped up as he ran his hands through my long locks, fluffing them around my shoulders. "That's better," he said.

He moved back to the camera and took another couple of shots.

"Much better," he said, his gaze shifting from the camera preview to me. "You look like an angel."

"Bah," I said, but my skin prickled with the compliment, and I couldn't control my smile.

"Sit sideways in the chair, with your legs over one arm," he suggested.

Wordlessly, I moved as he asked, bracing myself with one arm against the back of the chair and looking at him.

He shot a few more shots.

"Don't look at me. Lean back, if you can. Stay sideways, but let your head fall back."

It was fun being the model for once. I didn't have to think. One of my friends who was into swing dancing once told me the best partners never made you think; they were leads in the true sense, never letting a girl worry about the next move. It was like dancing on a cloud, in the arms of a perfect guide. The rest of life was full of having to strategize and plan, but as the "follow" in an ideal dance — and now, as the model — I could just go with the flow.

I leaned back as he'd asked, and I shifted so the position was tolerable. "Like this?"

"Wait." Wyatt walked up to me and regarded me at close range. I breathed in his scent and closed my eyes. Then I felt his hands running through my hair again, shaking out the tresses so they flowed free.

He took my left hand and lifted it so my arm pointed up, the palm flat against the back of the chair. The other arm he extended so my fingers were pointed toward the floor. And then, just for good measure, he ran his hands slowly down my legs, as if he were smoothing the jeans, and gave my feet a squeeze through the socks. That didn't do anything at all for his picture, I knew, but it lit a low fire in my belly. I felt him move away.

"Just like that, with your eyes closed," he said, his tone persuasive and hypnotic, and I heard the shutter go off a few times. Then the sound changed. He was moving, off the tripod, the shutter clicking.

"That's going to change your lighting," I said.

"Hush," he whispered, and I felt him moving closer, the camera talking in a voice I knew so well. The moment was creating itself. It happened sometimes in photography. I wondered if he felt it the way I sometimes did, or if he was just playing.

The clicking stopped, and I spoke. "Are you — "

Before I could finish the sentence, Wyatt pressed his warm lips upon mine. He moved in a sweet rhythm, echoing the clicking of the camera moments before, only more slowly, at a languorous shutter speed that blurred my senses. I opened my mouth under his, letting his tongue in, and then I felt one hand in my hair, the other working its way up under my shirt to my cotton bra, pinching one nipple through the fabric. I moaned at the brief pain and the rush of pleasure and moved to embrace him.

"No," he whispered. "Stay still. You are my sleeping princess, and I've come to wake you up."

Oh. I was awake, all right. He kissed me again, on my mouth, my cheek, my neck, tonguing the lobe of my ear. I felt him working to pull up my shirt. "You're asleep," he whispered. "Limp as a doll. You're not awake yet. You let me do this, because you are having a sweet, irresistible dream."

His words were even more seductive than his kisses, and I relaxed, letting him lift me slightly to pull the shirt over my head. He gently unclasped my bra; I heard it drop lightly to the floor. And then I felt his mouth at my breasts, a delicate touch at first, brushing each nipple with feather-light kisses. I was afraid to move, afraid he might stop, as he closed his mouth over one nipple and suckled there, teasing me with his tongue. He rolled the other between his fingers, stretching it, and I moaned again, feeling wet desire between my legs.

"And now, you wake up," he murmured, "and I hope you like what you see."

I opened my eyes and lifted my head. He leaned over me, one hand grasping the back of the chair, his eyes glittering in the lights, persuasive in his desire. He'd doffed his shirt, revealing his surfer's physique, broad shoulders, muscled arms and chest, narrow waist. The lights brought out every beautiful mound and valley.

Wyatt brushed a hair away from my face. "Yes?" he asked.

"Yes." *God, yes.* It was the first time I'd really seen him, his glowing skin, in the light.

"I want to photograph you," he said.

"Not now. Not like this."

"Please."

"No," I said, not ready for the camera. I knew from experience how personal a photo could be, clothes or not.

"Then let me have you," he whispered.

As if, at this point, he had to ask.

He leaned in to embrace me, kiss me again. Feeling his warm skin against mine, I sat up, wrapping my arms around him, my hunger his answer. He reached down and unfastened my jeans, pulling them off with my socks, and then pulled off my underwear. I felt so vulnerable, raw, naked under the lights in the quiet studio.

Wyatt sucked in a breath as he paused and took me in.

"Cali, my angel," he said. "So pale. So pretty."

I didn't trust myself to speak. I reached out to unfasten his jeans. He helped me pull them down; they were tossed aside with his sandals, and he was hard and naked before me. I wanted to side-light that taut body, bring out every muscle. But not now. I gestured him closer, then ran my hands up his chest, standing, grasping his shoulders, twisting him, pushing him back so he sat in the chair. The spotlight cast his unruly hair in fiery relief; his eyes, burning like coals, were almost in shadow in comparison. We were stars of an exotic drama, both of us bathed in light in the dark room, as if we were on stage. I was playing a role, a reckless role that felt more real than any staid relationship I'd ever had.

I knelt before him and touched the tip of his cock with my tongue.

"Cali," he said hoarsely, leaning back, clutching the arms of the chair hard. I looked up at him, meeting his enraptured gaze as I took his cock into my mouth, slowly at first, rimming the head with my tongue. He released an animalistic sound as I worked my tongue around the ridge. I clasped the base of his shaft with one hand and guided him up and down to meet my lips, feeling him pushing against me, hearing his sounds of pleasure as my long hair gently brushed his skin. The velvety, thick feel of him filled my mouth. His groans turned me on as much as his kisses, knowing I could drive him to this state of abandon. I could feel the slickness between my legs as I sucked harder, tasting the first salty dewdrops of his pleasure.

"Wait," he muttered, gently pushing me back. He lifted me and sat me in the chair, running a finger over my lips. I knew they must be swollen and wantonly red, and he leaned in and kissed me deeply, thrusting his tongue where his cock had just been. He released me, reached for his jeans on the floor and pulled out a foil square. He ripped it open and rolled the condom on his engorged erection. I shivered with anticipation, leaning back.

Wyatt reached under my behind and pulled me forward, to the seat's edge, then reached under my knees and lifted my legs, spreading them wide, so they were draped over the arms of the chair. He stood over me, watching me hungrily, holding his thick cock in one hand, and a wicked smile crossed his lips.

"You would be a beautiful picture right now," he said, "my devilish angel."

I felt so exposed like this, my sex wide open for his viewing pleasure. I felt naughty. I felt free. I'd never done anything like this with anyone, never revealed myself in quite this way, hot under the lights, at the center of what felt like a dirty movie, my yearning on display for a man. He reached out and touched my clit, gently rubbing until I was almost mad with desire.

"Wyatt," I hissed, throwing my head back, gripping the chair's arms as he brought me to the edge.

"Yes?" His tone was mischievous. I had no idea how he was restraining himself. I was ready to explode. "What?"

"You know what," I gasped.

"Say it."

"Fuck me," I begged. "Fuck me now."

"I was only waiting for you to ask, my princess," he said, and he pressed his tip against my wet folds for just a moment, teasing me. Then he thrust into me. I fell back in the chair, my legs still spread wide as he pushed in and out.

"Oh, God," I moaned. I'd never been screwed this deeply by any of my string of boyfriends. In comparison, they'd seriously lacked enthusiasm. And I was vibrating, perilously close to coming as he picked up his pace. He grasped my waist with one hand, clutched my hair at the nape of my neck with the other. He pulled me to him and kissed me hard, his tongue penetrating me almost as deeply as his cock.

And I shattered, crying out, feeling him ram into me and hold himself there, submerged, as I clenched ferociously around him.

He reached under my legs, pulling me up and forward and, *God,* even deeper, and then he was bucking against me, groaning through his teeth, coming like a runaway train.

He released me with a gasp, pulling out, and I collapsed against the chair, pulling my aching legs together, shaking. And then he did the oddest thing. He reached under me, picked me up, and sat on the chair with me in his lap. I curled up against him as he caressed me, soothing my shivering body. I buried my head in the crook of his neck, feeling his strength, his skin hot against mine. I didn't know why I was trembling, only that my limbs had turned to jelly. My senses were overwhelmed.

After a few minutes, he lifted my chin and kissed me slowly, sweetly, and I drank him in. The cool air of the almost empty room enveloped us, and we tangled ourselves together in the pool of light, drawing heat from each other.

Maybe twenty minutes passed, and then sanity came knocking politely at the door of my brain, asking if it might resume residence. It had some nerve, given I was still wrapped up in Wyatt's arms. The kissing had ended, but he still stroked my arms, my back, my breasts.

I shifted, looked into his eyes. He wore a small, ethereal smile.

"I was hoping for this," he said.

I didn't know how to feel about that. Was I such a sure thing? Or could I take his statement as a compliment?

I slid off his lap and looked around for my clothes. My panties were draped over my camera on the floor, several feet away from the scene of the crime. I started there and hastily dressed.

"Cali?" Wyatt called uncertainly as he donned his clothes at a more leisurely pace. "Are you OK?"

Oh, damn my hormones. I could only nod, but it felt like something wet was in my eye.

"I'm fine," I said, thinking I'd just laid another brick on his road out of town.

I put my camera back on the tripod for something to do and stole a glance at him. Now in jeans, he was grabbing his sweater off the floor when I saw an intriguing shape on the left side of his back. A tattoo, curling over one elegant shoulder blade.

"What's that?" I asked, my curiosity curing my reticence.

"What?"

"On your back. Is it a fish?"

"A shark," he said with a small smile, "patterned in the Maori style. Something about Polynesia gets into your blood when you spend that much time in the Pacific."

"Why the shark?"

"Always moving," he said simply, pulling the sweater over his head. He walked over to me, laced his fingers through my hair, embraced me, kissed my neck. "It's good to be here, Cali."

I hugged him back, wanting to feel his solid physique

against my slighter one. I inhaled the fresh scent of him and a lingering whiff of sex.

I looked up at him. "Why can't we have a normal evening together?"

Wyatt laughed. "Isn't this normal?"

"Not for me."

"So what's normal?"

"I don't know." I shrugged. "A nice, long talk, for one thing."

He released me, still looking amused. "You want to talk? Let's talk. Why don't we go out? You have a diner around here?"

I searched my mental database. "As a matter of fact, yes. It's kind of an after-hours drunk spot, but it's still early enough that it won't be overrun by clubbers."

"Then let's go," he said. "I skipped dinner."

"So did I," I replied, pretty sure the Oreos didn't count. "Give me one sec."

I ran upstairs to the apartment, brushed my hair into a ponytail, and grabbed my purse before coming back down to meet him.

"Where'd you go?"

"Got my purse," I said. "I live upstairs."

"Good to know."

"Where are you staying?" I asked as I led him out of the studio and to the lobby.

"Bohemia Beach, with one of my old surfing pals from California who moved here for a job. I'm renting a room and some garage space for my boards."

His mention of rent made me think of something. I walked over to the desk, opened a drawer and pulled out his check. As I walked back to him, I ripped it in two and handed it over.

Wyatt looked puzzled as he realized what it was. "Why?"

"Don't be stupid," I told him.

"It's for the photo lessons."

"That was not a photo lesson," I said.

"Don't you want me to come here anymore?"

"That's not what I said." God, he was dense. "If you think this is some kind of transaction, you can leave right now."

"Not at all!" he said, his dark eyebrows knitted together. "I just wanted to be fair. You're giving me your time to teach me."

"That line has been blurred beyond all recognition," I said. "Either we proceed as — friends, or not at all."

"I'm sorry," he said. "I didn't mean — I just wanted to be fair."

"You are. The fairest in all the land," I said drily. "So?"

"Friends," he agreed softly, and he kissed me in a way that said so much more. Or maybe that was just me wishing. "Are you OK?"

"Yes. Fine." Maybe. I opened the front door for him, hearing the jingle, wondering if an angel was getting her wings.

I locked the door behind us, and Wyatt took my hand as we strolled down the street toward the heart of downtown. I was so far beyond confused. I remembered the wave — the one I was supposed to ride and see where it took me, at least until I got lost in the crash and foam. But when I got emotional, the surf was rough.

Double Diamond Diner, or just The Diamond, as most of us called it, had been tucked into a side street of downtown

Bohemia as long as I could remember. We used to go there after high school dances and football games. Later, it was a great place to get fries and burgers to soak up the alcohol after a night boozing with my friends from *The Bugle*. It wasn't the best restaurant in town, but it was reliable, comfortable and good, with big windows that overlooked the street. It had streamlined walls and silver trim. A great old neon sign above the door put a slanted, cursive "Diamond" in pink across the blue outline of two diamonds, the shape you see on playing cards, with "Diner" in smaller pink capitals below it.

It was pretty busy, still late dinnertime for a lot of folks, though the seniors were melting away in favor of a younger crowd. A waitress greeted us at the door, and I realized it was Millie, the girl in my photography class.

"Ms. Goode!" she said. "Table or booth?"

"Calista, please," I said, "and a booth would be great."

Wearing a cute pink uniform dress that showed off her curves, Millie cheerfully led us to a booth and handed us menus before bustling off to take care of another table. I shot Wyatt a morose look.

"What?" he asked, looking as though he were trying not to laugh.

"She's in my class."

"So what?"

"So she'll know you and I aren't just — she'll know we know each other outside of class."

"We've been over this," Wyatt said, flipping open his menu. "You worry too much."

"Maybe," I said, focusing on my menu. Greek specialties reflected the heritage of the owners, mixed with such diner classics as meatloaf, burgers and breakfast, available around the clock. "So, how'd he take it?"

"Who?"

"Ron, when you told him you were out."

"Honestly? He was pissed." Wyatt put down his menu. "I drove everybody to the airport yesterday and told him then. At that point, he didn't have much time to react. He tried to talk me out of it. I tried to tell him that he had plenty of guys he ran with and one of them could take over the logistics. He didn't need me."

"Is he still pissed?"

"I don't know. By the time he left, he seemed pretty calm, almost cheerful. He shook my hand and told me he'd see me soon. 'We'll talk when you're back on the circuit,' is what he told me, as if this was just a phase I'm going through."

"But you are going back on the circuit, right?" I asked, trying to sound blasé. "I mean, you aren't really leaving the game. You'll be surfing. Going to tournaments."

"Not in the same way. Probably." He shot a glance at me, then looked around, catching Millie's eye and waving her over, as if he were trying to avoid talking about it further. But I couldn't let it drop.

"What do you mean, not in the same way?"

Millie beamed at us, notepad in hand. "Do you know what you want?"

"Tuna melt," Wyatt said, "with a Coke and fries."

"I'll have the French toast with bacon and a scrambled egg on the side," I said. "And orange juice. You still have the fresh stuff, right?"

Millie nodded, taking the menus. "Fresh squeezed every day. I'll be right back with your drinks."

"Fresh orange juice?" Wyatt asked as she walked away. "I should've gotten that."

"It's the best. But you were saying? About not being on the circuit in the same way?"

Wyatt sighed, not answering, and after a minute, Millie dropped off our beverages. Damn, she was fast.

He swirled his Coke and took a sip. After several more seconds, and a leisurely perusal of the mini jukebox at the table, he spoke.

"I will always surf," he said. "I love it. It's in my blood. It got me through a bad time in my life and helped make me who I am. But I just don't have the heart to chase the Big Wave anymore. Maybe it's all the injuries. Maybe I'm getting cold feet at twenty-five. I don't know. I saw one of my friends killed last year surfing the Pipeline on the North Shore. Hawaii. He mistimed a wave and was smacked by a heavy lip. He was knocked out by his own broken board. By the time we found him, it was too late."

"That's awful."

"You know going in that it's dangerous. One of my worst days was at Teahupo'o three years ago. Tahiti," he said to my questioning look. "It means 'broken skulls,' and that's just about right. Sometimes the waves are reasonable, but when we went, they were fucking monsters."

"How big?"

"Fifteen, twenty feet and higher. Catnip to the crowd I was running with. It only took a twelve-foot wave to mess me up. It sounded like an animal growling behind me when I was in the barrel. I got caught inside. My feet were strapped to the board, but the board was blown off my feet, and I couldn't kick out in time. I broke an ankle. I was out for months."

I shook my head, seeing the waves in my mind's eye, fluid but hard as stone.

Wyatt looked thoughtful. "I was just lucky I wasn't driven into the reef. It's hard to imagine the power of that wall of water until you're inside it. It's a clean wave, but it's heavy, like a building curling over you, crashing down on you. Ron surfed a twenty-five footer that same day, shot through it perfectly. It was like he'd touched God. Afterward, he sat on the beach and cried."

I tried to picture Ron Raker, the big, insanely confident surfer, overwhelmed by emotion after conquering such a beast. In a way, that image made me understand the appeal more than anything. These surfers were in thrall to the power of nature. It was a hierarchy they could understand. Given my fear of the water, perhaps I understood it more than I realized.

Millie delivered our food and vanished again, and we dug in.

"It's still beautiful to me, you know," Wyatt said, "looking down the barrel, the light shining through the wall of water, even as the water embraces you with its shadow. That rush when you hit it just right. I still crave the speed, that sense of flying through something so ephemeral that its like will never be seen again. But I can get that feeling with less pressure. And I can capture it for other people so maybe they can understand why we love it so much."

I nodded, swallowing a bite of the delicious French toast. "Photography can do that. It can help share a feeling, an experience. It's one reason why I love it. I think a camera can give you intimate insights into a subject." I put aside a sudden image of our encounter in the studio. "It can also put distance between you and the subject. Still, I think photography is getting more immersive all the time, with wearable cameras and all the live photos and video people get with their phones. It's like they experience things *through* the camera now."

Wyatt smiled between bites of his sandwich. "I suppose I'll do the same. And in between shoots, I'll surf. Gently."

I laughed. "Why don't I believe you?"

"I'm getting old," he said. "Creaky and cautious."

"Oh, right. You're so ancient." I grinned at him, sipping the tangy juice.

"Old for my years," he joked, but there was something dark and steely in his tone.

"Tell me about California."

"Some other time," he deflected me. "Tell me about you. You're from here?"

"I grew up here, went to UF, came back here to work at the paper."

"You ever try surfing?"

"Never," I said, adding salt and pepper to my egg. "Though I used to be inseparable from my skateboard."

"Then you should be a natural at a surfboard."

I just shook my head.

"Hard to believe you never surfed," he continued. "So many surfers got their start on Florida's east coast. I thought everybody here surfed."

"Not me," I said in what I hoped was a bright, cheerful voice that would stop his line of inquiry.

"Why not?"

So much for that idea. "I don't like the water."

Amazement transformed Wyatt's face. "You don't swim?"

"I can swim. But I don't like the ocean. I mean, I love the ocean, but not for swimming."

He looked at me thoughtfully as he munched a fry. "So when Ron tried to throw you in the water — "

"Yeah," I said, newly embarrassed by the memory of my freak-out, of Wyatt rescuing me.

"So what happened to you?"

"Nothing, I just don't like — "

"Something happened to you." His eyes narrowed, but they shone with interest, too, as if he were a detective enjoying an interrogation.

I shivered, a rush of amorphous fear coming back to me, making me cold. "It's stupid. I don't want to talk about it."

We ate in silence for a couple of minutes, and I focused on finishing my French toast.

"Cali." His expression was kinder now, and he reached across the table and touched my hand. "You wanted to talk. So talk."

Not about this, I thought. "It's irrational."

"Most fears are."

"Let's go get a drink."

His eyebrows rose, and he flagged down Millie for the check. I let him pay, feeling kind of annoyed that he would press me but glad that he cared enough to ask. And maybe I needed to get over it, this stupid fear that had kept me out of the water for so long. It was a habit that I'd learned to coddle and cultivate. I'd been building that wall between me and the waves for years. And here was a guy who lived in them.

WYATT and I walked for a few blocks in silence, looking around at the burgeoning club crowd. It was pretty thin tonight, on a Monday, but no matter what night it was, there was always carousing in this part of town. On impulse, I grabbed Wyatt's hand. He squeezed it as I led us toward the harbor and Plumeria Bar.

The red walls and rich woods were welcoming, a womb of comfort that took us in gladly. Behind the bar, the windows showed friendly lights twinkling on the harbor. Maybe a dozen customers clustered in small groups around the bar, which resonated with soft piano jazz from the speakers.

We stayed away from the bar this time; I led Wyatt to a couch where we could sit close to each other and talk without being overheard. He seemed happy to be there, and he entwined his fingers in mine and kissed me, shooting fire through my body, nestled against his. For a moment I forgot everything except the feel of his lips on mine, until I sensed the presence of a server hovering in range. We broke apart, and I looked up. It was the young bartender who'd made our drinks last time.

"Old-Fashioned," I told him.

"Gin martini, two olives," said Wyatt, and the bartender left us.

"Ooo, liquor this time," I teased Wyatt.

"I didn't drive," he said. "At least not to the bar."

He kissed me again, and I followed his lead, tasting, delving, wanting him more with each second. I wondered how many couples had made out on this couch. I pulled away in time to see the bartender set our glistening drinks on the coffee table in front of us. I took a long, cold sip of mine, savoring the whiskey, and Wyatt tasted his with an appreciative murmur.

"Now," he said, sitting back with the martini, "you were going to tell me what happened to make you scared of the ocean. Was it 'Jaws'? I can't believe how many people don't go swimming because of 'Jaws.' "

I laughed. "You're making fun of me. It wasn't 'Jaws.' Look, anyone except me will think it's stupid."

He didn't respond. He just watched me, waiting, sipping his drink, holding my hand. I took a sip, too, and then, finally, I caved.

"I was six. Actually, it was my sixth birthday. My family took me to the beach as part of a fun day they'd planned. A hot June day."

"Brothers? Sisters?"

"I just have the one brother, Damien. He wore that crazy suit to the art museum gala."

"Oh, yeah, I remember that. So you were all at the beach. Did you go in the water then?"

"I couldn't wait to go in the water. I'd gotten this inflatable unicorn Pegasus thing for my birthday, and I loved it. It was white. It had a unicorn head and handles on the neck, and wings that stretched out to either side, and I could ride it in the water. Float in it. But, of course, it was not meant as a flotation device, according to the fine print. Probably not meant for the ocean, either."

"Of course not," Wyatt said drily. "Did it pop?"

"*No*. Shut up," I said to his grin. "There are some rocks under the water here, and you have to be careful, but the Pegasus was fine. So my parents were there with other parents, and they were kind of distracted, I guess. They always brought beer to the beach, and they didn't get to go out much with us bratty kids around, so it was a chance for them to unwind. They let Damien look after me."

"How old was he then?"

"He'd just turned ten. So they kind of kept half an eye on us, but you know, we were in the shallow water. It wasn't anything to worry about. Except Damien had his friends with

him, too, just a couple of other boys, and they thought it
would be cool to push me on the unicorn. See how fast they
could go. See how far out they could get me. It was really fun
at first. And then they got to screaming and pushing each
other under the water and moving away from me, and I was
out pretty far from shore on this stupid unicorn. I had only
learned some really basic swimming at that time, so I was
afraid to just hop off and go back in to shore. I remember
thinking the waves would push me back in eventually. But
this group of waves came in that was big. It tilted the unicorn
up, and I just slipped off. And that might have been OK, if I'd
just doggy-paddled to shore, but I didn't want to lose my new
toy. I paddled after it through the waves. It kept moving away
from me, and the water was just deep enough there that I
couldn't put my feet down. And then I got caught in a rip
current."

Wyatt's expression darkened. "Where was your family?"

"It all happened so fast, my parents didn't even see I was
in trouble at first. I didn't know what a rip current was, and I
kept fighting it, and it kept pushing me out. I didn't know you
were supposed to swim parallel to shore, and I was so little. I
wasn't much of a swimmer. I started calling out. I remember
feeling hysterical. I swallowed ocean water, that horrible salt
water." My voice choked on the memory, and Wyatt put an
arm around me.

"Did a lifeguard rescue you?"

"No. There wasn't one on duty at that part of the beach.
Believe it or not, it was Damien. He was small, but he was
wiry and strong. He dragged me out of the rip current and
pulled me back to shore, where the stupid unicorn was sitting
on the beach, waiting for me. By then my dad had waded into
the water, and he scooped me up and took me to the sand,

but I was exhausted, and I threw up. I'd taken in a lot of salt water. There was a long moment out in the waves when I really thought I was going to drown. I was so scared." I heard how thready I sounded, and I looked up at Wyatt. He pulled me close to him, and I worked to regain control. "I'm still scared, I guess," I added in a more neutral tone.

"You don't have to be scared anymore," he said, kissing my hair. I took a long drink of my cocktail, imagining that he was talking about more than the ocean. "I want to get you back in the water."

"Good luck with that."

"Don't dismiss the idea. Doesn't part of you want to get back in the water? I mean, you would, if you weren't so scared of it, right?"

"I like the idea of it," I said. "I'm good in a pool. I like watching surfers like you ride the waves. But I can't see any point in me getting into the ocean."

"I think all our fears come from one place," he said.

I raised my eyebrows.

"The fear of losing control," he continued. "But the real secret is that you're never in control. On a highway, a boulder can roll down a hill and hit your car. A plane can fall out of the sky and land on your house. In calm water, you can run into a rock or a shark."

"This isn't helping," I said.

"What I'm saying is, because you're never in control anyway, there's really no barrier between you and risk. Or at least reasonable risk. It's all the same. You might as well take the chance."

"You said yourself the risk was getting to you," I pointed out.

"It's all relative," Wyatt said. "There's killer waves, and

then there's Bohemia Beach. I'm talking about reasonable risk here. I want to take you to the beach. Maybe you can shoot me surfing sometime."

"It's cold!" I said.

He laughed. "Not like California water. But I'd wear a wetsuit, since it's winter. You wouldn't have to get wet, but I want you to start thinking about the idea." He leaned in closer. "I'll keep you safe," he whispered in my ear, and how I wanted to believe him. He brushed a hand along my thigh. "Besides, I want to feel your body against mine in the water."

"Hmm, water fetish?" I teased, feeling a flush of heat, trying to change the topic.

"Actually, yes." He shot me an arch smile. "I have a special relationship with the water. And it has a special relationship with me."

"Then you hardly need me. Three's a crowd."

"That's where you're wrong." He took a long drink of his martini. "Especially because I can't find a mermaid to save my life."

"You won't feel much through the wetsuit," I joked.

"We'll practice for summer."

"You'll be gone by then."

Wyatt didn't answer, a faraway look in his eyes. He finished his drink and caught the bartender's eye, flashing him two fingers and pointing at our glasses for refills.

I took a long sip of mine to try to catch up, to blur my rational mind. I already knew he'd be leaving. And my body, warm against Wyatt on the couch, didn't care. We sat there for a few minutes in silence, and I listened to the piano music, enjoying the mood of this place, the feel of the man next to me.

"Do you teach tomorrow?" he asked.

"Not again till Wednesday. Our class. I only teach the one."

"Good," he said, taking a sip from the new martini our bartender had brought.

"Why?"

"It's not a school night." He grinned at me over the glass.

"What's on your mind?" I put down my empty first drink and picked up the fresh Old-Fashioned. It tasted as if there were even more whiskey in this one. "Mmm."

"I like that sound you make. I want to hear it again."

"Mmm," I said into his ear, feeling the warmth, the dopey deliciousness of the whiskey in my veins.

"Oh, yeah," he said, and he kissed me, a dreamy, tipsy kiss, his tongue languidly probing my mouth, my tongue answering in kind. I squeezed his leg, pressing against him.

"Mmm," I hummed against his mouth, this time from him, not the whiskey.

He released me, mischief in his eyes.

"I want to hear you moan for me," he whispered.

"You already have." I looked around. The other patrons were wrapped up in their own conversations.

"I want to hear you moan as I fuck you again tonight," he said softly. "I want to hear you cry out my name again and again."

"Wyatt," I breathed, looking into his dark, shining eyes. He turned me on like no one ever had. I casually ran my hand up his leg and brushed my fingers over his crotch.

He gasped at my touch. I withdrew my hand, but I knew he was as hard as I was wet.

"What do you do to me?" he murmured into my ear. "I can't get within a yard of you without wanting to fuck you."

"Then you'd better keep to the back of the room in photo class," I quipped.

He knocked back the rest of his martini. "Drink up."

"Why?"

"You know why," he said. "I want to take you home."

I knew what he meant, but I played dumb. "I know. You need to get your rest."

"Cali. This is no joke."

"Isn't it?" I took a long quaff of my Old-Fashioned, eyeing him playfully, trying to be cool.

"Drink up," he hissed. "I'm going to get a cab."

"It won't take that long to walk."

"Yes, it will. Barkeep! Bill, please." The bartender came over with the slip of paper in a leather folder, and Wyatt stuffed a wad of money into it. "And call us a cab, OK?"

"There's one outside now, sir," the bartender said, looking pleased with his tip.

"Excellent. Cali?"

I looked him in the eye, thinking that I'd started the evening wanting to be in control and was ending it — well, I wasn't ending it at all. I'd given in completely to the madness.

I drank down the cocktail, bit into its drunken cherry, savored the burst of sweetness in my mouth and followed him to the door.

IT TOOK MAYBE ten minutes to get to my place by cab. Wyatt paid the driver, and I climbed out of the back seat with him, feeling more than a little tipsy from slamming my second drink.

"My apartment's a wreck," I said, trying one last time to

be reasonable as we stood outside my gallery. "You should go home."

"I don't give a damn," he said, his deep voice powerful, enthralling. "Let me in."

I stood there wavering, feeling the cooling night air around me, hearing the light traffic on the street, the distant shriek of a giddy drunk girl and the shouts of ebullient boys. Here we were, playing out the same story, girl meets boy, only I'd never read the story this way before. I was supposed to know what was next in my predictable plotline, but our book was all mixed up, the chapters out of order, and the ending was not going to be satisfactory. Then again, all my other predictable stories, all my sweet, sensible relationships, had ended unsatisfactorily, too. And they didn't have Wyatt in them, his eyes flaring, his dark eyebrows broadcasting his intense focus on me. That laser-hot gaze shot through me, penetrating my soul.

I pulled my keys from my purse and let us inside the front door, hearing the jingle as if from a great distance. I locked the door behind us and led him through the studio, where I had one dim light keeping watch, to the space in back and the staircase. He grabbed my hand, and I led him up; I unlocked my apartment, let him in, locked the door behind me.

I dropped my keys and purse as he pushed me against the wall, his mouth on mine, his hands on my hips. I moaned as I met his tongue, his hunger, and he made a noise almost like a laugh.

"That's right," he said as he came up for breath. "I want to hear you."

He clutched my mound through my jeans, and I did groan, not because he told me to, but because it almost hurt, even as it felt so good. He electrified me with his touch, with his need as he rubbed me through the thick cloth. I wanted no barrier between us. I wanted him. Oh, how I wanted him.

He held my face between his hands, kissed me again. "Where's your bed?"

"This way." I turned and walked quickly through the crowd of boxes in the living room to the airy bedroom. *Box-free,* I thought thankfully. I flipped the light switch; a lamp and the fairy lights on the headboard came on. I turned off the lamp and turned back to Wyatt.

He stood in the glimmer, tense, coiled, ready to pounce. I could feel his craving. But he walked toward me slowly, deliberately, and put one hand behind my neck, pulling the elastic loop out of my hair, pulling me to him. This kiss was even more beguiling than the others for its languor, a shot of hot honey.

"Listen," he murmured. "I'm safe. You?"

I knew what he meant. "Yes. And on the pill."

"Good. Because I want to feel you with my cock. With every inch of my skin."

Oh, God, yes. He kissed me harder, his lips bruising mine, and I moaned again, wanting to feel him inside me. And I didn't want to wait. I reached under his shirt, pulling it up and off. I ran my hands over his delicious musculature as he drank of my mouth. He mirrored my motions, pulling off my shirt, and I unclasped my bra and tossed it aside. We were chest to chest, skin to skin, mouth to mouth.

Wyatt pushed me toward the bed and onto it. As I lay on my back, he quickly pulled off my shoes, socks, jeans and underwear.

"I can't get enough of you naked," he said, running his hands over my shoulders and down to my breasts, where my nipples were already hard. He licked each one, pinching them gently, and then he kissed his way down my belly to my triangle. I closed my eyes as his tongue found my clit. He teased it lightly at first, and it stood to attention, aching, wanting more. I lifted my hips to meet him and heard his amused murmur as the work of his tongue intensified, teasing me, bringing on tingling waves of pleasure until they magnified and screamed through me.

"Yes, Wyatt, yes." I remembered my fantasy of the day before in this very bed. And here he was, the man of my dreams — my dirty, onanistic dreams — sucking and licking at my clit until I could barely stand the ecstasy. "I'll do anything . . ." I said, not knowing how to finish the sentence as I came hard, angling up to his worshiping mouth.

He teased out my orgasm with his tongue before he stood, taking a breath, and I opened my eyes to see his sly smile.

"You'll do anything?" he asked. "I'll have to give that some thought." He was unbuttoning his jeans, pulling them off with his briefs; his sandals were already on the floor. His freed cock stood, red and engorged. "But for now, I just want to fuck you senseless."

"You already have," I whispered, drinking in his beautiful form in the fairy lights. He would have made a stunning photo.

"Oh, no, I haven't," he said, his voice low and dangerous as he climbed up on the bed over me, lowering himself to me. He pressed the thick head of his penis against my already oversensitive bud, rubbing against me until I made small cries of agonized delight. "That's what I thought," he said, and he eased his cock inside my slick folds.

"Oh, *yesss.*" Without the condom, he slid smoothly inside me, filling me with such undeniable power that I wanted him to stay there forever, fucking me, pleasuring me — and himself, because his own groans betrayed his gratification. He thrust deeply inside me and lifted himself, just shy of withdrawal, only to plunge again and again and again. My cries became louder, wilder, and I clutched at his back, bucking up to meet him, taking him to the hilt and begging for more.

His release triggered my own heavenly orgasm as he convulsed inside me, once, twice, and pulled out to spill the rest of his seed across my stomach, possessing me, marking me. As he sat back on his knees, panting, watching me, I stretched, sighed and repositioned, on my hands and knees in front of him, and bent to lick the come off his cock.

"Oh, Cali," he breathed. "Oh, God. Stop."

I lifted my head and smiled. "Stop?"

"Too much," he said, pulling me down to the mattress with him, our heads nestled on the pillows. He grabbed a tissue from the nightstand to wipe off my belly. We kissed, a kiss to get lost in, and I tasted both of us, a mingled essence, or maybe it was my imagination, the delusion of desire. I was one with him, kissing him, caressing him, steady and warm and comfortable against the bed, and I was falling, falling dizzily, aroused and ecstatic and scared out of my mind.

I AWOKE to gray light leaking through the blinds, and I heard the low buzz of early morning traffic. Wyatt touched my shoulder, and I looked up. He stood by the bed, dressed.

"I have to get going," he said softly. "Good waves this morning."

I was confused in my fatigue. "How do you know?"

"Text alerts."

"OK," I murmured sleepily. "Hey, um, go out the side door so I don't have to unlock the gallery. It'll lock behind you."

"No problem." He leaned over and kissed me, a brief, sweet kiss, and smiled. "I'll call you later."

And then he was gone, and I was alone in my bed, more alone than I'd ever felt. Whenever I'd had a man in my bed for the first time before, we'd already had a relationship. I'd known he'd be around the next day. This was different.

He'd said he would call. That would have to be enough. Because the alternative was too painful.

I rolled over, pulling one of the pillows to me, breathing in the ghost of his scent, and went back to sleep.

The next time I opened my eyes, it was 9:30. Just seeing a clock reminded me I'd have to work on setting my hours, or else I'd never get any walk-in business. Mostly, I'd be shooting on location or in the studio, but I had to be available for appointments to scoop up the brides and others who needed a photographer.

I took a shower, dressed in jeans and an ice-blue sweater with matching crystal jewelry, pinned up my hair and headed downstairs with a cup of tea and my laptop.

I turned on some music so it wouldn't seem so quiet, unlocked the door and started working at the gallery desk. I printed and posted my hours (select Tuesdays, Thursdays, by chance and by appointment), updated my website, and thought far too much about Wyatt.

After a quick takeout sandwich for lunch, I went back to the studio to work on my gear. A text pinged into my phone as I was rolling and stacking my cloth backdrops, and I wandered over to the table where it sat, hoping it was him.

It was Sloane. "How's it going?"

"Fine," I texted back.

"I mean how's it going with the boy?"

"Don't ask."

My phone rang a moment later, and I sighed, sat in one of the black leather chairs and answered. "Hi, Sloane."

"What happened?"

"What *didn't* happen?"

She laughed. "Good."

"What do you mean, good? I've officially gone insane."

"No, you haven't. It's good for you."

"Insanity? Or randomly screwing surfer boys?"

"Not so randomly," Sloane pointed out. "You keep meeting. Maybe it's fate."

"Maybe I'm desperate."

"Don't sell yourself short," she said. "Besides, I saw him at that gala, and he was several levels above desperate. 'Yummy' might be more accurate. Are you seeing him again?"

"I think so." That was true. I should see him in class, even if he didn't call. "But look, I don't want to think about boys all the time."

"They *are* distracting." Sloane's tone was mischievous and a little dreamy. Then again, she had Alex.

"What I mean is, let's get together, just us girls," I said. "Ez is playing at The Junction Box on Friday. And I'll ask Thea."

"Oh, yeah. I liked her. Anyone else?"

"I'll talk to Damien and see what the deal is with his friend Penelope, this fabric artist I met at the gala. She seemed kind of interesting. And I need all the contacts I can get."

"Sounds great," Sloane said. "I'm in. Eight o'clock?"

"See you then if not before, coz."

"OK, coz. Keep me updated." I could hear the wink in her tone.

As I hung up, I heard a jingle at the door and went out to the gallery to find a desperate mother whose daughter's wedding photographer had a family emergency. She needed help this Saturday. Could I do it? Money was no object.

Hell, yes.

The day was really starting to look up.

We spent an hour at the front desk going over details and my portfolio, and she left me with a healthy deposit check. I went upstairs, grabbed a celebratory soda and went back down to the gallery to sit on the mod couch and bask in my success. I cracked open the cold Pepsi, took a long sip and looked at my phone. I'd missed one call, from Wyatt.

"You would have liked the beach this morning," he said in a voice message. "The light was beautiful. Can we do a lesson tonight? Call me."

A lesson. There was something about the way he said that word that made me smile.

Nervously, I called him back.

"Wyatt Brooks," he answered.

"How formal."

"Cali! Sorry, I'm trying to sound professional in case any clients actually call me. I didn't look at the caller ID."

"I like it. You sound all grown up," I teased.

"What, I haven't proven my manhood to you yet?" he countered.

I felt a little thrill at his joke. "I'll need more evidence on that."

"Glad to hear it." His voice sounded husky. "Want to teach me something tonight?"

"About photography? Sure," I said, thinking about almost anything but. "Are you available this afternoon? I thought we might try a time-lapse, unless you already do those."

"No, that would be great! I'll be shooting video, too, and it's always cool to get dawn breaking over a surf spot."

"This would be sunset, but we can still do it beachside," I suggested. "I could pick you up about 3:30, if you tell me where you live."

"Sure. I'll text you the address. And then, Cali?"

"Yeah?"

"Maybe we can get dinner or something."

"Sure," I said, feeling shy for no reason at all. "Great. See you then."

Or something. I hung up with my heart beating like a schoolgirl's.

His text came in a few minutes later, and I almost choked on my Pepsi when I saw the address. He was staying on the street where my parents lived.

I FIGURED I might as well get in a quick visit on my way to Wyatt's, so I stopped at my childhood home, a 1960s house like so many others in Bohemia Beach, a few blocks west of A1A and the ocean.

I knocked on the door. My mother answered it, flour in her highlighted brown hair, a flowery apron covering her black stretch pants and clashing flowered knit shirt.

"Cali, you don't have to knock, honey," she said impatiently. "Come on in. Are you wearing jeans? I wouldn't think that would make such a great impression on your customers."

That was my mom, always quick with ego-skewering advice.

"It's not like I'd wear this to a wedding," I said as I followed her into the kitchen, where she was in the middle of making chocolate chip cookies on the Formica island. "I'm shooting a wedding on Saturday, as a matter of fact."

"Well, don't wear jeans."

"OK," I said, trying to take her scolding in good humor. "What are the cookies for?"

"Your father needs them for some potluck at work. It's not like I have time to make them. It's not like I don't have a job."

"And how's that going?" I asked. Mom had a morning job as a receptionist in the guidance office at Bohemia High School.

"They're still giving kids terrible advice, as usual. Most of them should not be going to college. They should be learning to weld or going to reform school."

I suppressed a smile as she finished filling the cookie trays and put them in the oven.

"So are you dating that surfer now?" she asked.

"*What?*"

"I saw in the paper that you had a date with Ron Raker. There was a picture."

Oh, shit. I hadn't looked at the paper in days. "No, it was a one-time thing. Do you still have the paper?"

She was shaking her head. "In the recycling bin. Now that boy, he definitely should have gone to college. Had a head for math. Instead he ends up as a surfer."

A head for math? Who knew?

"He's a world-champion surfer, Mom," I said, rifling through the bin by the door to the garage. I found *The Bugle* for Sunday, and there on the local news section was a photo of me with Ron at The Mix at Trifles. I looked bewildered and slightly squished by Ron's muscular arm. Bart's byline was on the photo.

I couldn't blame Bart for getting a couple of shots. At least he hadn't stalked me all night.

"Surfers are trouble," my mother said, wiping down the kitchen island, shooting me a skeptical look. "You can do better."

"We're not dating, Mom. He's halfway around the world this week." Of course, I didn't mention that I was dating — if that was the word — a surfer who lived right down the street. "Anyway, I've got to go. I just wanted to say hi."

"You can't stay for a cookie?" It was the kindest she'd been since I got there.

"Wish I could, but I have an appointment."

"Well, that's good news, since you're unemployed."

"*Self*-employed, Mom. See you later."

She smiled dolefully at me as I waved and got the hell out of there. I could see why my cousin Sloane freaked out any time she came over for a meal. Last Thanksgiving had been positively grueling.

In a couple of minutes, I pulled into the driveway at the address Wyatt had given me. It was a really cute house a block from my parents', on the other side of the street. It was from the same era but had been updated with white paint, black trim, and accents that added an Asian feel — a red Japanese gate, a small rock garden and a couple of very large red vases with beautifully trimmed topiaries. Just who was this friend of Wyatt's?

I didn't have time to give the question much thought, because Wyatt emerged from the front door with a tripod and a camera bag, wearing loose khakis with lots of pockets and a grayish-brown sweater that brought out his eyes. I got out of the SUV and popped open the back so he could stow his gear. He did so and gave me a kiss, short and sweet. He looked me in the eye, his expression unreadable, and then he slipped an arm around my waist and gave me another kiss, not so short, and not so sweet. It unfolded into something dark and delicious, and I closed my eyes, opening my mouth to him, lost in it before I heard hoots and shouts and looked up to see a school bus going by, the kids hanging out the windows, taunting us.

"Oh, God," I said with dismay, wondering how soon this would get back to my mother as the bus stopped and let out a dozen kids. Everybody knew everybody on this street.

"Sorry," Wyatt shrugged with a smile. "Couldn't help myself."

"You're fine. It's just that my parents live down the street. The jungle telegraph will have me humping you on the front lawn in no time flat."

"Now there's an idea," he joked, but his eyes sparked with more than humor. "When do I get to meet them?"

"Ha," is all I said, wondering if he really meant it. "Be careful what you wish for. Let's go while the light is still good."

"Sure," he said, heading for the passenger door.

"So who's your friend?" I asked as I backed out the car and headed down the street.

"Who?"

"The friend you're staying with."

"Oh, Jen. She's somebody I knew in California. She's an engineer with one of the aerospace companies up at Cape Canaveral."

"Oh." Whoa. A woman. A woman with a real job. And how had she known Wyatt? Or how did she know Wyatt now?

"Do you have your own room?"

"What?" He gave me a funny look, and then he laughed. "Of course I have my own room."

"Oh," I said again, hoping I wasn't turning pink.

"Besides," Wyatt said, "I think that's the way her husband prefers it."

"Oh, she has a husband?"

"Yes. He spends about a week a month in D.C. and commutes back and forth." Wyatt sounded amused at my questions.

"How did you know Jen in California?"

He paused a beat too long. "Surfing."

"Oh," I said again, wondering why my vocabulary had become so limited. Wyatt wasn't telling me everything. Maybe they'd dated before. Maybe Jen and her husband had an open marriage; after all, it sounded as if her husband was gone most of the time.

Maybe I didn't want to know.

I tried to put her — them — out of my mind.

"So," I said, "I thought we'd go to the public dock on the river side and do a sunset time-lapse from there."

"The lagoon, you mean?"

"The lagoon, the river, it's the same thing, unless you want to get technical," I said, hearing an edge in my voice. "Everybody calls it the river."

"That's cool." Wyatt's tone was neutral, soothing, responding to my friction. I knew I was way too touchy about what was probably nothing. I took a deep breath.

"Have you shot time-lapses before?" I asked.

"I've been meaning to with the GoPro but haven't. Definitely not with my DSLR."

"Do you know if it has a built-in intervalometer?"

"I think so."

"Great. We'll figure it out. I brought one along, too."

We parked near the small city hall and walked the half-block to the dock, which stretched far out into the river, a covered pavilion at its end. Instead of treading on the dock, though, I led Wyatt through the thick foliage of the park at the river's edge until we came to a bench facing the river in a densely shielded clearing among the oaks and palms.

"What do you think?" I asked him.

"I like that we can get palm trees and the dock into the frame on one side and the causeway bridge on the other. Very Floridian."

"My thinking, too. You have a wide-angle lens?"

"Of course," Wyatt said, pretending to be affronted.

"Awesome." I smiled, feeling myself clicking with him again, trying to forget whatever he wasn't telling me.

We set up the cameras on tripods, facing the river — I had one of my old Nikons and a device that let me program the repeating shots, and he had a newer model that had the same function built in.

"Every frame goes into the video later, so you want completely manual settings so you don't get a flicker as the light changes," I said. After a few minutes of tinkering, our cameras were clicking away, capturing a shot every five seconds in the mellowing light of late afternoon. A thin layer of scattered clouds drifted overhead, their edges aglow with the western light.

We sat on the bench behind the tripods. I heard the familiar cry of an osprey above, fishing, and admired a sunlit sailboat making its way down the Intracoastal Waterway, the channel at the center of the lagoon. I saw the flash of fins as a couple of dolphins curved through the water.

"This is a really beautiful place," Wyatt said, taking my

hand, entwining his fingers with mine as we looked out at the water. "Really peaceful."

"Do you miss the big waves?"

"Not yet. Actually, that was some nice surfing this morning. The waves weren't that big, but I got in some good rides. And I like that it's warm enough here I can surf all year 'round."

"Except you won't be here all year 'round."

"You seem pretty sure about that," he said lightly.

I looked at him sharply. "Aren't you?"

"Well, it's winter now, and I can surf, and that's what I'm talking about. It's great."

He was seriously fucking with my mind. I withdrew my hand and walked over to my tripod, ostensibly to check my camera and the intervalometer.

"It's still working," he assured me, and I turned around to watch him eyeing me from the bench.

"Yes, but doing this can really eat batteries," I countered, feeling contrary. "It should last until sunset, anyway."

"That's a lot of time to watch the river."

"Don't you mean 'the lagoon'?" I asked with mock innocence.

"Whatever you say. Come here."

I crossed my arms and looked at him, not moving.

"Cali." My name, the way he said it, was a beacon of persuasion. The light burnished his rakish hair in copper; his cheekbones, his lips were shaped and shadowed by the descending sun as a brilliant sculptor might carve a statue. He crossed his long legs in front of him, relaxed, but his chocolate-diamond eyes snapped with fire in the afternoon's golden glow.

"Come here," he said again, reaching out a hand, palm up, open, inviting.

"Why?"

"Because you want to." He licked his lips, once. "Because I want you."

I sucked in a little breath at the tone of his voice, the need in it. Something inside me began to liquefy, rock melting into lava.

"Please," he said.

My legs took me to the bench before my brain had a chance to say no. He pulled me to him, onto his lap, holding me around the waist with one arm, caressing my cheek with his other hand.

"My golden angel," he whispered.

I leaned in and kissed him. How could I not? He set off all my synapses, cooked all my chemicals. His response was immediate, hungry, his mouth devouring mine, almost savage as he pressed me close to him and pushed his tongue between my lips. My limbs turned to jelly, and I felt an unfathomable longing, an ache between my legs that his kisses only intensified.

"I want you here," he whispered, kissing my throat, circling a spot of intensely sensitive skin with his tongue, lapping like a cat.

"Not here," I choked out, feeling a flare of panic. I wanted him, but this was a public park on the river. No one was in sight, but I could hear voices through the cover of trees, not all that far away.

"No one will know," he said into my ear as he kissed it, as one hand strayed to my breast, squeezing.

"Oh, God. No. No, I can't." My mouth said no. My body said yes.

He kissed me again, and I felt a hand at my waist, unbuttoning my jeans, tugging on the zipper.

"No," I moaned into his kiss.

"Trust me," he whispered, pushing his hand into the gap, pushing aside my underwear, thrusting a finger inside me.

Still on his lap, I grabbed his shoulders, groaning into his neck as he spread my legs apart, moving his finger in and out, teasing my most sensitive spot.

"Do you want more?" he asked.

"Yes. No," I managed to gasp. "Not here."

"Then I'll fuck you with my voice," he intoned in my ear, still fucking me with his finger. "Because this is what I want to do to you, Cali, my angel. I want to pull those jeans all the way down and rip your panties off you. I want to see your beautiful ass lit up by the sun as I bend you over this bench. I put my fingers inside you" — now two fingers were inside me, and I let out a low, guttural, animal sound as he pleasured me — "until you are wet enough for me to take you. I can see how wet you are. The sun is warming your skin, and I pull down my pants and push my cock up against you and push it so far inside you, you scream with rapture."

I groaned into his neck, wanting him so badly, all of him, in my pussy, in my mouth. But not here. Not here . . .

"And then I fuck you relentlessly. I fill you up with my hard cock over and over again. And you love it. You love it, don't you, Cali?"

"*Yesss,*" I hissed, on the verge as his fingers thrust inside me, as his thumb grazed my clit.

"Come for me, Cali," he commanded, and I detonated in frenzied waves, gushing wet around his hand.

God. I'd never done that before.

"Wyatt," I moaned in his ear, arching against him,

crushing myself against his hard body. He held me tightly as my shuddering slowed and stopped.

He withdrew his fingers and brushed them against my lips. "Suck," he whispered, and I did, tasting my own desire. His eyes were as hungry as ever. I could feel his shaft through his pants, against my leg.

"You see how hard you make me?" he asked, withdrawing his fingers.

"Yes." I kissed him, a vulnerable, reverent kiss, in awe of the carnal magic between us.

Looking into his eyes, still on his lap, I shifted and unbuttoned his loose khakis. I reached inside, released him from his briefs, and grasped his length. He inhaled sharply, but he didn't look away as I stroked him, as I teased his tip with my thumb. We were suspended in a gossamer cocoon of perfect light as I intensified my caresses. The crimson sun teetered on the horizon, slipping into the water and beyond the low, dark skyline of Bohemia in the distance. The underside of the thinning clouds lit up purple and gold. A cool breeze spiraled around us, and still he watched me, his face strained with desire, his mouth slightly open, and then he came under my hand with a long gasp.

He enfolded me in his arms. We sat there for several minutes, wrapped up in each other, the cameras still clicking methodically, as the blue and orange twilight deepened to purple. At last, I looked up and saw the first stars of the evening shining brightly against the violet darkness. One of the cameras had stopped.

I kissed Wyatt's neck. "It's time," I whispered in his ear.

We disentangled and put ourselves together. I stood, shaky, trying not to think too much about what we'd done, what we hadn't done. My camera's battery had run out. I packed it up, and Wyatt stopped his, stowing it in his bag. With tripods and gear, we made our way through the darkened trail and to my car, putting our stuff in the back. When I closed it, Wyatt pressed me gently against the car, his hands on my waist.

"Was that OK?" he asked. "I get carried away with you. I've never had that feeling with — are you OK?"

"God, yes," I said, running my hands through that irresistible hair. He kissed my lips delicately, and we got into the car.

I started it up and turned on the radio. As indie rock played through the speakers, I looked over at Wyatt, feeling something new and powerful forged between us. Or maybe it was my imagination.

He smiled innocently. "Dinner?"

I took him to one of Bohemia Beach's more famous burrito hotspots, a hole in the wall with a diner counter, four tables and corrugated metal accents. We sat at the counter and watched surfing videos on the TV while we ate. Wyatt had a story about every location, about every event, about almost every surfer. He had a great memory and a dry sense of humor. And listening to him was an effective reminder that surfing was his whole life, and it was crazy for me to expect anything else.

He asked to come home with me, but I told him no. We had class in the morning, and I needed to think.

It wasn't easy to say no after his kiss goodnight outside his temporary home in Bohemia Beach. Whenever he kissed me, it seemed as if the world around us froze and faded into darkness. But I had to get ahold of myself, especially because I didn't especially like that I was dropping him at his friend's house. His female friend. I didn't think I was the jealous type until I started to contemplate anyone else making time with Wyatt.

By the time I got into the digital photo lab the next morning, I felt ready to play teacher again. But to minimize distractions, when Wyatt finally rolled in at 10:01, I pointed to the back of the room. He winked, nodded and sat down, completing my baker's dozen of students. His eyes were bright and his hair was wet. I wondered if he'd been surfing. He carried that passion with him; it drove him. And it was intensely, annoyingly attractive.

I spared him the briefest nod and scanned the room.

"Welcome back, everyone. Did you bring your thumb drives with your favorite people photos? Pass them up to the front, please. OK, I have an assignment for you. You have forty-five minutes to go out into the world, find a stranger and shoot a portrait of them that says something about who they are. I'm not looking for corporate head shots. I'm not looking for cute little kids. I want sentient beings." There was a laugh. "I know. Kids are sentient beings, but not until they're at least teenagers." Another laugh. "Find someone with personality and capture it with your camera. Be brave. Be interesting. Shoot as much as you want, but I want you to bring back one brilliant photo. There should be context; there should be personality; and there should be light! I've left releases on your desks; make sure they sign, in case we want to use any of the images in our exhibit. And by the time you're done, I'll have organized your favorites here into a slide show. Any questions?"

Wyatt's hand shot up.

I pursed my mouth at him. "Yes, Mr. Brooks?"

"Can we take photos of our lab partner?"

"No," I said emphatically, pinning him with a laser stare before looking around the room. "You shouldn't be with your lab partner at all. Today, you're cold-calling, my friends. Show your school ID if you have to. Pick a stranger, but don't take candy from them and *don't* get in their cars." Murmurs and giggles. "OK — go!"

Wyatt smirked at me, but he followed the others out the door, and I sat at the desk at the front of the room and set to work copying students' photos from their thumb drives to my laptop.

Fortunately, everyone had submitted photos in the correct format, though the sizes varied widely. I shrank some of the big ones and placed them all in a folder, numbering them so each student's was grouped together for the slide show. I had a few minutes as the students began straggling in, and before I turned on the projector, I reviewed the images so I could think about what advice to give them while finding something nice to say about each person's work.

I wasn't paying much attention to whose work was whose; in fact, I didn't know.

Except Wyatt's.

The color and light in his photographs of surfers blew me away. They had to be his; there was even one of Ron Raker kicking back in a hammock under a coconut palm on some tropical beach, beer in hand, grinning, shirtless, his golden tan glistening. He lived up to his reputation as a heartbreaker. The photo wasn't perfect; it was shot from a little too far away and could have been framed better. But it had an undeniable spark of life and a great sense of light.

I clicked past a shot of a surfer sitting on his board on a

beach at sunrise, opened photo No. 10 and snapped my laptop shut. I looked around. Only two students had returned, and they were ignoring me, comparing photos on their cameras. I opened the laptop again and looked carefully at the image on my screen.

It was me: me sideways in the chair in my studio, my head thrown back, one arm up, the other dangling. My cascading blond hair shimmered in the light, and my eyes were closed, my cheeks flushed, my pink lips slightly parted. This one clearly wasn't shot from the tripod. This must have been shot when Wyatt was moving around me, toward me, clicking away as I abandoned myself to the moment.

It was a beautiful photo, strange and arresting and inti-mate, tilted as if I were falling. It was the best in the bunch.

And even with my clothes on, I looked unapologetically wanton, as if I were inviting the viewer to ravish me.

Quietly, I moved the photo out of the folder and into another one. The class was filling up. I took a deep breath, skimmed through the rest of the photos, and then connected the laptop to the projector.

Wyatt was one of the last to enter, again, though he was chatting with another of the guys. *Good. Making friends. Yes, all good. This is all perfectly normal.*

He shot me a secret smile as he sat down.

I wasn't sure whether to be pissed at him or flattered. Probably both. But right now, mostly, I was pissed.

"OK, it looks like everyone's back," I said as Millie entered and sat in the front row, looking worried. "How'd it go? Who'd you get?"

Subjects ranged from a local baker to tourists to a home-less man. Wyatt had shot the owner of the local hardware store in his milieu. The shop was practically a museum, since it had been around since the founding of Bohemia, so the portrait had a lot of potential.

"Millie?" I asked. "What did you shoot?"

She looked nervous, her dimples noticeably absent. "I had trouble finding someone who would talk to me. And I didn't want to talk to the men. They're so rude."

The students laughed, especially the guys.

"They certainly can be," I agreed, glaring at them, especially Wyatt. "Did you find someone?"

"Yes. I found a lady who was shopping."

I tried not to let my skepticism show. "Can we look at it? I realize these photos haven't been edited yet — we're going to talk about that next week, about how to pick the right photo and make them better in the digital darkroom. But maybe we can take a peek?"

"OK," Millie said quietly, popping the memory card from her camera and handing it to me.

I smiled at her, took the card and plugged it into the reader hooked up to my laptop. My photo software opened, reading the card, and I blew up the previews, skimming through the images.

The woman was frail and ancient. She wore an elaborate hat that probably dated from the 1950s. It perfectly matched her pea-green wool coat with brown fur collar. She had a curve to her back and clutched a vintage purse tightly in her wizened hands — though it probably wasn't vintage to her. In her face, furrowed with wrinkle upon wrinkle, her lips were lines of bright red framing tiny teeth in a sly smile, and her green eyes sparkled like a twenty-year-old's. Millie had shot her in front of the old five and dime, which still had the art deco lettering over the door, making it an image out of its time. It was a tender, beautiful portrait.

"Millie, this is lovely," I said, meaning it. "You've really captured her. I love how the morning light is kind of winking from the side, giving her a glow, picking up the lines in her face. The setting is perfect. Very nice."

"Thanks, Calista." Millie's face relaxed, and her eyes crinkled at the corners. She took her card gingerly and tucked it back into her camera.

"But now," I said to the class, "we're going to go over your favorite portraits and talk about why they work and why they don't. Wyatt, could you hit the lights?"

"Sure, Ms. Goode," he said, the tiniest tease in his tone as he got up and flipped the switches.

"Please, everyone, you may call me Calista," I said, deliberately addressing the entire room as I loaded the slide show, a colorful parade of faces on the wall in the comforting darkness.

We had a good discussion of distracting backgrounds and clothes, the rule of thirds and lighting. We talked about capturing natural posture and expressions, about keeping eyes sharp and backgrounds less so, about letting the subject dominate the photo in almost every situation. And we had fun, laughing at some of the images, expressing awe at others. For each group of ten, we counted down, and at the end of each set, I asked the student to identify him- or herself.

With Wyatt's set, a gasp greeted the photo of Ron Raker.

"This photo shows that even if your portrait isn't technically perfect, having a hunky celebrity in it doesn't hurt," I said, and the women in the room answered with approving murmurs. *A palpable hit,* I thought, wishing I could see Wyatt's face.

And then we'd gotten through his pictures, and Wyatt got a round of applause.

"Where's the tenth photo?" one of the guys in the front row asked.

"Corrupted file," was all I said.

Take that, Wyatt.

He was back there in the dark depths of the room, invisible to me, but I didn't feel victorious. Somehow, even though I knew I'd pricked his ego and had discovered his land mine, I felt defensive. It seemed as if he'd won a battle, and I hadn't known I was fighting a war.

WHEN CLASS ENDED, I focused on breaking down my laptop and the projector. By the time I looked up, the room was empty. So was I. As annoyed as I'd been by the photo, I felt a need to confront Wyatt about it. Was that his intention? Was he just pulling my pigtail on the playground, looking for attention? I didn't think he was being malicious, trying to expose me, even though that's how I felt when I saw the image.

Outside, the day had turned cloudy, and a cold mist kissed my cheeks as I pushed my bag up on my shoulder and started to walk toward my studio. We didn't have much winter in Bohemia, but it looked as if we were in for a day or so of nasty weather. The sweater I'd put on this morning felt too thin. The fronts that were dumping blizzards up north were dragging chilly fingers across Florida, reminding us that nowhere was entirely safe.

I shivered as I walked past Ponce De Leon Square, a pretty little park that was a perfect place on a warm day to see art students and others having a bite, painting a picture or lazing about on the grass. Now it was nearly empty, its denizens chased away by the turn in the weather.

Only one young couple sat at the edge of the central fountain, where a low wall encircled a bubbling two-tiered pedestal with a conquering Ponce de Leon on top. They looked serious, as if they were having a quiet argument, while Ponce stood above them, pointing toward the east, rakish feather on his hat, his sword at his hip. He seemed pleased, as if he indeed stood atop the fountain of youth.

A tiny bird alighted on his outstretched finger, a goldfinch. It eyed the trees and walkways around it with bright eyes, calm, alert.

The girl below whirled and walked away from her lover, and in a twinkle, the finch was gone, a flash of yellow in flight. The boy hung his head and walked in the other direction.

My camera never left my bag. It was a moment I could not freeze. For a second, I saw all the moments tumbling downhill through time and realized that I couldn't stop them, couldn't make them all neat and square.

God, it was getting cold.

I moved on, stepped up my pace and, ten minutes later, found myself at my studio door. I let myself in with a jingle and turned on the lights, trying to beat back the gray. I stood over the desk, wrestling my laptop out of my bag, when the bell rang again.

I looked up to see Wyatt, his face inscrutable.

"Hi, Cali." He put his bag down on the couch that faced the wall of photos and sat on the armrest with that innate grace he had, all lanky muscle barely concealed by a T-shirt, sweatshirt and jeans. "How you doing?"

"Quite well, thank you. And you?" I rummaged through my bag, pretending to search for something.

"I guess that depends on you." I looked up to see him run a hand through his hair, which had dried during class only to be dampened by the weather. It stuck up, the blond streak shining in the gallery lights.

"I have no idea why it would depend on me." I gave up on my bag and leaned against the desk, facing him.

"You didn't like my photo?" He was calm on the surface, but something like worry glinted in his eye.

"Which photo?" I asked innocently.

"The corrupted file."

I nodded and matched his sardonic tone. "It was an excellent photograph. Just a little much for Portrait Photography 101."

"Ah, I'm glad you saw it. I was afraid it really was corrupted," he said, his tone belying his statement.

"The only thing getting corrupted around here, apparently, is me." I was getting emotional, exactly what I didn't want to do. "I'm not myself around you."

Wyatt got up and moved toward me.

"Don't say that," he murmured, laying his hands on my shoulders. "Maybe it's the opposite."

"What are you talking about?"

His dark eyes were hypnotic. "Corrupted is not the word. You're expressing yourself. So am I. There's something pure about that. Pure angel, pure devil, pure you. The real you."

"Are you a poet as well as a surfer and a photographer?" I asked drily. "What a Renaissance man you are."

"Listen," he said. "Maybe I shouldn't have put the photo in my set. But why would you have a problem with it? Why not reveal the fire under that icy exterior? Let it go."

"Are you calling me an ice princess now? Great. I would think recent events suggested otherwise."

"You tell your class to take risks and be brave," Wyatt said. "But are you?"

"Bullshit. I don't want to be exposed like that, to the class, to everybody."

"Why not?" he asked. "That photo was perfectly decent. And it's not about you and me. It's about the art. Everything you do here is about the art. I see it in some of your work. Not all of it. Don't frown at me. That's not an insult. You can't be a genius all the time. But there's something you're keeping locked inside. Let it out."

He moved his hands down, clasped mine. I looked to the side, looking everywhere but at him. He leaned into me. I tried to think with my brains, not my body — my body, which was always ready with an answer to Wyatt: *Yes.*

"Look," I said, turning back to him. "You're the one who's taking classes from me. Don't you find this lecture a bit ironic?"

"Not at all," he said. "You're doing exactly the same for me. You're letting in light I haven't seen in — haven't seen ever. You help me see differently. And not just through a camera."

Wyatt bent over me, slow and inexorable, and kissed me. I breathed in the scent of him, fresh air and mist and the distant salty tang of ocean. I made a small, plaintive, involuntary sound as my mouth opened under his, and he wound his fingers into my twisted-up hair, removed the clip, tossed it and pulled me closer to him. After a moment, I pushed him away, trying to stop this roller coaster.

"You're muddling me," I croaked, looking down.

"Then why is it you're making everything clear for me?"

He lifted my chin. "I wouldn't say this stuff if I didn't believe in you, didn't admire what you do. Is this all just work for you?"

"The photography? I shoot pictures for the joy of it, if that's what you mean. But I also need to make a living. I'm shooting a wedding this weekend. It's called a job."

He laughed and took a step back. "But it's not just a job in your hands, Cali. It's art. It's life. Both together. Or at least, that's what it should be."

"What do you mean by 'it' in this scenario?"

"Everything."

I shook my head. "You make no sense, Mr. Brooks."

"You think too much, Ms. Goode."

"Not around you."

"That's what I'm counting on." He walked over to the front door and turned the lock.

"What are you doing?" My heart raced.

"Come with me into the studio."

"I need to keep my office hours."

"I know," he joked. "They're beating down the door."

"Wyatt," I said in a warning tone.

He advanced toward me again, grabbed my hands and pinned them to the desk as he leaned into me, kissing me harder this time.

"It's either here or in the studio," he murmured in my ear, his voice low and dangerous and sexy.

"You wouldn't."

"I would if you let me. And you want to let me." He kissed my neck, licking that sensitive spot he'd abraded the night before. One of his hands strayed to my jeans and popped open the top button.

"Studio, then." I yanked away from the desk and broke

into a sprint, a wild laugh escaping my lips, Wyatt hot on my heels. I really was going insane.

We were through the doors in a rush. The one dim hanging bulb barely illuminated the space — though I'd upgraded the bulb to the vintage filament type, which cast a soft, amber glow on Wyatt's cheekbones. It shone as an ember in his dark eyes as I turned to face him, slightly out of breath.

He scanned the room and walked toward me slowly, maneuvering me toward the black leather chairs in the shadows. I stood before him, weirdly elated at giving in to this overwhelming need, a need I'd only ever felt with him.

He kissed me, and then he began to strip me of my sweater, blouse and jeans, slowly, deliberately. Every time he touched me, it was as if an electric charge skated across my skin. A low fire built and flared in my core, and I could feel the ache of wanting him, as fresh as ever.

I stood before him in my bra and underwear — one of my nicer sets, light blue satin — and his eyes flared in appreciation. He reached out to caress my breasts, then lifted them from the cups so they perched above the bra, round and pale, nipples hard before him.

He still hadn't removed a stitch of clothing.

"You are exquisite," he said, pinching my nipples as he claimed me with a hard kiss. I gasped as he released me and deftly reached around my back to detach and remove the bra.

"Your turn," I said softly.

Wyatt began to strip, the sweatshirt, the T-shirt, the sandals and jeans, the briefs. Oh, but he was beautiful in the dim light, a sepia-tone statue, not cool marble, but hot-blooded and irresistible.

He moved toward me again, placed his hands on my hips, kissed me deeply.

"Turn around," he said. I did, and he pulled down my underpants. I stepped out of them and waited, my heartbeat running away with itself.

He ran a finger lightly down the crevasse of my behind, causing me to shiver, and pushed it inside my wet cleft, stroking me, priming me. Using the same finger, he brushed my clitoris, the bud hypersensitive in my aroused state. I was breathing hard as he pushed me forward toward one of the wide leather chairs.

"Kneel," he whispered, and I did, kneeling on the seat cushion, holding on to the back of the chair as he stroked my ass, pressed his hard shaft up against me. I moaned as it grazed my skin.

His cock entered my slit with a firm sweetness that became almost painfully pleasurable as he seated himself. He was a hot slab of muscle against my back. As he pulled out slightly and thrust in again and then again with terse, purposeful movements, he reached around me and caressed my breasts, teasing them until I groaned with the sensations taking over my body. He built a powerful rhythm, and I began to thrust back against him, my hands flat on the soft back of the chair as my cleft gripped his cock, over and over. He growled with the satisfaction of it.

He erupted inside me, and I cried out, pounding back against him, wanting all of him.

"Cali," he groaned, now holding me by the waist as he pumped the last of his seed into me. An orgasm throbbed wildly through me in response, and by the time we were done, I was shaking, my palms sweaty against the chair.

He pulled out of me. I could feel his wetness against my

leg. I was overwhelmed by the primal force and release of our coupling. He turned me around and pulled me against him, sinking into the chair, and I curled up next to him, wrapping an arm around his taut stomach, kissing his neck, his ear, our earlier conversation filed away for another time when my heart wasn't about to burn from the fire.

I WOKE from a doze to find Wyatt sleeping beside me on the wide leather chair. I slipped out of his arms, and he turned over, mumbling something as if from a dream. Good. I didn't want to wake him. Not yet.

I watched him as I dressed. In the dim light, I could just barely make out his expression. It was one of peace, a peace I'd never seen on his face before. It was as if he always carried with him a subtle tension, a subconscious worry that only eased in slumber. I draped his sweatshirt over his shoulders and went out to the gallery.

It was late afternoon already; I could tell by the way the light had changed. I unlocked the front door, just in case a customer dropped by. Wyatt was right. They weren't exactly banging down the door. I knew much of my work would be on location, but I needed to come up with strategies for marketing studio shoots. An online ad might be a start. I found my clip and pinned up my hair, then sat at the desk, opened my laptop and made a list of the possibilities. I'd just finished a half-hour's worth of ideas when I heard a noise. I looked up to see Wyatt entering the lobby gallery, clothed as he'd been when he came in, as if nothing had happened. As if we'd reset to zero once again. But then he smiled at me, a warm, broad smile, and my heart melted a little.

"Have you worked on the time-lapse yet?" he asked.

"No, but I ingested my photos. Have you looked at yours?"

"Yeah, they look pretty good, but I want to see you make the video first. Do you have time now?"

He was so polite, so natural. No demands, no challenges.

"Sure," I said. "Let's move to the couch so we can both see the laptop."

We sat side by side on the low, modern couch with its thin, not terribly comfortable seat cushion, facing the wall of photos. Wyatt put an arm around me as I opened the photo software, and for the moment, my angst faded, abolished by his comforting warmth. Looking at the photos of twilight descending over the lagoon, I relived what we'd done behind the camera. I snuck a glance at Wyatt, and he smiled, giving me a squeeze. So this was his sweet side.

I showed him how to go through the photos and eliminate anything that might look wildly out of place — like the frame that had a blurred bird swooping by the lens — and how to kick off the process that would put all the frames together into a movie.

We watched the progress bar slowly count up toward a hundred percent, usually one of my least favorite activities as an impatient person, but I didn't mind so much. Being here next to Wyatt, just talking, felt so pleasant.

"So tell me about the wedding you're shooting. Is it Saturday?" he asked.

"Yeah, Saturday afternoon, at a barn in west Bohemia."

"There are barns in Bohemia?"

"Once you get west of I-95, there's some farmland before it all goes to swamp. You'll find horses, cows, all sorts of things."

"Ostriches?" he asked.

"I can't say for sure, but I know at least one family raises emus."

"But not the wedding people."

"Right," I said. "They just rent out their barn for weddings and similar events. I've never been there myself, but the mother of the bride assures me it's beautiful, and I love old structures. The contrast between the formal wedding and the rustic barn should be really pretty."

"I know barn weddings are all the rage," Wyatt said. "I saw an article about them in a photography magazine. But I think most of the people getting married in barns wouldn't know a horse from a cow."

I laughed. "Probably not. But they're living the dream."

"The manure," he said with dreamy sarcasm. "The horseflies."

"More like mosquitoes, except this cold front should kill most of the bugs."

"Can I help?" he asked.

I turned away from the progress bar — at seventy-seven percent — and raised an eyebrow at him. "Not really your thing, is it?"

"I'm expanding my repertoire, and it would be educational. Besides, isn't it better to have a second shooter?"

"Usually," I said. I liked having backup for a wedding; it was insurance against missing any big moments. And a second shooter added richness to the final photo story.

"Are you worried I can't handle it?" Wyatt asked.

I answered thoughtfully. "No, I'm not worried. I've seen enough of your photos. You're good. I just hadn't thought about having help, is all. Do you have a decent flash?"

"A couple."

"Good. I only use a flash when necessary — we'll have to see what the light situation is."

"So you'll take me?" he asked.

"Sure. And I'll pay you."

Wyatt shook his head and smiled. "No 'transactions' between us," he said, echoing my own word.

"But I have to compensate you. It's, like, six hours out of your day."

"Consider me an intern. I'm here to learn." His tone turned flirtatious. "Plus, I think it might be fun to go to a wedding with you."

"It's not like we'll get to drink champagne."

"Maybe after," he said lightly. "Look, the video's done."

I tapped over to the laptop's desktop screen and opened the video file.

A short, elegant silent movie unfolded before us, as a blue sky deepened into orange and purple, clouds rushed by and the water reflected the gold of the smoothly sinking sun, all highly accelerated as part of the time lapse. The palms and oaks on the fringes of the frame trembled with unnatural speed, and the river's low waves twinkled just as fast. A hint of stars shone in the dark sky as day turned to night and the video ended.

"That is *so* cool," Wyatt said. "I hope mine looks that good."

"I have a feeling it will," I said, catching his eye. "You seem to have the touch."

He leaned in and kissed me. "Glad you think so."

"You want to do dinner?"

"I can't. I promised Jen I'd go to dinner with her. And tomorrow night I'm supposed to go bowling with her and her husband."

"He's back in town?" I tried not to sound too relieved.

"He will be tomorrow."

Oh. So Wyatt was having dinner with his old surfing girl-friend, or whatever she was, tonight. I wasn't sure how bohemian his lifestyle was, and it's not like I'd asserted any claims — except with my body. I knew I was suffering from an irrational outbreak of jealousy, but I had it just the same. And I had to ask him about his association with Jen before we hooked up again. There were some things that weren't worth taking a chance with, and I wasn't going to be the other woman in a sexual relationship.

He must have seen my thoughts spinning across my face.

"How about Friday?" he asked in a conciliatory tone that just irked me.

"I can't. Girls' night. I'm meeting friends at the Junction Box."

"I keep hearing there's a great band that plays there."

I nodded. "My friend Ez is in it. She's one of the people I'm meeting. On our *girls' night,*" I emphasized.

He looked like he was hiding a smile. I got up, out of the warm curve of his arm, and put my laptop back on the desk.

"So," he said, "what is this girls' night mystique, anyway? Guys don't have guys' nights, do they?"

"All the time. They're called football."

He laughed. "Women like football, too."

"You know what I mean. Women need to define their space. Our lives don't revolve around you, you know."

"Thank God," he said. "We're pretty dull creatures, really. Primitive, Cro Magnon beasts who want only one thing." He got up, too, grinning, and picked up his bags.

"Savage," I said, but I couldn't hold back a little smile.

"We'll talk. I'll see you Saturday, OK? For the wedding. Should I meet you here?"

I sighed. This was so *not* going according to the Calista Goode Relationship Playbook. "Meet me at 3. We have to be there at 4. What are you doing, renting a car?"

"Jen has an extra she lets me borrow when I need it. I wasn't ready to buy one."

"Of course not," I said. Because that would be just one more unwelcome thing tying him to Bohemia Beach.

FRIDAY, I got to the Junction Box, in a flapper-era building near the railroad tracks in downtown Bohemia, after Ez's first set had already started. She and the Emeralds were in the midst of a raucous tune when I strolled in, and I didn't want to distract her. She'd join the rest of us between sets.

I was running late after nabbing a last-minute job at a dance studio, thanks to Bart. He'd had a call at the paper from the proprietor, who'd wanted to hire a photographer to shoot the little girls and their teachers during a dress rehearsal for a recital. It was loads of fun. The girls ranged from cute little chubby princesses to elegant sylphs straight out of a Degas painting. The natural light flowing into the studio windows made for gorgeous candids.

I hauled lights for the formal shots and had to rush home with all the gear before I got to the bar — which meant I'd skipped dinner once again. I'd just had time to change: navy-blue leggings, suede boots and a white tank top. Over it, I wore an oversized, button-up gray and blue sweater tunic that reached halfway down my thighs. I'd worn big, dangly blue glass earrings and a long, matching necklace. I left my hair long and wavy. I was ready to let loose.

I saw Sloane, first. My cousin was at the dark-wood bar, talking to my black-clad brother under one of the Victorian gaslights. He had a particularly bitter look on his face, along with the premature signs of excessive gin and tonics.

Sloane was wearing one of those cute dresses she had, russet brown, along with brown tights and boots, and a pretty green and brown chiffon scarf that seemed to float about her and bring out the green tendencies of her blue-green eyes. She smiled when she saw me and gave me a big hug.

"How's the photography coming?" she asked.

"Great!" I said. "Two jobs this week, plus class is — interesting."

Sloane winked at me.

Damien's smile was acidic. "Dating any more surfers?"

I narrowed my eyes at him, then looked at Sloane. She shrugged, as if to say she hadn't told him anything. He was probably fishing after the Ron Raker incident.

"How about you, Damien?" I asked. "Still seeing Javier?"

Damien's expression became even more grim, and he knocked back his drink. "Neil, another!" he shouted over his shoulder to the suspender-wearing, mustachioed barman. "Javier went back to Miami, his return to the fleshpots of Bohemia Beach TBD. *To be determined,*" he slurred into Sloane's ear.

"I know what it means," Sloane said.

"That ended almost as fast as one of *your* relationships, my dear sister." Damien took a swig of the fresh drink Neil handed him.

"Not fair." He was baiting me, and I refused to get angry.

"Mine have often lasted more than two weeks, and more typi-cally four months to a year," I declared.

"OK, then," he said, "let's say it lasted slightly longer than the *excitement* in your average relationship."

"As if that's something you would know," I said icily.

"I have eyes, my dear sister."

"Stop calling me that."

Sloane giggled. "Forget it, Cali. He knows not of what he speaks." She wiggled her eyebrows at me, and I thought of Wyatt. Talk about excitement. "Let me get you a drink. It's still happy hour. You can have my second Old-Fashioned."

The call of the whiskey calmed me, and in a moment, Sloane and I each had a generous glass in our hands. It was a drink I'd introduced her to.

Sloane gave Damien an undeserved hug, which he shrugged off, looking sheepish, and we found a table as he wandered unsteadily around the bar to a cluster of his artist friends.

"So you have two jobs this week?" Sloane asked.

"One today and a wedding tomorrow," I said. "And I have a few ideas on how to market the studio. I thought I'd run it by you all tonight."

"Awesome. Who else is coming?"

"Thea — you met her at my studio. And Penelope. In fact, here they are now."

The two women entered. Thea wore jeans and a cowl-neck black sweater, a pretty contrast to her braided red hair and pale skin. Penelope's fine features were precisely made up. She'd worn a low-cut pinup dress only slightly less juicy than the one she'd worn to the art show opening. This one was pink with white polka dots and a wide white belt, acces-sorized with a white sweater. Her yellow and pink hair was coiffed in a perfect vintage wave. I did introductions all around.

"Penelope is a fabric artist," I said after introducing Sloane, "and Thea is a graphic artist who does signs and more mysterious things that she will tell us all about."

"If you talk about it, you take the juice out of it," she said, somewhere between cryptic and humorous.

"Well, I'll talk about what *I'm* doing," Penelope said. "I'm in the middle of designing costumes for the Chamberlain Theater's production of 'Alice in Wonderland.' "

"What an opportunity!" I exclaimed.

"Exactly," Penelope said, waving over a server. "My imagination is running *wild.* Vodka martini, dirty," she told the waiter.

"Gin martini, dry, one olive," Thea said.

"Gin! *Nooooo,*" Penelope exclaimed.

"Vodka? What's the point? It's flavorless," Thea said.

"Yes, but once, gin and I had a very awkward one-night-stand," Penelope said in a stage whisper, pursing her very red lips. The waiter seemed nonplussed.

I laughed and pointed to Sloane. "Another Old-Fashioned for both of us. Better make it three, so we have one ready for Ez when she has her break. Is it still happy hour?"

"Afraid not," the waiter said before leaving us, "but I'll tell Neil it's for Ez. You know what he's like."

I nodded and explained to the group that Neil had a soft spot for Ez, or at least for her cocktail demands.

"So what are you doing with the 'Alice' costumes?" I asked Penelope.

"Lots of shimmer and color and checks, checkered and striped *everything,*" she said. "And a dizzying number of diamonds and spades and hearts and clubs. Big collars. Short skirts. Extremely silly shoes."

"I can't wait to see the play," Sloane said.

My wheels were turning. "Do you think maybe I could photograph the cast in their costumes? Like, pro bono work for publicity? Unless you already have someone lined up."

"Oh, *please,*" Penelope said with dramatic desperation. "The director's uncle thinks he's God's gift to photography with his fucking cell phone. *Please.* I'll put in a word, and we'll have you out next week. I could really use photos for my portfolio anyway."

"That brings up something else I wanted to ask you all about," I said. "I'd like to do some shoots in my studio, sell them as women's nights or parties, with wine and cheese and music. And I'd like to get one under my belt, as it were, so I can put examples on my website. Would you be interested? A freebie to get started?"

Penelope's eyebrows arched. "Would we be naked?"

Now everyone laughed, and the drinks arrived, adding to the happiness of the table.

"Nudity optional and not necessarily encouraged," I joked. "It would be a girl-only thing, so we could easily do lingerie or sexy poses or just some really bitching portraits. Business suits. Costumes. Whatever you want."

Thea intoned, "We will have the most incredible social media profile photos in the history of the Internet."

"I could cover myself in clay," Sloane joked.

Everyone laughed, except Penelope. "You would look *fabulous,*" she said. "You should do it. And I have a few of my pinup friends I could bring. Trust me, they will not hurt your portfolio," she said to me, "and they're always looking for new shots. If they like you, they'll come back and tell their friends, too."

"Excellent!" I said. "Sloane, what are you thinking?"

She blushed. "What Alex would think of a photo of me entirely painted in clay."

"He wouldn't be thinking at all," I said. I'd seen how Alex looked at her fully dressed.

"Which leads me to a confession," Sloane said. "He's here."

"For girls' night?" Thea asked.

Sloane smiled. "He promised to keep to the other side of the bar. He has a couple of new friends he's chatting with. And Gary and Damien, too," she added, pointing out her fellow potter and my brother in the group.

"Oh, who cares," Thea said. "I never did understand the point of girls' night, anyway. It's just a night. Not a girls' night. Right? It's our night, but we don't have to label it, as if it's some Amazonian ritual."

"That's odd," I said. "Wyatt said something similar."

"Wyatt?" Penelope asked.

Sloane said, "Funny you should mention him." And our eyes all followed her gaze toward the door, where Wyatt had entered with one of the guys from the photo class and another guy, maybe a surfer, judging by the bleach-blond hair and the build.

"The one in the black leather jacket and the clingy jeans? Are you seeing that tantalizing bit of man flesh?" Penelope asked. I let slip a nervous giggle. "You go, girl."

I recovered myself. "I'm sort of seeing him."

"There is no sort of with that boy," Penelope continued. "Mark my words. You must pin him down and have your way with him."

At that moment, Wyatt's eyes found mine, and he shot me a salacious grin before he turned back to his friends.

"I think she already has," Thea quipped.

Everyone laughed and drank, and I joined in, feeling my face go hot.

The band paused, and Ez said into the microphone, "We'll be back in a few minutes, amigos. Drink a lot and tip Neil *really* well." She blew the bartender a kiss, and a smile lifted the curled ends of his handlebar mustache.

Ez headed our way and pulled up a chair. "Cocktail?" she asked pleadingly.

I handed her the Old-Fashioned we'd ordered, and she drank half of it down before smacking her lips and releasing a satisfied sigh. "Penelope, how you doing, girl? And Sloane? And who's this?"

I introduced Thea, and another round of drinks mysteriously appeared.

"Thank Neil," the waiter said, nodding at the bartender.

Ez blew him another kiss.

"If you're dating him, then almost everyone at girls' night has a guy in the building," Thea said.

"I am not, but it doesn't hurt to have a friend behind the bar," Ez said, pushing back the long bangs that habitually covered one of her almond-shaped brown eyes. "Are all of you dating someone?"

"Absolutely not," Penelope said. "I'm dating several."

"I'm waiting for her leftovers," Thea joked.

"I'm happy," Sloane said, typically shy, looking over at Alex.

"I have no idea what the fuck I'm doing," I said, feeling the effects of the whiskey on an empty stomach, "but he's cute."

"To cute!" Ez bellowed, holding up her glass. We clinked the glasses together and drank.

"What about you, Ez?" I asked.

"Oh, just playing with the boys in the band."

"That sounds saucy." Penelope's plucked eyebrows rose.

"Only one at a time," Ez said. "Right now, I'm into percussion." She looked over at the drummer, who gave her a nod and a sly look before heading out the back door.

"I do love musicians," Penelope said, sipping her martini. "As soon as I get a spare couch, I intend to add another to the stable."

We laughed as our waiter delivered another Old-Fashioned.

"From Gary," he said as he put it down in front of Ez.

"Which one's Gary?" Thea asked.

Sloane subtly pointed to the corner. "Tall. Curly hair."

"Don't forget cute," I pointed out.

"To cute, goddamn it!" Ez toasted again, and we lifted our glasses and drank. "So much cute, so little time."

I felt a wave of dizziness. *Oh, shit.* I was getting drunk. I waved down the waiter. "Can I have an order of cheese sticks?"

"I have a terrible craving for smoked salmon, crème fraiche and caviar," Penelope announced.

"You won't get it here," our waiter said. "How about fish dip?"

"All right," Penelope said. "One must live with disappointment."

Thea and Sloane ordered fries and calamari. Soon we were eating our snacks and listening to Ez's second set, which started with a melancholy solo piece, a lament about always searching but never finding light and love. Ez's deft fingering on the baby grand piano offered a mournful counterpoint to the bleak, emotional vocal. The bar was spellbound.

"Damn, she's good," Thea said as we applauded at the end of the song and the rest of the Emeralds came out and picked up their instruments, chased through the back door by the faint smell of doobie. "Look, I hate to do this to you, but I have an early-morning job. I should get going."

"We'll talk again soon," I said. "I'll ping everyone about scheduling the photo shoot."

"Sounds good." We exchanged hugs, and the activity at our table seemed to stir up motion in the corner. As Thea paid and left, Alex approached.

"May I have Sloane back now?" he asked, comically plaintive, his gray eyes dancing.

"I suppose," I said with mock severity.

"Mmm," Penelope said, looking Alex over, from his wavy dark-blond hair to his admirable figure. "You need to let me design you a suit."

"As long as it's not like Damien's art-show outfit," he said. Sloane chuckled, put down some money and led him away by the arm.

"He did *not* just insult my couture," Penelope said, but she was holding back a smile.

"If you can't beat 'em, join 'em?" I suggested. She nodded, the smile lighting up her delicate features, and we paid the last of the bill and headed for the bar and the art crowd there. I tried not to look as if I was looking for Wyatt, but of course, I was. Maybe he'd left already.

Penelope went to hug Damien and scold him for being morose, and I contemplated my next drink. At least I'd walked to the Junction Box — one of the benefits of living in

Bohemia proper. So I could have one more, I thought. I would choose later between staggering and cabbing it home.

I felt a hand on my shoulder and turned around to find Wyatt behind me, a beer in his hand, a warm spark in his eyes.

I COULD'VE LEFT at the same time as Thea, had a good night's sleep before the wedding. But it would have been hard to leave the bar knowing I hadn't even said hello to Wyatt. I was glad he'd found me.

He surprised me by leaning in and kissing me, the sensation of his heated lips competing with the band's loud chorus in my ears. I realized it was the first really public kiss we'd had, and it felt strange. Especially because I wasn't sure where we stood.

"Not out with Jen tonight?" I asked as he released me, then grimaced at my own sharp, alcohol-loosened tongue.

His brow furrowed. "She's happy to get rid of me. Finally, she has a night alone with her husband."

"I guess she already had her nights alone with you."

He looked at me with disbelief. "You can't possibly be thinking what you're thinking," he said.

"What am I thinking?"

"Cali." I heard low, simmering anger in his voice. "We need to clear this up right now."

"Let's not," I said, still feeling tipsy. "Let's talk some other time when I can hear you."

"You can hear me now. Outside."

"It's cold," I protested, not wanting the confrontation.

"Not that cold." He didn't touch me, just gestured toward the back door.

I reluctantly led the way to the courtyard, with its picnic tables and strings of lights. On the east side, a black iron fence separated the space from the train tracks. A packed parking lot hid behind bushes and palm trees on the other, and a gate led to an alley in back. A few hearty souls were drinking and smoking out here at the tables, but it was relatively quiet. The band's notes blended softly with the noises of Bohemia on a busy Friday night.

I sat, realizing I didn't have a drink and kind of annoyed about it. Maybe I was just annoyed with everything. Wyatt sat next to me on the table's bench and put down his beer, and I reached for it and took a sip. He looked at me with his own brand of irritation.

"Sorry," I said.

"You can drink the damn beer," he said. "I want to clear the air about Jen and David. Whatever you've cooked up in the hot wires of your brain is nowhere close to reality."

"How do you know what I think?"

"I just know you can't possibly know the deal," Wyatt said simply. He leaned his elbows on the table, put his face in his hands for a few moments, then sat up and looked at me. He seemed tired. "Jen was a real friend when I needed her, and when she married David, he was my friend, too. *Friends.* Who happen to be twenty years older than I am, if that makes any difference."

"Oh." My image of the sexpot surfer girl eroded somewhat. "How do you know them?"

"When my stepdad kicked me out of the house when I was fifteen, I had nowhere to go. I slept on different friends' couches for a few nights at a stretch. But my high school friends, they couldn't talk their parents into a permanent guest. I could see it in their faces. They didn't want me hanging around all the time.

"I ran out of couches. For about four months, I just slept on the beach or in the back of this ice cream stand where I got a job. I stayed away from the shelter so I wouldn't end up in some foster care situation. Sometimes a surfing friend took pity on me and let me spend the night. My last friends were in the surfing community. It had always been my escape, and then it was all I had."

"Wait." My head was spinning. "Why did you get kicked out?"

Wyatt took a sip of his beer. "No good reason. I was an OK student, a decent kid, if a little wild. I just didn't get along with my stepdad. My mom was a really needy person, and when she married him, she cared a lot more about pleasing him than protecting me. Their relationship was unhealthy at best, and my relationship with them deteriorated the older I got. I got tired of him hitting me. I started to fight back. Truth was, if he hadn't kicked me out, I probably would have left anyway. Or been in jail or dead."

"Oh, no, Wyatt. I'm so sorry." I felt sad and guilty for misjudging him. "Was your dad around? Couldn't he help you out?"

"My real dad? I have no idea where he went. He left when I was two. My mother said he was dead, but that might have been a lie. She lived on lies."

"Shit."

"Yeah, well." He took another sip of his beer. "At my lowest point, I was out on the beach one day, where I spent most of my time when I had nowhere to go, and this woman came up to me. She was a surfer, too. I'd seen her around.

And she asked me if I was OK. She bought me a hamburger. She said she had a lanai where I could spend the night — it was a hammock, actually, on her back patio. That was Jen. I think she was testing me, wanting to see if I was bad news. But I wasn't on drugs or anything. I was just shit out of luck. And she let me stay a few more nights, and then she let me move into her spare room in exchange for doing stuff around the house. She really adopted me, though not officially. She's just this super-nice, generous person. She started dating David soon after she took me in, and he was good to me, too. He's the one who introduced me to Ron."

"Really?"

"Sure. David was an organizer of a local surfing tournament and arranged for me to meet Ron when he came to town. I was pretty good by then, had even won some prize money. Whenever there were big waves within driving distance, I was on them. Ron and I hit it off. I graduated and hit the circuit. He helped me get sponsors right away, since I was one of his crew. Jen and David and Ron saved my life. They really did. It's only been in the last year that I saw I was going to have to part ways with Ron, but he'll always be a really important friend to me."

"Damn, Wyatt," I said. My eyes moistened as I watched him staring out into space. "I'm an ass. I'm sorry."

He looked over at me. "No, you're not. I should have told you sooner. I thought you girls liked men to be mysterious." His attempt to make light of what he'd told me didn't quite work.

I nudged closer to him and slipped an arm around his waist. I lay my head on his shoulder and held him close. The chill in the air intensified with a passing breeze, and he shifted, straddled the bench and wrapped me up in his arms. He pulled back just enough to look into my eyes.

"I love your hair like this," he whispered, running one hand through my mane.

"Since you never let me wear a hair clip more than five minutes, I figured." My comment failed to coax a smile from him. "I'm sorry about what you went through, Wyatt. I think you're the bravest person I know."

"Hardly." His eyes were shadowed, conflicted. He fisted his hand in my hair and pulled me toward him, pressing his mouth over mine, opening me, devouring me slowly, his tongue possessing me. He drew me closer, and I closed my eyes and fell into his kiss, holding him tightly, wanting to burn away his sorrow. A rushing noise seemed to build in my ears as our kiss intensified, as our bodies pressed into each other. The ground seemed to shake, tension vibrated through my frame, and then a mighty horn shattered the air and a train was roaring by, making the tables tremble, drowning out the band, whipping the air with a wind of its own making. Wyatt broke the kiss and laughed, looking into my eyes, and I laughed, too, immersed in the exhilarating, visceral noise.

Finally, it passed, fading into the night.

"If the train was heading into a tunnel, it would be perfect," I joked.

He kissed me again, then whispered into my ear. "We can make that happen. Who needs symbolism when we have each other?"

"Rascal. Let's have a drink."

"At your place," Wyatt said. "If you *have* something to drink."

"I'm a journalist," I said with mock outrage. "Of *course* I have something to drink."

He grinned, the uncertainty gone. "Good. Let's go. Let me tell the guys I'm leaving."

We went back through the bar. As he said goodbye to his friends, I stopped to give Sloane and Alex a hug and check on Damien. His eyes were lidded, and he slumped on a barstool, barely following the conversation.

"You OK?" I asked.

"Almost numb enough," he said, an acerbic smile taking over his face as Wyatt came up behind me. "So you *are* still dating surfer boys. He's a pretty one."

"Shut it, Damien. And get a ride home."

"You know me. Always looking for a ride."

I frowned at him. I'd never seen him like this. I kissed his cheek despite the waves of hostility coming off him.

"Don't worry," Alex said quietly. "We'll get him home OK."

I nodded at him and Sloane, and then I accompanied Wyatt out the door.

"Your brother? What's wrong with him?" he asked as we walked toward my place, past the busy clubs of downtown Bohemia.

"I'm not sure, but it might just be a broken heart," I said. "This is assuming he has a heart."

"Probably. Some people are better at hiding it than others."

It was a funny thing to say. I leaned into Wyatt, still tipsy, trying not to think about broken hearts. At least Wyatt was mine right now, if not forever. I tried to tell myself that was enough.

"You ever talk to your mom now?" I asked.

His reply was cold. "She died of cancer a couple of years ago. We were completely estranged."

"No siblings?"

"Nobody," he said. "And that's fine with me."

We walked the rest of the way in silence, me trying to reconcile his moments of fire with the ice in his words. He still had his arm around me. He felt warm. But I wondered how cold his heart might be, a heart that needed nobody.

In my apartment, which now was officially free of boxes, I lit the candles in the fireplace and brought a bottle of bourbon and two glasses with ice from the kitchen to the living room. The soft, flickering light glimmering in the glasses made me happy as I filled them with the whiskey. They, with Wyatt sitting on the couch behind them, would have made a beautiful picture.

He shed his leather jacket and threw it on top of the gray and white fleece blanket draped over my stuffed chair. His tight black T-shirt was revealing and alluring. I swallowed at the sight of him and sat next to him on the couch, drunk and delighted to have him all to myself.

He took a sip of his whiskey and watched me watching him. I reached out and ran a hand through that wild hair of his. "How do you do this?"

"What — the streak?"

"Yeah. Bleach? Color? Professional hair stylist?"

"It's actually been that way for a long time," he said. "Since I was a teenager."

"You mean you've been dyeing it all that time?"

"No. A chunk of it just turned white, and it's been that way ever since."

I raised my eyebrows. "Since you left home?"

"Yes. It's natural."

I took a long sip of my whiskey. "Figures you would make a symptom of stress look sexy," I teased him.

"Maybe it wasn't stress. Maybe I'm just that sexy," he said, matching my humor.

I put down my glass and took his, setting it next to mine. I ran both hands through his hair and leaned forward, kissing his forehead, kissing his cheek, inhaling his warm breath and the scent of whiskey. But he spoke before I could touch my lips to his.

"I have to tell you something," he said.

I sat back. He was stopping me? *Oh, shit.* And he had to tell me something?

"I'm leaving Sunday," he said.

"What?" My heart slammed to a cold stop.

"It's for a gig. Mavericks. It's hard to say for sure, but there's buzz about big waves in the next few days from a powerful storm, and some of the surfers are planning to go. There's a new magazine that's trying to gain traction in the scene, and they're hiring me to shoot some of the guys for profiles they're doing. They want artsy stuff and also surf. I can't say no. It's going to be awesome for the resume."

I nodded numbly. "Of course you can't say no." I picked up my whiskey again and drank deeply. I glanced at him. He was searching my eyes, trying to figure me out.

"I'm going to finish the class," he said. "I'll be back in less than a week. I'll make up the classwork, or even if I don't, I don't need the certificate — but I still have more to learn. Maybe you can help me catch up."

"Sure," I said as coolly as I could. "I can help you finish up before you leave again."

"Before the next gig? It might be a while." He picked up

his drink, too, and took a sip. "Story of my life. I never know where I'm going next."

"That's funny," I said, thinking it wasn't funny at all. "I always know where I'm going next. Or at least I used to, until this year."

He chuckled. "You're only two weeks into the year."

"Tell me about it." I drained my glass, set it on the table and leaned back.

"It's only a week, Cali," Wyatt said more softly, putting his glass on the table, leaning closer to me. He took one of my hands and drew circles on my palm with his fingers.

"I know I'm not one of those hip girls you're probably used to dealing with, but I guess I'm not used to being with a rambling man." I glowered at him. "But I hate to get all maudlin on you. The whiskey's making me talk."

"What about New Year's Eve?"

"What about it?"

"Did you think you'd ever see me again?" he asked, his hand wandering to my knee, caressing it through the thin leggings.

"I — no, I didn't."

"I didn't see you running away then."

"That was different." His hand, now traveling up my thigh, was *really* distracting. I swallowed. "It was a kiss. A moment."

"You were using me," Wyatt teased.

"No! I just wanted to kiss you, is all. And you started it."

He ran a hand through my hair. "Did I?"

I pondered this thought. Maybe I did start it when I looked at him over the champagne glass, giving him the eye in the middle of the party.

"And at the bar by the beach," he murmured in my ear,

the hand on my thigh creeping higher, "that room in the dark — did you think you'd see me again then?"

"I don't know," I said softly, wavering. "I didn't care."

"You don't know, or you don't care?" He kissed my neck, that sensitive spot right below my ear. "Maybe only the moment matters, Cali."

"Oh, fuck, Wyatt," I said. "Maybe nothing matters." I turned toward him and put a hand on his knee, turnabout being fair play and all. I slid my hand up over his crotch, cupped him and squeezed through his jeans.

I felt a quake pass through his body, and he closed his eyes.

"Cali," he breathed.

I wanted to show him what he would be missing when he left. I wanted to communicate, somehow, even half of what was going on in my mind, my body. My heart.

I stood, a little unsteadily thanks to the whiskey, and pulled off my boots. And then, slowly, as he watched from under lowered eyebrows, I worked off the leggings under my long sweater. I tossed them aside. My sweater covered my hips; I reached under it and slid off my underpants, dropping them as his eyes followed my movements. Still the sweater hid much of my body. I pulled my arms inside the sweater, wriggled out of the tank top and dropped it to the floor as Wyatt's eyes widened. My arms slid into the sleeves again. The button-up front of the soft sweater left a deep "V" at my neckline that revealed the curves of my breasts.

"See?" I held out my arms and smiled. "Magic. I'm half undressed, and you can't even tell."

"Show me," he said, his voice low and urgent.

"Take off your shirt first."

It was off in a flash, revealing the rolling muscles and

lines of his torso, the valley that led my eyes down to his jeans. He sat forward, watching me, his eyes dark, flecked with golden candlelight.

The whiskey was really making me loose. I'd never done a strip-tease for a boy. But Wyatt was no ordinary boy. And his skin, his chest, were beautiful, as golden as the light.

I grasped the bottom of the thick knit and lifted it ever so slowly, pulling it back down and up a little more, but not quite enough for him to see everything. And then I unbuttoned one button from the top, and another, and another. The gap extended the open "V" halfway to my belly button, but still the sweater concealed me.

I reached under the hem and touched myself. Wyatt licked his lips. I let out a little sigh as I rubbed my bud, watching him as I fanned the flame of arousal — mine and his. He started to get up.

"No," I whispered. With one hand I pulled up the sweater just enough so he could see my triangle. With the other, I penetrated myself with my finger. I was wet as I performed for him, releasing a soft moan as I moved. My excitement increased as I observed him.

Wyatt's mouth opened slightly, those curvy lips red in the flickering light, his eyes glittering, his face a mask of desire. He unbuttoned his jeans, unzipped them slowly, and I saw the bulge in his briefs. Still penetrating myself with my finger, I revealed one breast, then the other, before letting the sweater conceal me again. He took off his sandals and jeans, watching me, and then he stood and shed his briefs. He was exquisitely nude in front of the fireplace, lit askance by the candlelight. He stepped toward me.

Drunk and high on adrenaline, I offered him my wet finger, and he took it in his mouth, sucking on it, much as I'd once done for him. And then, unstoppable, he reached his hands up to my shoulders, pushed the sweater open and let it drop to the floor, revealing all of me. The rosy peaks of my breasts fully betrayed my arousal. He crushed me to him, pushing his tongue inside my mouth, fucking me with it. I pushed back on his chest, hard, and he landed on the couch lengthwise, a look of surprise on his face.

I fell to my knees and looked up at him, saw the fire in his eyes. I opened my mouth and took in his cock, all of it, drawing out, laving the head with my tongue.

He exhaled, half breath, half moan, leaning backward as I sucked. I took him deep, my hair falling around him. He reached for me and grasped my tresses, pulling me toward him as I sucked, as I licked around the red tip.

He sighed as I released him. I climbed up and straddled him on the couch. He looked up at me, at my long hair swinging down over him.

"Ride me," he whispered.

He helped guide his shaft toward my opening, his tip teasing my folds. I lowered myself slowly, easily, I was so wet. He filled me, hard and hot, as I clenched him, tight and slick. We both groaned as I squeezed around him, as I felt him stretch me.

I began to move, slowly, and he grasped my behind, making low, guttural sounds. My God, he felt good like this. He touched my nub and began playing with it, teasing me into short breaths, rapid heartbeat and, *oh, yes,* waves of aching pleasure from inside and out. He watched me with a tiny smile, enjoying the view of me lost in desire, of my breasts swinging over him.

Abruptly, he lifted me, flipping me onto my back, and I was looking up into his dark, intense gaze. He pressed his moist lips to mine in a long, ornate kiss, as plush and layered as a rose, his tongue touching mine in a mating dance of whiskey and firelight.

A wicked gleam entered his eyes.

"Did you think you were in charge?" he asked.

A slow grin took over my face. "Maybe, yeah."

"Put your arms over your head," he said.

I looked into his eyes, questioning.

"Do it," he said, and I felt a tremor of excitement. I complied, and with one strong hand, he grabbed my wrists, pushing them back into the pillows of the couch. With the other, he pushed two fingers into my slit and began to stroke my sweet spot with sinful dexterity.

I dropped my head back, trying to buck against his fingering, squirming under the steely grip of his hand. "Please, Wyatt."

"Please, what?"

"You know what. Don't tease me."

"Say what you said that other time."

"What?" I pled ignorance. His fingers moved to play with my clit and slid back and brushed my anus. I shivered. In a moment, he teased my nub again. I clenched. I wanted all of him inside me. *"Please,"* I groaned.

"Say you'll do anything for me."

Maybe if I were sober and fully clothed and cold and alone I would scoff. But right now?

"I'll do anything," I whispered. "Only — give it to me."

"Oh, I'll give it to you." He deftly manipulated my clit with his fingers, sending me right to the edge of ecstasy.

"Yes, yes, yes," I moaned, not caring how I sounded, wanting more, *more.* "I'll do anything!"

He abruptly released my hands, straddled me, grabbed my hips. And then he plunged his cock inside me.

I cried out with his size, the force of him, my sensitivity already somewhere in outer space as he pounded me, opening me still more, every cell screaming with the hard, painful pleasure of it. I shuddered against him, grabbing his hips, trying to pull myself to him, to crash into his hard body with all my energy. And then I was coming, milking him, contracting around him as he made an animal cry of pleasure, of power. He had power over me, but I knew, looking into his scorching eyes as they locked with mine, that I also had power over him. We were an electric circuit, lit up, sizzling and sparking together, on the verge of conflagration.

We ground to a halt slowly, small tremors still moving through me as he withdrew. He bent down and licked one nipple, sucking gently, and then sucked the other, sending sparks across my skin and through my already molten core. He released the nipple, finally; wet and red and hard, it popped out of his mouth, aching sweetly.

He stood and pulled the fleece blanket from the chair, wrapped it around us and spooned me as we lay on the couch. He pressed his mouth against my neck and licked.

"I'm going to take you up on it, you know," he murmured.

"What?"

"That anything that you'll do. But I'll play fair."

"How?" I rubbed myself against him, and he grunted.

"More fair than that," he said. "You'll be able to refuse me twice. But the third time, you'll have to do it."

"What?" I was ready to dismiss his game, but I found myself curious about his challenge.

"Whatever I ask."

I could hear the provocation in his voice, and a pulse of desire went through me.

"Whatever you say, surfer boy." High from our lovemaking, I burrowed against his hot body, my eyes closed, breathing in the scent of him, of us, as we drifted off to sleep.

WAKING up with Wyatt was so different from going to sleep with him. At some point during the night, we'd moved to my bed, and as light seeped through the blinds on the window, I roused to the sensation of comforting heat against my back and an arm slipping around my waist. As he pressed against me, memories of the night before rushed back into my body, fueling my arousal. He pulled me even closer, and I could feel him, hard and ready behind me, as we lay sideways against the pillows. Still sleepy, I shifted to give him access as he spooned against me, as he pushed his erection between my legs. He kissed my neck and caressed my breasts and I opened more, until his shaft slipped inside my wet slit and he moaned softly in my ear, taking me gently, with deliberate thrusts, until he came in slow motion inside me. I groaned in answer to his sigh, shuddering against him, drowsy with pleasure.

He eased out of me, leaving me soaking wet with his seed, with my own desire. I turned toward him, then, and our mouths touched in dreamy kisses until we simply nestled against each other, spent.

"Are you sure we can't stay here all day?" he murmured.

"It'd be kind of hard to shoot the wedding from here."

"We could send a drone." He showed his dimple, and I ran a thumb over it, kissed it.

"That'll be all the rage next year. For now, we're grounded."

"Too bad." He slid a hand over the curve of my hip under the blankets, giving me goose bumps.

I *wished* we could stay in bed all day. Especially since he was leaving tomorrow.

"I think it'll be fun," I said. "You ready?"

"I will be."

"I'll take the lead and let you know what to shoot, at least at first," I said, thinking it through. "We can be more creative in the reception, after the ceremony."

"I'm ready to obey your every command, my lady."

I chuckled. "Ha. Don't tempt me."

"But my job is to tempt you." And he kissed me again.

Several kisses and caresses later, Wyatt rolled out of bed. I tied on my short, ice-blue satin robe, followed him to the living room and watched him get dressed.

"I've got to run to the house, get ready and get my gear," he said. "I suppose I can find a cab this time of day?"

"Take my car." I found the keys and handed them over. "Be back by 3, and we'll head over together."

A look passed between us, one of those telegrams of trust and good feeling that must come from a girl being willing to lend out her wheels.

He smiled. "I'll be here."

"Before you go —"

"Yeah?"

"Do you have anything other than sandals? Rubber soles are fine — just something not so, um, beachy. And black is always a good rule of thumb for the clothes. I mean, to shoot a wedding. Otherwise, I wouldn't dream of giving you fashion advice."

He grinned. "A wise man always takes fashion advice from a woman. I'll see you at 3. Or before, in case you want to remove my clothes and dress me properly."

I licked my lips involuntarily, and his smirk transformed into a look of pure lust. He took two steps toward me, unfastened my robe in one motion, slid his arms around my naked waist and kissed me as if I were on fire and his mouth was the only thing that could quench me. My whole being quivered as he released me, as his eyes raked my flesh, my exposed body under the open robe. And then he headed out the door.

I sat heavily on the couch, rubbing a finger over my swollen lips, listening to the silence that filled in around his parting, like the fading wake of a powerboat. I needed a shower. I needed clothes. Or I would never get dressed again, waiting for his return.

"Do you take this man to be your lawfully wedded husband?"

The question hung in the cool, purple twilight, and the wedding guests seemed to hold their breath. They were seated on white folding chairs under tall, gnarled oak trees, whose broad branches were draped with fairy lights and candle lanterns. Well-dressed relatives watched as the ceremony took place against a backdrop of a formal fountain, flowers and flaming torches.

From the back, I snapped several shots as the cherubic blond bride said "I do." I snuck a glance at Wyatt, several feet away from me. At that moment, he looked at me and grinned, and a thrill ran through me.

Geez, Cali. Don't get all traditional now.

I tried to keep my expression professional as I nodded at

him, and he slipped up the side of the crowd to the front to get another angle.

I eased up the center aisle, staying out of the videographer's way, and crouched as the preacher pronounced the couple husband and wife. I shot a flurry of exposures, taking advantage of the ambient light, as the couple kissed and the crowd cheered. The next forty-five minutes were a blur of shooting the bridal party and formal photos.

When we'd shot everyone's grand entrance into the lofty barn, which glowed with candles and strings of white lights reflected in haphazardly hung antique mirrors, we went out to the garden to take a ten-minute break.

"Half-time," I said, dropping into a folding chair on the center aisle in the front row. Now it was dark, but the torches were still lit, and the fountain gurgled pleasantly.

"Maybe three-quarter time," Wyatt said, sitting across the aisle from me. "We got the formal shots done. That was a bitch."

I nodded in agreement. "Three-quarter time," I echoed. "Waltz time."

"Do you dance?" Wyatt asked, rummaging in his bag and switching memory cards in his camera. He looked gorgeous in black — black slacks, black button-up shirt, even a skinny black tie. And black high-top sneakers, a lot like the ones I favored — though I'd gone with comfortable leather flats tonight.

"I dance, but I don't waltz," I said.

"It's easy," he said. "Want to?"

"I think they're playing Frank Sinatra inside. I can almost hear it. Not a waltz."

"And soon it will be 'The Electric Slide,' I'm sure," he said.

"That's OK. I can hum a waltz." He'd finished with his camera and turned to me with a smile. "Waltz with me?"

"What waltz are you going to hum?"

"Um," he said, looking a little lost. "I know 'The Blue Danube.' Everyone knows that one."

"You're crazy."

"Come on," he said.

"Have you been drinking?"

"Not yet, but I intend to drink heavily later."

I laughed and got to my feet. "OK, you asked for it."

He stood and reached out his hand, and I took it. He pulled me to him, and I regarded his angled features in the torchlight, that expressive mouth, the dark eyebrows. Now he didn't look as if he were joking.

Wyatt put a hand on my waist and lifted the other to clasp mine. He began to guide me in the measured one-two-three of the waltz.

"Da-da-da-da-da — dum dum, dum dum," he hummed, and I giggled as he continued.

"Love the lyrics," I whispered.

He laughed. "Shut up. It's Strauss. Da-da-da-da-da — dum dum, dum dum," and suddenly it wasn't just a goof. It was sweet and warm and delightful in his arms as he swept me around the fountain, humming in his rough baritone under the trees, under the sparkling stars, twirling through flickering pools of firelight.

I pitched in a couple of "dum-dums" as he hit the higher "da-da-da-da-daaaaa" notes, and finally, he ran out of "da-dums" and stopped. We both stood there, still in our dancers' pose, breathless as the chilly breeze flowed around us, and then he dipped me, his lips brushing mine sweetly before he lifted me and let me go.

I swayed, almost dizzy, definitely carried away.

"I think I like waltzing," I said in a small voice.

He watched me in the delicate light. "I like waltzing with you."

I held my breath for another moment, and then I heard the DJ's obnoxious bellow straining the barn's sound system.

"Speaking of dances, we still have to shoot all that stuff. And then some reception candids and the bride and groom leaving in that pretty Silver Wraith they rented."

"Right," Wyatt said, and the moment was gone. "I think some boards would look great on top of that Rolls."

"Maybe at *your* wedding," I said offhandedly, picturing his surfboards, then felt a rush of chagrin. His wedding. To whom? Almost certainly not to me. "So yeah, have some fun, get crowd shots and details, and I'll focus on the bride-dad dance and all that."

"OK," he said, hefting his bag, his voice flat and uncertain. I felt the same way as we headed back inside. But soon, the demands of the job had me energetic and attentive, and we swung through the next few hours in what almost felt like a dance, as he backed me up when I shot big moments, as he worked the tables and the crowd and the dance floor while I shot the principals, as we ganged up on the cake-cutting and the bouquet toss. We worked together like butter on popcorn. His presence made the evening so enjoyable, I wondered how I'd ever shot weddings solo.

Still, it was a long night, and I was all too relieved to capture the fleeing taillights of the Silver Wraith as it rolled down the gravel drive. The guests started to leave as we packed our gear in the back of my car. I tucked the check the mother of the bride had given me into a secure pocket of my camera bag and breathed a sigh of relief. That was rent for one more month.

"Take this," Wyatt said, handing me a memory card case. "That's everything I shot tonight."

"Do you want me to dump the cards so you have them for your trip?"

"I have plenty. Don't worry about it tonight," he said.

"When do you leave tomorrow?"

"Early."

"Oh." I tried not to let my disappointment show, but it leaked into my voice.

He smiled in the dim lights of the parking area. "I can sleep on the plane."

"Oh," I said, brighter this time. "Want to go out?"

"Want to look for meteors? Since we're out here in the boonies? I think there's a minor shower. We might see one or two."

"That sounds cool, but I'm kind of hungry, since they only let us inhale a few appetizers during our break."

"I've got it covered," he said. "That other bag isn't a camera bag. It's a cooler. I was hoping we'd have time for a snack."

"Clever man." I smiled. "Let's find a spot."

I drove us away from the barn and onto one of the lonely roads that meandered among the ranchland well west of Bohemia. I found a dirt side road and parked by a dilapidated shack.

I backed up my SUV toward the dark western sky, and we pulled out the simple snacks Wyatt had brought — cheese, crackers, grapes, oranges, even a thermos with hot chocolate — and arranged them on the tailgate. We sat and enjoyed the repast and the view of the star-spangled realm above and the nearly flat landscape — but not so much the increasingly cold night. We finished eating, wrapped a beach towel around our shoulders, huddled together and watched the sky, still and calm, no meteors in sight.

"You do this a lot?" I asked.

"When you hang out on the beach, you watch the sky. It passes the time between waves, or at night — I've spent a lot of nights on beaches."

Because he'd had nowhere else to go.

"So you know all the constellations?" I asked.

"Only a handful. There's yours." He twisted and pointed to the northeast.

"No way. I don't have a constellation. I would have heard of it. There's no Calista up there."

"There's Callisto. That's what she used to be called, before she became a bear."

"Now you're just making stuff up."

He grinned. "Seriously. It's a long story, but she had sworn to remain a virgin forever until Zeus seduced her and got her pregnant. This ticked off her goddess, who turned her into a bear."

"So — I'm a virgin or a bear."

"Bear with me," Wyatt said, and I groaned at the pun. "Her son was given away and became a king, and he was hunting one day and came across his mama bear, only he didn't know who she was. To prevent him from killing her, Zeus turned them both into constellations — Ursa Major and Ursa Minor. Big bear, little bear."

I looked back to where he'd pointed earlier. "How can I see her?"

"The best way is to look for the Big Dipper. It's right in the middle of Ursa Major."

"So really, I'm a big dip, is that what you're saying?"

He laughed. "I prefer to think of you as the easily seduced nymph, if that's OK."

"That sounds better. Hey." I snuggled against him. "Are you as cold as I am?"

"At least," he said with a shiver. "Let's go back to your place."

"Thought you'd never ask."

It was almost midnight when we got home, and once we unloaded the gear in the studio, I was exhausted.

"Tired?" Wyatt asked, reading my mind as I unlocked the apartment upstairs and let us in.

"Yes," I confessed. "But don't go."

"Get comfortable. Put on your sweats. I'll get us something to drink."

"Thanks."

He headed for the kitchen. I went into my room and rummaged around for something that would be comfortable and yet not offensively grungy. Of course, I could always go for a notch above that — like comfortable and irresistibly sexy. Did I have anything that would do? Because I might be tired, but I wanted to make the most of this last night with Wyatt.

I dug through my PJs drawer and found something I'd worn once — like maybe two boyfriends ago — and that guy hadn't appreciated it at all. It was somewhere near the end of a dull three-month relationship, and he'd barely glanced at me when I put it on. Instead, he watched a particularly crass episode of "South Park" while drinking beer and dozed off.

I hoped Wyatt might be a more appreciative audience. It was a chemise made of stretchy cornflower-blue lace that barely came to mid-thigh. The triangular pieces of fabric over each breast narrowed and tied in a knot behind my neck, accentuating my cleavage. The lace hugged my breasts, making every mood of my nipples obvious. I had a feeling Wyatt might be interested. And if he wasn't, I'd kick him out.

I stripped of everything except the chemise, brushed my hair into a cloud of blond and wandered out to the living room to find him pouring two glasses of cabernet. He'd even lit the candles in the fireplace. And he still looked sleek in his elegant black clothes.

He lifted his head with a startled expression.

"That's not a sweatshirt," he said.

"I do own other clothes." I grinned at his reaction.

"I can't wait to find out what else." Scanning me boldly, he handed me a glass of wine, and I took a deep sip. "I want to take your picture."

"Haven't you taken enough pictures tonight?"

"You said you'd do anything for me," he reminded me.

"Sorry," I said. "Not tonight." *Or ever,* I thought.

"That leaves one more refusal."

I set down my glass and curled up on the couch. "You're not really holding me to that, are you?"

"I absolutely fucking am." The emphatic way he said it made my hair stand on end with anticipation. He sat next to me, took a sip of his wine and set the glass on the table. "Come here."

He pulled me to him and bodily shifted me so that I straddled him. I could feel his bulge under my naked pussy. Now I was getting wet.

"Don't you want to take some of those clothes off?" I asked, kissing his neck, letting my tongue linger there, tasting his pulse as I licked.

"Not yet." He sounded almost hoarse. God, he was hard

under me.

"Like torture, do you?" I licked his earlobe, then nipped it.

"If this is torture, yeah, I like it." He pinched a nipple through the lace. I gasped. He pinched the other one, and I moaned. His finger moved lower, circling and rubbing my clit before easing inside my slit.

"You are so wet for me," he whispered. "I like that. Do I make you wet, Cali?"

"Yes." I was barely able to breathe the word.

"How bad do you want it?"

"I want you. I want you inside me."

"Tell me exactly," he said, loosening and removing his tie with the hand that wasn't fucking me into a frenzy.

"I — I want your cock inside my pussy."

"I like those words," he whispered. "Dirty words. I want to fuck your cunt. Do you hate that word?"

"Not when you say it." Sometimes that word was an infuriating insult, but the way he said it, in this heated context, it was like a reverential tribute to my sex, and I was breathless hearing it.

"You tell me." He was still whispering. "Tell me what you want in the dirtiest way you know how."

I was about to come just listening to him, and now I was supposed to talk? I rocked slowly against his hand. "I — I want you to fuck me with your hot, hard cock," I murmured as my pleasure grew. "Deep. Until I moan." His eyes blazed, and I grew more confident, moving as his fingers probed me, grasping his shoulders, whispering things in his ear I'd only thought to myself. I almost felt him grow beneath me.

"Is that all?" He laughed, a low, wicked chuckle, and lifted me, pushing me aside. "Touch yourself while I get ready for you."

I groaned, feeling vulnerable, missing his fingers inside me, and leaned back against the pillows, lightly fingering my bud, crackling with sensation. This was so much hotter, so much weirder with him watching me. But I was watching him, too, as he slowly unbuttoned his shirt and took it off, revealing the rippling muscles of his torso. He did the same with the black slacks and his briefs, and finally, he was naked and beautiful and hard all over, staring at me with fiery intensity. I stretched, hoping he was ready for me now. My body was one hot pool of desire.

"And do you want my mouth on you, too?" he asked, his voice low and enticing. "Because you look so delicious, I want to taste you." He knelt in front of me, pushed up the fabric of my chemise, grasped my buttocks and began to lick my clit, to tongue me until I was wild with want, until the pulses inside my core had grown to power surges.

"Please fuck me, Wyatt," I moaned. I was all about the dirty talk now that he had me again on the brink of orgasm.

He lifted his head. His lips were wet. "Open wide for me."

I stretched my legs wide and he grasped me under my knees, turning me so he stood in front of the couch, tilting me up toward him, completely in control. He probed me lightly with his tip, and then he plunged his cock inside of me. At this angle, he reached farther than he ever had, than anyone ever had. I clenched with each profound thrust. I began to cry out with each powerful penetration as he lifted me to him. I braced myself with my arms and pushed back.

Wyatt's irresistible strength, his focus on me, were intoxicating as he sped up his rhythm. He gasped as he came, driving inside me, triggering an engulfing orgasm that spurred my otherworldly cry.

After a few more exquisite thrusts for good measure,

Wyatt slowed and eased himself out of me. He leaned over me and slanted his lips over mine. Then he scooped me up and carried me, luscious and limp, to my bed.

"I'll be right back," he said. "I'll blow out the candles."

He was back in a minute, and as he got under the covers, I wriggled against him for warmth in the cool, dark apartment.

"How do you do that to me?" I whispered as he wrapped his arms around me.

"Something inside you wants to let go, and with me, you let it." He kissed me, lightly probing my mouth with his tongue. "Thank you for that."

He was right. With him, I had let go more than I'd ever done with anyone. In that moment, his possession of me was complete. And it scared me.

WHEN I AWOKE in the morning, he was gone, but he'd left a note: "Check your email. ~ W."

When I did, I found a photo he must have taken with his phone at the wedding. It showed me laughing as I coaxed someone to pose, with Wyatt reflected in a mirror behind me, holding the phone-camera, grinning at the shot. First, I was simply impressed with his eye, his unique way of seeing an unusual photo. And then I was captivated by his grin. And last, I saw how sweetly he had captured me, how joyful he looked.

"See you next weekend," the email said.

"Be safe," I wrote back, and then I wondered how to sign it. Finally, I settled on: "XO, your nymph."

Sigh. A week without Wyatt.

A week to find my head and reattach it to my shoulders.

I started with processing the wedding pictures —
between the two of us, there were thousands of them. I was
struck by not just their quality but the differences in our
style. I was what one might call an inspired documentary
shooter. I captured the truth, and sometimes I did so with a
touch of inventiveness, even with style. But I was hiding
behind the camera.

Wyatt *felt* his images. Even if his technical skills occasionally faltered, his eye found a way to make his images moving
or bright or entrancing. In his most exceptional photographs,
I saw a challenge, a motivation to look inside myself and
expand my vision. My heart. It hadn't been in my work in a
long time.

Maybe my life was full without Wyatt, but I still found
reminders of him everywhere as the week progressed. Our
class did digital darkroom work one day and played with
lighting on another, making me think back on our heated
night in my studio.

At a rehearsal for the play Penelope was costuming, I shot
joyous photos of the actors in their colorful garb, working
with the lighting director to get just the right look on stage,
and I remembered Wyatt's eyes lit by the torches outside the
wedding barn as he waltzed me around the fountain.

And then there were his texts. There were no words. The
images seemed almost random, but I could see he was telling
the story of his trip as he sent messages back to me: the
gaggle of boats and press covering the Mavericks competition
out on the waves; a couple of young surfer boys worshiping
their heroes as they sat on their boards on the beach; the
California shoreline at sunset, ruggedly beautiful, so much
rougher than our own. There was even a shot of Ron Raker,
grinning and wet against a blue sky. His old friend Ron. So

they were hanging out again, just like old times. The photo reminded me that I'd only borrowed Wyatt from his life.

I returned the favor, sending him bits of whimsy and color from my days, and just once, a photo of myself. I wore the Queen of Hearts' crazy headdress from the theater, with gigantic, sparkling playing cards sprouting from my head, and glowered at my phone camera with one eyebrow raised.

It was the only time he replied with a photo of himself — of his mouth and eyes wide open in cartoonish shock. I laughed when I saw it.

The highlight of my week was speeding toward me, Thursday, my first women's night at the studio, and I wanted it clean and comfortable. I added a few extra chairs and lights and painted the scruffy studio bathroom sky-blue. I expected an eclectic crowd: Penelope and four of her pinup model friends; Thea; Sloane; and Ez. Eight guests would be plenty for my experiment. I stocked up on champagne, fruit, chocolate, cheese and crackers, because there really is no such thing as a party without cheese and crackers. And I wholeheartedly endorsed the cliché that a gathering of women also required chocolate.

Thursday morning, I called Penelope and asked if she could bring something special to the shoot, a perfect prop, and I was ready when she arrived before everyone else.

I opened the back door to reveal Pen in a fabulous, puffy white dress with red polka-dots and a black leather jacket. She pushed the centerpiece of the evening: her turquoise Vespa scooter.

"Damn, that's beautiful," I said as she wheeled it in.

"I do hope you're talking about my dress," she joked.

"Of course. The scooter is hideous."

"Exactly," she said, but her tone was full of love as she

looked down at the gorgeous little motorbike, with its brown leather seat and chromed mirrors sticking up like bug antennae. "You're lucky it's not raining. I have to keep my baby clean and dry."

"Bring it on into the studio," I said, and we parked it under the lights, in front of the black paper backdrop I'd set up that rolled all the way out on the floor to the camera. Energetic rock music was already pumping through my speakers. "Are all your pinup friends coming?"

"Yes, and I hope they don't wear you out with costume changes. I brought three myself."

"Cool! We'll do whatever we have time for," I said, hearing the bell ring on the front door. "Help yourself to champagne while I get that."

"I thought you'd never ask," she said, pursing her bright red lips in mock reproach.

I laughed and went to the lobby to find the four pinups in wild '50s getups, along with Thea, who seemed distinctly out of place, a demure robin among a flock of scarlet tanagers. She was taller than them, even though they were in heels and she wasn't, and she wore light-blue jeans and a sweatshirt. Her red hair was tamed in a plain ponytail. I guess I looked at her strangely.

She looked herself up and down and then at me with a smile. "I have something in mind."

"Great," I said, wondering how this group would come together.

At that moment, Sloane and Ez arrived from opposite directions, and I corralled the women into the studio. The pinup crowd greeted Penelope with lilting voices and air kisses. She introduced them, and they grouped around a mirror I'd set up in one corner to get ready.

"So," I said to Sloane, who'd opted for a sweet look with a long, floaty maxi-dress in black and a light green scarf that perfectly matched the scooter. "Did you bring the clay?"

She laughed. "I think we'll save the clay shoot for another time. I can't tell you how interested Alex was in what we were doing tonight. I don't want to get his imagination too riled up for next time."

"You mean you'll be the pure, innocent one tonight?" asked Ez, who wore black leather pants, a draping, silky amber tank top and a snug black leather jacket.

"Not entirely," Sloane said, lifting the hem of the long dress just enough so we could see the stockings and garters underneath.

"Whoa," Thea said.

"I see you've been to the Velvet Glove again," I noted.

"Oh, no. I already had these," said Sloane, who then turned bright red as Ez asked, "Oh, really?"

I laughed. "OK, everyone," I called, getting the attention of the crowd. "This will be a really free-form night. We'll make sure everyone has the chance to be photographed in at least two outfits, if you want them, but there are no real rules. I'll make sure everyone gets in front of the camera. In the meantime, help yourself to champagne and snacks. Who wants to go first?"

"Let me," Ez said. "I'm not going to be taking my clothes off." She nodded with a wry expression at the pinups, half of whom were already scantily dressed.

"Thanks," I said to her as we moved toward the lights and the others drifted toward the snacks. "Then I can get over all my natural prudishness in time for everyone else."

She grinned and pushed back those floppy, dark bangs. "I

can't believe you're naturally prudish with that surfer. He's your guy, right?"

"He's Mr. Right Now, anyway." I knew it was a flippant answer. I focused all my attention on my camera as Ez crossed her arms and looked closely at me.

"You really like him, don't you?"

"Of course not. I don't get attached to guys. Especially boyfriends. And he's not a boyfriend."

"Then you're unusual, but I applaud your approach," Ez said. "Getting attached to one guy is death. That's why I keep dating losers."

I laughed uneasily. "You do not."

"Losers are easy." She shrugged. "I never want to keep them around. It makes life simpler. Where do you want me? I don't think that scooter is my thing. Can I drag over one of those black chairs? I'm looking for a new publicity shot for the band. Maybe a CD cover. I want to look like a cool, elegant badass."

"No problem." Ez made me feel better about being relationship-challenged. Though her situation sounded worse than mine.

In a few minutes, Ez was lounging in one of the low leather chairs, giving the camera serious attitude. Despite her devil-may-care exterior, she was a performer through and through, and she responded well to direction. I tried dramatic side-lighting and back lighting and started to relax as the other women egged her into poses from silly to stern to seductive.

Finally, she'd had enough, and she walked away to pour herself a glass of champagne. She downed it in one go and poured another. *OK, then.*

"Next victim?" I asked.

"We're next!" came a chorus of two. It was a pair of pinups, dressed identically in black leather corsets, fishnets and frighteningly tall high heels. They weren't twins, exactly, but with their matching, dramatic makeup, they could have been sisters. Maybe they were. We introduced ourselves, and they took up provocative poses with the Vespa.

"Damn if they don't look better with it than I do," Penelope said at my ear. "You'd never know they were engineers at the space center, would you?"

Soon all the pinups joined the mock-twins in crazy, sexy group shots, and then we did single shoots with each of them as Thea and Sloane looked on. Penelope adopted tortoise-shell cat's-eye sunglasses and looked positively adorable in her polka-dot dress and black jacket on her beloved scooter.

As the pinups went for a costume change, and Ez worked on her fourth glass of champagne — good thing I had several bottles chilling in a tub — Sloane shyly approached.

"I'm not sure I'd ever ride a scooter in this dress," she said.

"Good thing you're not riding it, then." I winked. "Just sit sideways on it and hold on to one handlebar." I got her comfortable and then had her move around, trying different poses. Finally, her nervousness seemed to fade.

"OK." I nodded at her. "It's time."

"What do you mean?"

"You didn't wear that underwear for nothing, did you?"

By this time, the pinups had mostly made their costume changes, and the five of them, including Penelope, were gathered around me with Thea and Ez, watching.

Sloane scanned all of them nervously.

"Go ahead," Penelope said. "Show us a little leg."

The others immediately joined her in good-natured exhortations, and Sloane, overwhelmed with positive reinforcement, lifted up the dress slowly, revealing the stockings and, finally, the garters and satin-and-lace panties. The women whooped and I barely stopped myself from giggling as I got a number of photos that I was sure would make Alex swoon.

The women — well, the ones wearing 1950s bathing suits — started shouting, "Take it off!"

Sloane shook her head, but she was smiling. And then, overwhelmed by approbation, she looked at me. "Get ready, because this is going to be quick."

"OK, ready!" I said with a chuckle.

Sloane lifted the long dress up and off her head, revealing a black bra that perfectly matched the rest of her lingerie. Ez took the dress, and my camera took in the sleek line of Sloane's form. It began with elegant high-heeled shoes and followed well-turned legs and sensuous curves that perfectly complemented the scooter, up to her lightly made-up face, red lips and reddish-brown hair. Amid the hoots and hollers, I snapped a series of photos, using side-lighting, taking the camera off the tripod so I could get fun angles as she looked toward the camera and away; as she straddled the scooter, then posed against it and in front of it. After a few swift minutes, she seemed to remember herself, grabbed her dress from Ez and pulled it back on to the applause of the group.

"You should do one of the car shows with us sometime, honey," one of the twins said.

"I'll leave it to you professionals," Sloane said, but she was grinning.

"Thea," I said. "You ready for this?"

Thea had been quietly munching on cheese and crackers and watching with amusement. "Where do you keep your ladder?"

I looked at her quizzically. "It's in the back. I'll get it."

I retrieved the folding wooden ladder, another item that came with the place. We rolled the scooter out of the way to make room for it.

"I was thinking about those old pinup paintings," Thea said, pulling a broad paintbrush from her pocket, "the ones in which women ended up showing off their underwear in improbable ways. I'd be a painter, and —"

My mind lit up. "I get it. Can you gals unroll the white backdrop? I'll just be a minute."

I went to the office in the back and brought out a stack of old *Bohemia Bugles*. With Thea and Sloane's help, I spread them out on the floor under the ladder, on top of the rolled-out backdrop. I went to the back again and returned with the nearly empty can of sky-blue paint.

"Oh," Thea said, her eyes twinkling. "Now you're getting into it."

She pulled the elastic loop out of her springy red hair, setting it free. She put on bright red lipstick to complement the touch of eye makeup she already wore. And then she pulled off her sweatshirt. She had on overalls, not just jeans — and only a lacy, white bra underneath.

"Wait a minute, girl," Penelope said, coming over with a handful of bobby pins. In a few minutes, she had Thea's hair pinned in a sweet, messy up-do.

Thea took off her shoes and socks and rolled up the pants of her light-blue overalls to her knees. She adjusted the overalls so they hung off one shoulder, showing more of her cleavage, demonstrating that, despite her penchant for boxy clothes and her large frame, she had a figure that would make most men goggle.

She climbed halfway up the ladder with the open bucket

of paint and the brush.

"If you don't mind," I said, "dip the brush in the bucket and do a little smear on your cheek and your, uh, chest."

Thea laughed. "Exactly. Why didn't I think of the paint, too?"

The other women looked on with interest as Thea daubed herself with a couple of strategic smears of the paint, which brought out her intense blue eyes.

"Now," I said, "I want you to lean toward me, but not so you'll fall. I want you to hold the paint can out as if you're about to drop it, as if you're about to lose your balance. And I want one of those priceless retro-pinup looks of surprise on your face."

Thea knew exactly what I was talking about, pouting in an adorable "O" that brought out her cheekbones and belied her tomboy vibe. I did a strong vertical photo that showed off her body, but it had an essential innocence about it. Unlike in most pinup art, her hips and thighs weren't showing, and she didn't have a come-hither look. But at the same time, she had a latent sex appeal that her modesty only enhanced.

"All right," I said after several variations on the pose, some with her holding the brush, and a couple with the brush in her teeth. "Everybody stand back. I want you to drop the paint can."

"What?" Now Thea looked genuinely surprised. "Are you nuts?"

"There's only a little paint in the bottom. I'm going to snap it in midair. In fact, you're going to tip it upside down and toss it in the air, up and slightly toward me, looking just as shocked as you have been, looking right at the camera. Tilt it so it's just starting to come out, and then try to flip it in a somersault."

"What about your floor?"

"Paper backdrop. I'll just roll out some more. It's all good."

Thea laughed in anticipation, and the women started buzzing as they backed up. I adjusted the lights so they provided a bright, flat illumination that, with the strobes, would allow me a fast shutter speed. I framed her and the ladder with plenty of air for the paint can.

"OK. Ready?" Thea asked, assuming her pose.

"Let's do it!"

She tossed the can, and it rolled up and over and forward, paint sloshing out as she looked on with her "O" of sexy surprise.

I snapped a staccato burst of photographs, and the can's bottom banged against the floor, shooting up a long spray of blue paint that had the women shouting and laughing as they jumped back even farther. Some of it splashed on Thea.

I laughed in delight. It was perfect. Thea laughed, too.

The others applauded, while Sloane came to look over my shoulder. "Did that work?" she asked.

I flipped back through the photos and found two or three with an almost perfect composition of can and paint and ladder and model.

"Oh, these are fun," I said to Sloane and Thea.

"Let me see!" Thea said, manifesting a heretofore unseen girlish enthusiasm.

"Just a quick preview — I'll do more with it in editing." I flipped through the images for her. "Pinups? Who's next? Get ready while I change the backdrop."

I mopped up the few drops that had escaped the paper and tore off the splotched piece, then found yoga pants for Thea to wear, since her overalls were spattered with paint. For the next shots, I rolled down a seashell pink backdrop that looked really '50s and decided to let myself enjoy the champagne, too. We passed the hours in a blur of fun and creativity that had me trying new approaches to lighting and poses and composition. Having willing subjects who dressed to the nines helped. I felt elated, energized. This was *fun*.

The crowd rolled out just before 1 a.m., with the sober driving the drunk. I shut down the studio lights and the music and, buzzed from the work and the bubbles, marveled at the dim quiet. And only then did I wonder what Wyatt was doing.

In his time zone, his night was just starting. He was so far away. His *life* was so far away. Or, more accurately, his life was fluid, always changing, and he was always on the move.

My offhand comments to Ez tonight had their basis in truth. I had to admit that my previous coterie of boyfriends had been more convenient than critical to my existence. A guy who only wanted to share some laughs and my bed should be right up my alley, and I should stop pretending I wanted anything else.

So why did I miss him so damn much?

I checked my phone for the first time in hours and saw he'd sent a photo. In the frame was a wide beach with a lone surfboard, stuck vertical in the sand, as the golden sun set behind it. The shot showed much of the ocean and the sky — a beautiful, austere, lonely photo.

Maybe there were a dozen people lurking behind him when he shot it, but I didn't think so. It conveyed something about him, some essential loneliness at his core, an isolation once forced upon him that he now maintained out of habit, or defense, or need. I wondered if there was room for me on his beach.

Or room for him on mine.

I AWOKE to a rhythmic sound that had me banging on my alarm clock and then sitting bolt upright in cold fear. It wasn't my alarm. It was a pounding on the door, the kind cops make when they're there to arrest you.

No one had ever come in that door — the door to the outside staircase. It was just after 7:30 a.m., definitely before my usual wake-up time, especially when I'd been up till the wee hours drinking champagne. I staggered out to the living room in my oversized "BoBeach" T-shirt.

"Who is it?"

"Wyatt."

Stabs of emotion, like beams of light in the dark, helped bring me to half-consciousness. He was here? He was back?

I opened the door, and there he stood, in jeans and that sexy, rough, gray-brown sweater that made it look as if he'd just stepped off a beach. But that wasn't right.

"God, it's good to see you," he said, stepping in, grabbing me around the waist, lifting me and kissing me hard and fast. "I'll be right back."

"OK," I mumbled as he dashed to the other door. I put a hand to my lips, wondering if I should brush my teeth. Wondering where the hell he went.

I went to the bathroom and brushed my teeth anyway, then crawled back under the covers and curled up against the pillows.

Perhaps I dreamed him.

A few minutes later, I heard doors slamming. And a few seconds after that, my bed bounced.

"Hey!" I rolled over and opened my eyes. "You really are

here." He lay on his side atop the blankets, propped up on an elbow, grinning at me. His hair was wild and irresistible.

"Come here," he said, and this time he pulled me in for a sweet, leisurely kiss, one that melted away my morning chill by achingly slow degrees. He released me and pushed my mussed hair away from my face, drinking me in as if he'd forgotten what I looked like.

"Where'd you go?" I asked, still sleepy and more than a little aroused.

"I had to bring my stuff inside."

"Stuff?"

"The shuttle brought me straight from the airport." He kicked off his sandals and snuggled closer.

"Red-eye?"

"Uh-huh."

"No more waves?"

"The really big waves were pretty much done after the first day, but I stayed and got more images. Portraits. Candids of the guys."

"Did you surf?"

The answer didn't surprise me.

"Yeah, but not on the big day. I was working. Though sometimes being on a Jet Ski is almost as crazy." He kissed me again, distracting me from the unwanted idea of Wyatt lured back to the big surf scene, never to return to Bohemia Beach. "Did you have a good week?" he asked, kissing my neck.

"Mmmm," I said, my brain warring with my body. "Yes, really good."

"Oh," he said, shifting back a little. "You didn't miss me?"

"I was pretty busy," I said, resisting an impulse to tell him just how much I'd thought about him. His thick eyebrows lifted. He wasn't really hurt, was he? I didn't want to be suckered any further into his whirlpool, not when he'd just leave again. "But yeah, I missed you," I couldn't help but add when I saw his eyes. There was someone far away and lost in them, a boy who'd never known what home was.

"That's good." Now I heard a note of triumph in his voice, saw the twitch of a smile on his lips. Was this just a game to him? He tugged on the blanket. "Do you have room for me under there?"

"Aren't you tired?" I protested, but he made me want to laugh, and he could see it.

"Exhausted." He pulled off his sweater and the T-shirt beneath, tossing them aside, then started to work off his jeans. "Well?"

"There might be room," I said, unable to keep my eyes off his body.

"Tell me when you decide," he said, stripping off his underwear to reveal his impressive member at full attention. I felt him watching me as I took in the chiseled manscape that was Wyatt Brooks. When I looked into his eyes again, he was grinning. Could I be any more obvious?

"I think I can make room," I said in a small, breathless voice.

"It might be easier if you take off that shirt," he said, eagerly slipping under the covers with me.

"I'm too tired." I feigned a yawn.

"Then I'll help you." His voice was quieter now, the joking over. He reached under the nightshirt, running a hand up my thighs, over my hips. His lips curved when he found no underwear there, and his hand kept traveling, slowly, lighting up my skin with electricity as he trailed his fingers over my belly, as he cupped one breast and squeezed.

I made a soft, involuntary sound and lay back as he

tugged the shirt up and over my head, tossing it to the floor.
He slipped on top of me, under the covers, pressing me into
the mattress, almost literally taking my breath away as he
grasped both my hands with his, spreading my arms, exquisitely holding me in place. He stared into my eyes for a long
time, and then his gaze strayed to my cheeks, my lips. He
brushed my mouth with his, then ran his tongue along my
bottom lip before lifting his eyes to mine again.

"So blue," he murmured. "Like the light through a wave."

If my eyes were light, his were dark, coal on fire. He
shifted, and I felt his erection pressing against me, his hard
body blanketing mine. I was suddenly aware of just how hot I
was under him, hot and needy. I closed my eyes and inhaled
the scent of his skin, of man and wind and sea.

He lifted himself slightly, never letting go of my hands,
and positioned himself so his tip teased my entrance. A tiny
gasp slipped from me, and I involuntarily strained against his
hands, wanting to touch him.

"Oh, no, my fair princess," he murmured, kissing my neck
just below my ear, sending my pulse thrumming. "This is
where I take possession of you again."

I looked up at him, saying nothing, but I felt my brow
furrow. That anxiety was creeping in again, even as he
rubbed his shaft against my clit and I breathed faster,
wanting him in spite of myself. One of his eyebrows lifted
slightly as he read my face, my eyes.

"Don't you want me?" he asked, though he must have felt
my response. I closed my eyes again and lifted my hips
slightly to meet his teasing cock as he moved against me. My
brain struggled to get a thought in edgewise, holding my
tongue in check.

He squeezed my hands, but he did not let go.

"Look at me, Cali." His voice was dark, sweet coffee, stimulating, deep and irresistible. "You missed me." It was a statement, not a question.

I opened my eyes and stared into his, biting my lip, wanting him so.

"You missed me," he repeated. He kissed my neck, my ear, my shoulder. He suckled on one nipple, drew on it with his teeth, and I bucked beneath him. "Say it, Cali," he whispered. "Give in to me."

I moaned as he repositioned again between my legs and my clit quivered with the contact.

"Yield," he said so softly I could barely hear him. He leaned closer, his whole body, his whole being a divine pressure on mine. *"Yield."*

"Yes," I finally breathed, opening my legs wide. He sank into me with a groan, filling me, stretching me.

"So wet and tight," he whispered, grinding against me, the force of him almost unbearably intense. "I've missed this. Missed you, Cali. God, yes."

And then he was lost in the movement, measured and profound and then harder and faster, his thrusts a sweet agony inside me as I moaned under his gracefully balanced weight, my hands clenching his as I pushed against him. I came, an explosion of lava under the waves, fierce and fiery and glowing as he continued to pump against me. Just as my high waned, I felt his release inside me, the completion of my shuddering pleasure, and then all of him relaxed. His hands released mine and he held me around the waist, kissed me, rolled me slightly. He held me close, still inside me, as he lay his head on the pillows, caressing me. I sucked in a little breath, feeling him snug within me, wanting him there forever.

No. I can't. He can't, and he won't.

As I watched his eyes flutter closed, as his hands stilled, I cursed my loss of control, even my momentary happiness, because it would be so hard to lose. This was something I couldn't want, couldn't allow myself to want.

In a minute, he was asleep, still inside me. I dozed off in his arms, warm, afraid to move, as fragile as a seashell.

AFTER A COUPLE OF HOURS, I slipped out of bed and showered. When I emerged from the bathroom, Wyatt still slept the sleep of the dead, worn out by his waves and travel. I snuck downstairs with a cream-cheese-slathered bagel and a Pepsi — my whistling teapot was too noisy — and opened for business.

There wasn't much, but it was Friday, and as I worked on my photos from the previous night's shoot, a few tourists wandered in to roam my small gallery space. They smiled politely and nodded at me as they took in my photographs. I realized I was looking at another source of income. Maybe I could stock some postcards I shot myself — creative, fun ones. I could create a photo book, a beautiful souvenir of Bohemia Beach. Maybe even set up a high-end photo booth where I could shoot quick portraits. And I could start holding shows in my space to bring in new people, to make a name for myself in the art crowd. I took notes, feeling a continuation of the inspiration I'd felt last night, trying not to think about how much more work I was creating for myself.

About noon, the double doors from the studio opened, and Wyatt emerged into the empty gallery with his hair wet, in his baggy khakis, a fresh surfing T-shirt and his familiar black hoodie. I guessed he'd raided his suitcase, which I'd seen among the huge pile of "stuff" in the back office that he'd mentioned this morning, including three hard Pelican cases for camera gear and, of course, a surfboard.

"Hello, gorgeous," he said.

"Oh, stop," I said, but I didn't want to admit I'd chosen my soft cotton shirt so carefully this morning. It was wide-necked, long-sleeved, clingy, sky-blue and nearly translucent. And my hair was down, finally dry and wavy after my shower. The hair dryer would have been even noisier than the teapot.

I always felt nervous when he walked into a room. He never seemed to have that problem. He seemed utterly relaxed, his easy confidence even sexier than his body.

"What are you up to?" he asked, wandering over to the desk, looking over my shoulder. He whistled.

"Oh, you probably shouldn't see that," I said, clicking away from the photo of Sloane I'd been editing, one of the ones where she was stripped down to her lingerie as she straddled the scooter.

"Now I see what Alex sees in her."

"What do you mean?" I felt a touch of defensiveness. "Sloane is awesome."

"I'm sorry. She just seems so quiet. Not like you." He grinned, leaned down and kissed the spot where my neck met my partially bared shoulder.

"She's my cousin. And you never saw that photo. She'd kill me."

"OK — a relative *and* homicidal. Got it."

I chuckled. "Well, I've never actually known her to kill anyone, but it took champagne and a lot of cajoling to get her in that state, and I'm not sure anyone but Alex will ever see those photos. Because *you never saw it.*"

"What are you talking about?" he asked innocently. "Photo? What photo?"

I smiled, relieved he wasn't going to pursue it. Except —

"What's it going to take to get *you* in that state?" he asked, gently rubbing his hands over my back.

"Tell me about your trip," I said, as if I hadn't heard him.

"Calista."

"Wyatt."

"Seriously." He put his hands on my shoulders, spoke low in my ear. "I want to photograph you. You're so beautiful. Consider it — part of my education."

"God, you make me feel like a dirty old woman."

He laughed softly. "At least I make you feel dirty. But you won't when I photograph you. You'll feel pure and free. I promise." He touched his lips to my shoulder again as he massaged the tight muscles there.

"No."

"That's twice. My third request is going to be a doozy, because that's the one you have to say yes to."

"Did I actually agree to that?" I shut my laptop and got up to face him.

"Sometime after you moaned 'I'll do anything' while I was fucking you," he whispered in my ear, and I felt myself melting from the inside out.

His hands traveled from my shoulders to my behind, and he pressed my hips against his and kissed me. I could feel his erection through our clothes, could feel my body's unbidden response.

"You are not dragging me away from my work again." I pulled away.

"Oh, come on, Cali," Wyatt coaxed. "You want me, too."

"I want my sanity back," I said, half-laughing, half-lying. I loved how crazy he made me. And that's why I had to stop. "I'm serious. Why does every conversation end up in bed?"

"Not necessarily in bed," he quipped. He got close again. His breath warmed my cheek, and my skin tingled. He slipped one hand inside the front of my jeans, caressed me through my underwear. His dark eyes caught mine, and they said it all. *You're wet. You want me.*

"No," I said, breathless, disentangling myself, pushing him away, envisioning a horrified customer stumbling into a tryst with a jolly jingle of the doorbell.

He sighed. "I'm so attracted to responsible women, I guess I can't blame you." But his face had the pinched look of a man who needed release.

I offered him a rueful smile and placed my palms against his chest — that hard, surfer's chest. "Look" — I stopped myself from saying *sweetie,* which was about to roll off my tongue — "I do want you. And I want to hear all about your trip. But I have to work a little between now and then. Why don't you do whatever you need to do, and we can go to the Junction Box tonight? And then — whatever you like?" I smiled at him. "Except pictures," I added.

Those dark eyebrows met, then relaxed. "You're killing me," he said. "But I do have a bunch of photos to edit and file. So I accept your offer. Um, I guess I'll get a cab ... "

"You can take my car." I shrugged. "Or you can work here."

He smiled, and I saw his hips do a slight movement, the prelude to a dance. "Do you have laundry?"

"Dirty clothes, yes. Washer and dryer, no."

"Ah. Then, if you don't mind, I'll take your car over to Jen's and come back and get you at six or so. And we can do dinner and then go to the bar. OK?"

Great. Laundry was the dividing line between which woman he spent the afternoon with.

"Sure," I said drily. "I'm sure she'll be happy to see you."

"Ironically, she's in Denver till tomorrow, and only her husband is in town. And he's at work. Which means I can take care of my blue balls without interruption. Tease." Wyatt grinned, whirled and went toward the inside doors, then turned again, a little more uncertain. "Keys?"

I couldn't help but laugh. "Kitchen counter. Come back soon."

"Oh, I'll come, all right." He lifted an eyebrow and made his exit, and I felt stupid for resisting him, stupid for being so enraptured by him. I sat heavily in my chair and pulled up the photo of Sloane, usually so modest on her exterior, so sensual underneath. Were we all like that? Maybe only those of us who allowed it to happen could go there, who were lucky enough to find someone with whom we felt comfortable enough to open up — to open everything: mind, body and soul. That was the dream, wasn't it? I didn't want to keep myself tied in knots. And I liked the new friends I was making. They weren't constricted by their beliefs. They were freed by them. Their bodies — their minds — their imaginations all were free to play in the worlds they'd created for themselves. I liked that. Was I too hung up on having one guy? Or had commitment become a habit?

I had to admit that it had become a habit, at least before Wyatt.

But what I wanted with Wyatt was everything.

Commitment? My instinct, my years of training at my mother's knee, made me want that, too. But if commitment wasn't something Wyatt could ever do, why would I spoil what we had?

Because commitment was part of the freedom. It was part of what I needed to be free in my mind, my body, my imagination. To open myself completely. To trust. And if he was only marking time until his next trip, his next move, then I still needed to guard myself. To guard my heart.

I touched the laptop's track pad, finding the tools I needed to soften a shadow, to darken a background, to create a beautiful atmosphere around my subject. Here, I could control the outcome, where my imagination met my vision. I was almost free enough.

I heard the back door close, settled into my afternoon and lost myself in my art.

I MADE myself stop working at 5 and texted Wyatt, offering to make him dinner in a rare flash of domesticity. He promised to be at my place by six-thirty, giving me enough time to change into my favorite butter-soft blue jeans and my ice-blue sweater with the scoop neck. I added the slender silver necklace and earrings with matching crystals and put up my hair in a simple twist.

The chicken and sweet onions were sizzling, the pasta was boiling, and I was almost done chopping the red bell peppers when I heard Wyatt enter the apartment from the inside door. I was confused for a moment until I realized I'd let him have my keys. At least for the day. I was struck by how this simple intimacy felt so — comfortable.

In a moment, he embraced me from behind and kissed my neck.

"Mmm." My body's response was immediate, but I fended him off with humor. "Careful. I have a knife."

"That's the only thing keeping me from ravaging you right now."

"You're so disarming," I joked, putting down the knife. I turned around and slipped my arms around his waist. He wore jeans, too, and a couple of layers of loose, faded sweatshirts, navy over white, that would have looked slovenly on most guys; he made the outfit look like something out of a catalog. I lifted my face to his and kissed him lightly, closing my eyes, savoring the fresh scent of him, the feel of him in my arms. His tongue flicked lightly at my lips, and I opened for him, just a little, before pulling back and breaking the spell.

"Don't stop me again," he murmured, putting his forehead to mine.

"Aren't you hungry?"

"You have to ask?" His eyes suggested it wasn't food he craved.

"You have to eat," I said. "You're a growing surfer boy and all. Want to open the wine?"

"All right," he said, releasing me with an exaggerated sigh and a smile. He hunted in my junk drawer for the corkscrew, opened the pinot noir and poured a couple of glasses. I added the peppers, portabella mushrooms and pine nuts to the chicken, along with more olive oil. The kitchen filled with delicious aromas as they cooked and Wyatt sat at my tiny bistro table and watched me, asking about my week, telling me about his trip.

"Corky almost had me convinced I should go out to California to stay," he said as I spooned the chicken mixture over the cooked penne on a couple of colorful thrift-store plates.

I almost dropped the spoon, then recovered and set it and the pan on the stove. "Really?" I served the plates and sat at the table. "Who's Corky?"

"Editor of the new magazine I was telling you about." Wyatt dug into the food and grinned as he quickly chewed and swallowed his first bite. "Damn, this is good. I'd kind of forgotten what a home-cooked meal was like."

"Don't get used to it. My repertoire is extremely limited." I took a sip of wine, not quite ready to eat as I tried to wrap my mind around the idea of him leaving, this time for good. "I thought you said you would never live in California again?"

He nodded as he ate, his expression more serious. "I know I said that. And I still feel weird going back there. But it's different now. I was so powerless as a kid. So — afraid." His voice dipped on that last word, as if it had cost him something to say it. "The place feels different to me now. Like I've changed it by changing myself. I know that sounds weird."

"No, it doesn't," I admitted. "It makes sense. You've made a success of yourself. You've built a new life, and you're reinventing yourself again." I took a bite of the food and felt only a small amount of pleasure in how good it tasted. The idea of Wyatt leaving was too distracting. I focused on my plate, toying with the pasta, digging out the tasty pine nuts, pressing a couple between the tines of my fork.

"Maybe we're always reinventing ourselves," he said. "You're doing the same thing."

I looked up into his eyes and drank more wine. Half my glass was gone already. "I don't know what I'm doing."

"Who does?" His laugh wasn't altogether happy. "Corky made a lot of sense. I know, it's hard to imagine a guy named Corky would make a lot of sense," he added wryly. "It's just that so much surfing happens there, and it's so much easier to get to Hawaii and the rest of the Pacific from the west coast." He shrugged. "He just gave me a lot to think about, that's all."

"Oh, for teleportation," I said, only a little sarcastic.

"But teleportation would take all the fun out of airport security checkpoints and fighting over the carry-on bins."

Wyatt's humor dragged a smile out of me. So there we were. He was thinking about his next move. And I was thinking about mine. *This* was why I needed to guard my heart.

I asked him for details on his gear for shooting in and on the water and learned he had a sponsor for at least some of the underwater cases — those could cost more than the cameras. And I had a better sense of what was in the big pile of luggage he'd taken with him.

"I'm starting to realize I could use a Sherpa to help me with all the gear," he said. "Now if you just worked on your muscles — "

"I'm plenty strong, but that's why we buy cases with *wheels,*" I said, finding the whole notion comical. "You probably want a Sherpa who actually likes to go in the ocean. I'm sure one of them is sick of Everest by now. They might enjoy following a warmer sport."

"Some people just love ice and snow."

"True. You don't see too many Sherpa snowbirds. Most of them are from Minnesota and New York," I replied, and he grinned.

"Dessert?" he asked when we'd finished the pasta and he'd taken the plates to the sink. *Points for Wyatt.*

"Alcohol for dessert," I said, determined to be of good cheer. "The Junction Box, remember?"

"Of course. Just checking to make sure you didn't have a Key lime pie stowed away somewhere."

"Publix makes a pretty good one. I'll remember for next time."

He practically lifted me out of my chair and kissed me

hard and fast. "You're sweet enough for me." The kiss left me breathless and dazed. "I'll hit the head, and then we can go."

In a few minutes, we were walking in the clear, cool night. The stars glittered overhead, brilliant white points — distant, fiery suns reduced to silver dust on black velvet. Florida skies only had this kind of clarity on the lowest-humidity days in winter.

"Look at that moon." Wyatt's voice was tinged with wonder as he gazed to the west. Despite the steely core under that surfer's demeanor, there was a dreamer in him, in the way he looked at nature. The way he watched the night sky.

"It's just a sliver," I said, admiring the way the delicate crescent slipped between the buildings, as if it were going to sink right into the street.

"Yeah, but if you look closely you can see the whole circle, deep in shadow."

He was right. Almost invisible, the dark remainder of the moon was barely a suggestion in the night. "So much more unknown than known," I said.

Wyatt looked down at me and smiled, putting his arm around me as we started walking east toward The Junction Box. "That's part of the fun, don't you think?"

"Tell that to the people who thought they would fall off the edge of the world if they sailed too far."

"Ah, but the unknown drove them to sail too far. The special ones, anyway."

"The greedy ones," I noted.

"Nonetheless, greedy or special, they discovered new worlds. Because they wanted to know what was unknown."

This side of Wyatt surprised me. Though I thought I understood his wanderlust a little, his thirst for adventure, I'd never heard him make it sound so — inspiring. With his arm around me, enveloped by the beautiful night, with the sounds of music and laughter rising as we passed bars and restaurants on our way to the club, the feeling was a little bit contagious.

I leaned into him, wondering when he'd leave for his next adventure, and made a decision to enjoy his company but not count on it. I could do this, this noncommittal thing. I just needed a little emotional distance so when he headed out the door, I was ready to deal with it.

I needed to be like that untouchable moon. You'd need a damn rocket to get to me, but you could admire me and bask in my light. I almost giggled to myself at the analogy. I'd had most of that bottle of wine, and I wasn't thinking entirely straight. *So, keep it simple. Casual. Cool. I can do this.*

Ez's band was in the middle of a hard-rocking tune when we entered. She was too busy to notice us as she banged on the keys of the baby grand piano and sang in a throaty, emphatic yowl that managed to be both primitive and tuneful. The lyrics were about always holding a part of herself back, and I wondered if she was singing about her own experiences. I knew she wrote most of the band's songs. I thought again of the moon, hiding so much of itself in the dark until those rare days when it beamed all of its reflected light on us, the river, the beach.

It was time to stop thinking and start drinking.

"Old-Fashioned," I told Neil, who wore red suspenders over a vertically striped shirt and black trousers cut in a high-waisted vintage style. With that handlebar mustache, he was in full retro bartender mode. "Wyatt?"

"What's on tap?" In a minute, Wyatt was taking a long drink of a dark red ale in a frosty glass and then licking the foam off his lips. Those lovely, sculpted lips.

"Let me lick them next time," I said without thinking.

"What?" After a second, he grinned. "Oh." He took another sip before the foam could dissipate and bent toward me with a full, frothy mustache and a wicked glint in his eyes.

I felt my face heat. But it was a bar, after all, and we were surrounded by jolly drunken people, and I wanted him. *Casually,* of course. I moved toward him, then slowly ran my tongue over his upper lip, so slowly I heard his breath catch. For good measure, I nipped his lower lip and salved it briefly with a kiss that filled my taste buds with the hoppy flavor of the ale.

His smile melted away in the fire of something hotter as he looked into my eyes. "We need to go back to your place."

I grinned at his expression, feeling a twinge of power at this new, casual me who absolutely did not need this quite literally delicious man. "Not yet. I want to hear the rest of this set. Ez is trying out some new songs tonight."

He ran a hand through that floppy hair and cocked his head at me, like a dog trying to figure out an unfamiliar noise. "I don't know what you're up to," he said, his voice low, "but you know how to drive me crazy."

"Doing my best," I said brightly, taking a sip of my drink, tasting the familiar, warm, sweet rush of the whiskey.

I took it easy on the alcohol over the next two hours, nursing my Old-Fashioned as the effects of the wine slowly wore off. I balanced on a fulcrum of near-sobriety while everyone around me, including some familiar faces — Penelope, Thea and new art school friends, along with a couple of local surfers Wyatt had met — became increasingly, wildly drunk. By the time Ez had a break and came over demanding a drink — Neil had set up two Manhattans for her consideration this evening, one of which she quaffed in a single draw — the others were calling for shots. Wyatt guided them in choosing one of the better tequilas, and I opted out, feeling that strange sensation I sometimes got: a contact "drunk." I knew that wasn't a thing, really, not like the contact high the folks out back were no doubt getting from the Emeralds, but I could feel myself adopting the loose, bubbling conversation of my inebriated friends. My brain went whirling out into the night, leaving nothing behind but a vacant, pleasant feeling as I watched them drink more and more.

"You OK?" Wyatt whispered to me after they'd done a round of shots to giddy laughter.

"Sure," I said. "Great. You?"

"I feel good," he said, though I thought I heard some off note in his voice. He wasn't nearly as drunk as he let on, either. And then he was laughing at something Penelope said, and I felt my phone buzzing in my purse. I saw a photo I'd shot of my brother at the regional show, grinning in his crazy suit, pop up on the screen.

"Damien? I thought you'd be here," I half-shouted into the phone over the Junction Box cacophony.

"It's not Damien, honey," came a cloyingly pitched tenor that could only belong to one person.

"Saffron? Where's Damien?"

"He's fucking unconscious, is what," Saffron drawled, as if she, or "he" as her dad had called her until his last breath, were talking about how pretty her hair was. I dimly heard a matching racket on the other side of our conversation.

"Is he OK?"

"Other than wavering between tediously angry and unconscious and threatening to cut his own throat after he cuts out some bastard's heart? Fuck if I know," she continued, sounding bored. "You need to come get him, honey. He's bringing the party down."

I felt a surge of ire, at Saffron for her insouciance, at Damien for whatever he was doing to himself. But he was my brother, and he could be kind of fucked up, and I had to go to him.

All my giddiness gone, I tried to seek a quieter corner. "Where are you?"

"The warehouse. Where else?" The warehouse. That was Saffron's quasi-legal loft apartment in the industrial district. "Get over here, honey pie, and take care of him, would you? And before you ask, no, I can't pour him into a cab. He's fucking hostile, honey. So get over here right now, OK?"

Damn it. I'd have to drive. "OK," I snapped, now more worried than annoyed.

Wyatt drifted to my side as I ended the call. "Who was that?"

"That was Bohemia's most famous drag queen asking me to rescue my brother."

"What's wrong with him?" Wyatt's eyebrows came together in a mix of confusion and concern.

"I think he's drunk. And depressed. Or maybe just being dramatic. Either way, I have to go." I was getting more anxious by the second. I hoped Saffron didn't have a lot of knives lying around.

Wyatt put an arm around me. "I'll go with you."

"No." His eyes widened in surprise, but my anxiety meter was spiking. "No. I have to deal with this myself. It's a family thing."

Wyatt withdrew his arm as if stung. He stood up straight. His face turned to stone. And I thought, *It's exactly as if I'd slapped him.*

I looked at him with only a trace of remorse as his eyes clouded over, stormy, terribly dark. I couldn't deal with whatever he was feeling right now. And it's not like he was a part of my life.

Not really.

That's what I told myself as I rushed out the door.

RATHER THAN DO the fifteen-minute walk to my place, I paid a cab to get me there in five, and I rushed through the alley to the back and my car. Fifteen minutes later, after hitting every red light in Bohemia, I was on the southern periphery of town among a small army of faceless, gray industrial buildings. One two-story structure of red brick stood out for its mid-century lines, rounded corners and large panels of glass brick, which broke up its facade. This old warehouse was Saffron's building, inherited from her parents, who'd hoped their son — er, daughter would sell it or make it a going concern. Instead, despite dubious zoning, Saffron had taken over the second floor and turned it into a vast apartment, the frequent site of jam sessions and poetry slams.

I had to park on the street. I pressed the buzzer and, after a full minute, finally gained admittance to the dark, cluttered first floor. The echoing space was filled with piles of random objects, from antiques to electronics, that Saffron sold online when she wasn't performing. Only one light hanging ahead of me indicated where to go — it cast a dim glow onto an elevator that looked suspiciously new for the space.

Though it had a vague feeling of abandonment, the whole building seemed to pulse subtly to a beat emanating from overhead. I knew there were stairs somewhere, but I decided I'd rather go for the light. The piles in the shadows gave me the creeps, or maybe it was the mannequins among them. I walked across the dusty cement floor to the sleek silver doors and hit the button.

Then I was in, and up, and the doors opened on a medley of music and noise and color. There were few walls in the space, just lots of square gray columns, strange objects (a suit of armor, a massive discarded neon sign from a bar that used to be downtown), and folding screens. There were plush seating areas everywhere. A crowd of musicians jammed in one spot under a half-dozen antique chandeliers. Another group lingered by a round art-deco bar in the middle. A few black-clad explorers foraged in the fridge in the kitchen at one end, framed only by a long counter from an old soda fountain.

They wore black, but they weren't Damien. I looked around anxiously and focused on a slim figure sashaying in my direction. Saffron wore a little black dress, a clingy, short, satin thing with netting that extended from just above her presumptive breasts and over her shoulders, even as a five o'clock shadow haunted her chin. But her lipstick was impeccable, and her black bob and black-rimmed geek glasses framed the hard angles of her face perfectly.

"Bedroom," she said, pointing to one end of the vast room, where there was indeed a wall with a door.

"Lucky him," I said, heading that way.

"Never in a million years," Saffron called out in her sing-song manner.

That's OK. She wasn't Damien's type, anyway.

"Bring coffee," I ordered over my shoulder, and I heard a "Hmph!" as I crossed the floor.

The wall at this end, gray like much of the interior of this place, was covered in large paintings. The door was red. I opened it.

To my relief, the bedroom was nothing like the circuslike main room. For one thing, it was smaller, almost the size of a normal bedroom, with a false ceiling of billowing swaths of silky white fabric. All the furnishings and art were a restful black or gray or white, with the exception of a handful of red pillows of varying sizes and textures scattered on the bed's lustrous gray cover. Among them, coordinating nicely in his all-black outfit, was a snoring Damien. He stirred and sat up with a groan when he heard the door shut.

"I'll fucking stab anyone who tries to move me!" he shouted. And then his gaze focused, and his face twisted into an expression somewhere between shock and embarrassment when he saw it was me. "Aw, shit," he said, and fell back against the cushions.

"Are you armed?" I asked, relieved to see that he wasn't bleeding and even looked a little abashed.

He moaned and sat up again, watching me with bleary eyes. "Am I in the kitchen?" He looked around, genuinely confused. "Then I guess I'm not. But if you have a knife, you can stick it right here." He pointed to his heart.

"Don't tell me you actually have some sort of feelings you want to cut out of there."

"Of course not. I just don't need it anymore. Can you get me a gin and tonic?"

"No," I said, setting my purse on the floor and sitting next to him on the bed. "God, you smell like a distillery."

"So maybe if you squeeze my armpit, gin will drip out. Get a glass."

"Gross!"

The bedroom door opened, and Saffron appeared with a

cup of coffee. "I'm not getting near him," she said, holding out the mug to me.

"I'll kick you in your precious swaddled balls!" Damien snarled, but I could hear a trace of humor in his tone, even if his syllables were a little slurred.

"Drama queen. You should have seen him twenty minutes ago." Saffron rolled one shoulder provocatively on her way out the door.

"Drink," I said, handing Damien the cup.

He took a sip and screwed up his face. "This isn't gin."

"You don't need any more gin."

"I need lots of gin."

"Are you OK? I mean except for being completely hammered?" I took the mug back from him as he swayed and gripped the bed.

"Room's spinning, kinda."

"I bet." Outside the bedroom, the musicians launched into a new song, and Saffron's distinctive, throaty vocal slinked around the rhythm instruments. My brother had paled to a bilious shade of eggshell. I put a steadying hand on his shoulder and silently prayed to Bacchus to steady Damien's stomach. "So — did someone break your heart?"

He was silent.

"Javier?"

"I'll stuff canned Spam down his pretty vegan throat!" Damien said, only this time, something like a sob sneaked into his voice.

"No, you won't. You're not violent."

"Why can't I be? Just this once?" He shook his head. "He's found some guy in Miami. Another artist, for Christ's sake. As if I'm not enough artist for him."

"I'm sure he didn't break up with you because of your art," I said.

"So it's my personality? Great. You're a real comfort." He grabbed the mug from me, sloshing a little on one of the red pillows, and took a long swallow before handing it back. He wavered, regarding the dark splotch in the red fabric. He poked a finger into the cushion. "See? Art."

"You're in love."

"Never," Damien said with mock horror. He lay back again and looked up at the swoops of fabric that served as a ceiling. They moved ever so slightly in unseen air currents, and I thought of clouds.

"Admit it. It's OK."

"You're only saying that because you're always in love," he said.

"Oh, Damien." I sighed. "You of all people should know that's not true. It's never been true."

He dragged himself up to a sitting position again. "Hey," he said. "Something's missing."

I lifted an eyebrow.

"Your surfer boy," he said. "Where's he?"

"I told him not to come."

"That's good," he said. "It's no good to be in love. And you're in love with that one."

"Ridiculous." I looked up at the ceiling so I wouldn't have to look at my brother.

"I'm not ridiculous," he said. "I'm an ARTIST!" he shouted to the ceiling, the gin still in his voice.

I turned back to him. "Yes, you are."

"And *you* are in love. Maybe you're not in love all the time," he conceded, "but you're in love with this one."

"No," I said, more emphatically. "I can't be. He's moving away."

He eyed me with a melancholy, drunken wisdom and reached out for the mug of coffee, draining it. "This is where I tell you it's not worth it. He's not worth chasing. You shouldn't try to keep him, because he'll just break your heart. If I were a good brother, that's what I'd tell you. But then again, I'm not a very good brother." He grinned, and then his eyes went fuzzy. He looked into the empty mug. "Where's my gin?" He was gone again, back in Drunk Land.

"You're coming home with me." I took the mug and set it on a nightstand.

"No way. I do not want to be with people in love right now!"

"We're not. He's not." I didn't want to think about this now. "He won't be there. I think he's pissed at me," I said, remembering Wyatt's icy expression when I left the bar.

"Are you sure?"

"Can you walk?" I stood, grabbed my purse and held out an arm.

"Fuck yeah. Let me OUT OF THIS FREAK SHOW!" he shouted.

The musicians outside the door faltered, then picked up again with the jazzy tune.

In truth, Damien could barely walk, but he managed to cling to my shoulder, and I got him to the elevator as Saffron, still singing, shot us a dirty look. Downstairs, my brother attempted to warn one of the mannequins against getting into a relationship. I tugged him away and was rewarded with a new round of cursing.

As soon as I got him in the passenger seat of my SUV, he fell asleep.

Poor Damien. I'd never seen him fall for anyone, ever. He was taking it hard.

As I drove toward home, Wyatt's face flashed in front of me, jaw set, that hurt in his eyes. I'd said something that really wounded him. It wasn't just that I'd wanted to go alone.

It's a family thing.

Wyatt didn't have a family. But he didn't have me, either, if he was moving to the west coast.

And he'd basically said he didn't need anybody, right?

That's what he'd *said.*

"Fuck." My turn to curse.

The moon had set, and the sky was inky black. I parked in back of my building and laboriously got Damien inside and up the stairs to the couch. His usually electric black hair was limp and sad, his eyeliner smudged. But his black outfit looked just fine. Artist. Waiter. Ninja. He had plenty of options when he woke up.

I checked my phone before I crawled into bed. No messages. I wondered if I'd been wrong. And then I remembered Wyatt's eyes again and felt vaguely sick. I'd pushed him away. That's what I'd wanted to do, right?

I was lousy at this cool and casual thing.

I opened a new message. "Damien's OK. See you tomorrow?" I typed.

There was no immediate response. I turned off the lights and lay there, clutching the phone to my belly. After ten minutes, I texted again. "You OK? Did you get home OK?" Because I'd not only left him; I'd left him with no wheels, too.

No response.

Nothing but the distant rumble of a train, and the chill of my empty bed, and the sound of my brother snoring in the next room.

PART 3

I awoke in the morning with the phone still clutched in my hands. Still no message, just a really low battery. I plugged it into the charger on my nightstand and rolled out of bed, alone again. Except for maybe my brother.

No, he was gone, too. The couch was empty. He could walk to his place from mine, or stagger, if he had to. I suspected he could walk fine this morning, but I didn't envy him his hangover.

I thought about last night, about extricating Damien from Saffron's. That went as well as could be expected. And then I thought about Wyatt and the strong possibility I'd been a jerk.

So what if Wyatt was leaving? Why not include him in my life? Embrace him while I could? I hated myself right now, not just for what may have been reactive, defensive behavior, but for all my second-guessing. I was never this way when it came to dealing with guys, and yes, I *dealt* with them. I set the rules. I determined the course of the relationship, right up until the moment the lights went out and I was only too glad to see them leave. The lights were never that bright, anyway.

Not till now. *Wyatt, under the studio lights. The shark on his shoulder, frightening, sinuous, art in motion.*

I needed to tell him I was sorry.

I showered and dressed in a long, soft, flaring black skirt and a blousy pull-over white shirt over a cotton tank top that hugged my torso, wanting that feeling of comfort. I texted him again.

"Are you busy? Can I see you?"

There was no reply. And then I was mad at myself again for my wishy-washy, un-Calista-like behavior.

But I still texted him an hour later. Two hours later.

I resigned myself to work at my lobby desk. Over a couple of hours, I saw only one visitor, a college-age guy who'd opened the door and closed it immediately after he saw what was inside, as if the pictures might bite him. At lunchtime, as I ate a peanut butter sandwich and lost myself in Photoshop, my phone buzzed on the desk next to me. I turned away from the image of Thea I'd been editing, picked up the phone with trepidation and looked at the screen.

"Thanks for getting me out of there last night. I can't remember much of it, but I know Saffron can be a total bitch."

Damien. I allowed myself a wry smile.

"Glad you're alive, bro," was all I typed back, all that he expected. And I was just chewing on my disappointment when the phone buzzed again.

I switched screens.

Wyatt! "Been surfing. Glad your brother is OK."

So Wyatt was alive, too. I felt a rush of relief, remorse.

And maybe a tad of annoyance at his half-answer to all my texts.

"You busy today?" I typed, willing my thumbs to be as nonchalant as possible, trying to forget how many texts I'd already sent him.

"Working on photos. See you in class."

Whoa. He was not only blowing me off today — he was blowing me off Sunday, too. Or forever. It sounded like forever.

No, no, no. My breath seemed to jam up in my lungs. The bottom fell out of my stomach. I couldn't let this happen. I couldn't let him walk away. Seeing me in class was not the same as seeing me. He'd slammed a door in my face — one, I had to admit, I might have closed first.

I felt something strange and uncomfortable flitting around in the back of my mind. I tried to figure out what it was. And then, I thought, it's *need.* Not just for his body, though there was that, too, a terrible aching void that cried out for him. It was something else, something intangible I'd only ever found in Wyatt.

It was lose him now or lose him later. I preferred later.

I closed up shop, got in my car and headed for Bohemia Beach.

Twenty minutes later, I was cruising slowly down the street where I grew up, hoping my parents weren't outside when I drove past the family home. I didn't think I could face the interrogation once they spotted me. To my relief, they were nowhere in sight, and I focused on finding Jen's house.

It was hard to miss the red Japanese gate. It gleamed in the sunny, cool afternoon. I pulled into the driveway next to an open-style, happily weathered black Jeep and saw a couple of boards leaning against the garage, one wood-grain with light green and dark brown accents, the other blue with a swirling white pattern. Eyeing the boards, I felt a little twist of regret. Thanks to my stupid fear, I could never connect with this huge part of Wyatt's life.

I walked to the front door and rang the doorbell.

Immediately, the high-pitched frenzy of a yappy dog startled me out of my worries. I hadn't known there was a dog here. And then the main door and the screen door were being pushed open by a lovely, tan woman of about forty-five with shoulder-length, frosted-caramel hair, wearing a skin-tight T-shirt and faded jeans. My mouth dropped open.

"Yes?" she asked, bemused.

Holy crap. This was *Jen.* And she was fucking gorgeous, the delicate lines around her eyes only serving to enhance the merriment in her expression. With one sneaker-clad foot, she nudged back a viciously barking black and white chihuahua mix, and it quieted instantly.

I tried to get myself together. "Hi. I'm —" Who was I? "I'm Calista. Is Wyatt available?"

Jen's eyes widened, and she broke into a broad smile, a beam of sunlight through the clouds. "Oh, *you're* Calista," she said, sticking out a hand. "I am *so* happy to meet you. Come on in. Wyatt and David are having a beer by the pool."

I gingerly entered, keeping an eye on the dog, but it just sniffed my sandaled toes once and trotted off, content that I was no match for its powers.

The house had a wide-open feel — 1960s but renovated, with restored terrazzo floors, colorful rugs, funky lamps and spare, modern furniture. I trailed Jen through the living room and dark dining room and dropped my purse on the table. I followed her through the sliding glass doors to a back patio furnished with oversized chairs and surrounded by large tropical plants. A lagoon-shaped pool sparkled among the palms at the heart of the fenced yard's lush, secluded miniature jungle.

A rugged-looking man with silver-blond hair sat in one of the comfy chairs under the thatched overhang, talking to a distressingly familiar figure who had his back toward me.

"We have a visitor," Jen announced with a touch of drama.

I ignored Wyatt and strode past him to Jen's perplexed husband. "You must be David," I said with as much enthusiasm I could muster. He switched his beer bottle from his right hand to his left so he could take me up on my handshake. His palm was still moist from the cold beer. "I'm Calista," I added.

"Oh!" he said, appearing even more surprised than Jen, and I saw them exchange a look — definitely the look of a couple who knew each other's shorthand. For some reason, even though their reaction suggested I had been a topic of conversation, this instance of marital harmony made me feel a tiny bit better.

At least until I turned to face Wyatt.

He remained cocooned in the overstuffed orange cushions of his wide, cedar-frame chair, outwardly relaxed but giving the impression of coiling like a spring. His knuckles were white over his beer bottle. His expression was neutral, too bland, I thought, to reflect whatever was happening in his head.

"Cali. I didn't expect to see you," he said evenly, not getting up, not holding out a hand, just regarding me with his dark eyes.

"I thought I'd drop by and see if I could catch you on a break. Which I guess I have."

Something flickered in Wyatt's eyes, perhaps a

microsecond of discomfort when he realized I was challenging the message he'd sent me earlier about working.

"Dave," Jen said — I'd honestly forgotten they were there — "would you help me with something in the house?"

"What?" David asked, clearly much more interested in whatever was going to happen between me and Wyatt.

Jen scowled. "You were going to help me hang those new blinds."

"Oh," David said, looking at her. "Now? Uh, OK," he responded to a deepening of her scowl. He shot me an awkward smile and followed her, taking his beer with him. They closed the sliding doors behind them.

I looked back at Wyatt, who seemed to have lost some of his surety, as well as his ability or willingness to speak.

I sat in the chair David had vacated and found it immediately comfortable and soothing. My whole body relaxed just being near Wyatt again, despite his chilly reception. The beautiful plants, Asian decor, a tinkling wind chime and the cerulean blue of the sky and the pool, with its gurgling, built-in waterfall, probably helped, too.

"So you went surfing this morning?" I asked awkwardly.

"Yes," Wyatt said. He took a long sip of his beer, his gaze never leaving mine. With a pulse of panic, I realized I had no idea what he was thinking. Whatever I was going to say, I had to do it without cues. I just had to say it.

Eventually.

"Those your boards outside?"

"David's. We both went."

"Longboards, right?"

"Yeah." Wyatt took another sip of beer and turned his eyes, unfocused, to the pool. "Waves were mushy today."

"Oh," I said. I couldn't wait any longer. "I'm sorry I said no last night."

His gaze snapped back to mine. "No to what?"

"No to you going with me. I could have used — I mean, I wish I'd had you along."

The corner of his mouth quirked up, and he took another long sip from his bottle.

"It's empty," I remarked.

I saw a hint of color in his face as he glanced at the bottle, as if to confirm what both of us knew, and he put it down on the pavers.

"You didn't need to come over here," he said. "I'll see you Monday."

"I needed to." I could feel tears threatening, and I willed them back with a swallow. *I need you.* "I needed to see you. I needed to say — I'm sorry, Wyatt."

"Nothing to be sorry for," he said, but the line of tension in his jaw eased slightly, and I wondered if — hoped that —I'd reached him. I watched him carefully. That current between us was still there, faint on this cool afternoon, like background radiation, and the more I looked into his eyes, the more I felt it grow and simmer. The more I knew that losing him would cause me profound pain.

Later, I told myself. *Don't think about that now.*

I don't know how much of what I was thinking showed on my face, but Wyatt's face softened another fraction.

He said nothing.

I got up and walked slowly over to him. I reached out to him, tentatively, as if he might bolt, and ran a hand through his hair, fluffing the white-blond streak, pushing it back and up, as if I had nothing better to do than style his mop. I heard his breathing change, and my body responded in kind, warming, wanting him. But I just brushed his hair with my fingers, slowly.

After a minute, I touched his ear lightly with one finger, tracing around the top to the lobe. For a moment, I thought of a seashell, the whorls that led into shadowed chambers that, for the fanciful, stored the sound of the sea. I was so wrapped up in this idea and in my own emotional state that I jumped when he reached up and grabbed my wrist.

I looked down and met his flinty eyes. His curvy lips had flattened into a line, somewhere between anger and lust. He pulled me roughly into his lap, still holding my wrist tightly, stiffly, as if I were a wild animal he'd caught that might bite him if he let go.

I relaxed into his grip and leaned against him, whispered in his ear.

"I'm sorry."

I just breathed there for a moment, my cheek against his.

"I'm sorry," I said again, and he released my wrist and pulled me to him. I hugged him tightly, going limp as the tension leaked out of me. Silent tears rolled down my cheeks. He had to have felt them.

"Nothing to be sorry about, Cali," he whispered back. So he wasn't going to acknowledge his hurt or even my transgression. We might need to work on that communication thing. "Shhh," he said, stroking my hair as he held me. "Shhh."

He twisted one hand in the thick fall of my tresses and pulled my head back. He focused on my face. My scalp prickled. I wanted this, his touch, his desire, his assurance. His eyes were like caves, dark and unknown, and they held mine, promising nothing, suggesting everything. His fingers still in my hair, he pulled me toward him and slanted his mouth across mine.

His kiss was a balm for my worry, warm and slow and deft, a sweet remedy for an ache whose depths I didn't understand. He released my hair and slipped his arms around my waist, a hand under my layers, lightly touching the skin of my back as he deepened the kiss.

I heard a rumble and the growl of a car, and Wyatt looked up and made a small sound of amusement.

"What?" I asked.

"David and Jen. They just left."

"Are you sure?"

"The Jeep is unmistakable, and yeah, I'm sure. That's something they would do."

"Because of —"

"Yes," he whispered. "Stop asking so many questions." He pulled me back toward him, and our kiss flamed hotter, like a campfire whipped up by a gust of wind. And then his hands were pulling my blouse over my head with the clingy tank and reaching under my skirt to pull off my underwear as I unzipped his pants, worked off his jeans, yanked off his sweatshirt; our sandals came off; we tore at each other, limbs tangled, until we were skin to skin, only my skirt still in place. My back was chilled gooseflesh, my front smooth heat as he put his hands on my breasts and squeezed and circled his fingers around my pebbled nipples with admiration. My heartbeat accelerated. I straddled him, hitching up my skirt, looking into his eyes, and his hands moved to my behind, guiding me onto him.

Oh, fuck, he was hard. He seemed to swell inside me as I slid over him, my wet sheath stretching, clenching the hard length of his cock as I held onto his shoulders and matched his gaze, now hooded with desire.

"Yes, Cali," he said, crushing me into him, plunging inside me.

I cried out with the agonizing pleasure of it, and then we were moving together. Something sizzled in his eyes as they burned into mine, an intensity that made the world go away. His mouth found mine again, his teasing tongue, as I ground against him. My core started to shimmer like heat over the sand. The world seemed to waver around us, the palm fronds swaying, the pool glinting, sensual and bright and complicit. Pleasure sparked and flared and amplified through me, a tentative wildfire whose flames licked higher with each thrust. The breeze lifted my hair and he grabbed it again, pulling my head back so he could lick and nibble at my neck. I pressed my hands against his chest, played with his nipples with my thumbs, and he hissed. We were each other's fuel, lighting every nerve until I felt us both blaze with desire, a want amplified by emotion. He slipped his hands behind me, squeezed, drew me hard and close. In a flash, my orgasm was a fireball, burning through my limbs, dazzling, overwhelming. He buried his face in my neck, still pumping into me, and he groaned as he came inside me, triggering a new spasm, an almost delirious pleasure in knowing we found this joy in each other, needful and exquisite and strangely inevitable.

We clutched one another as our bodies quieted, drawing warmth from each other, caressing and kissing until Wyatt shivered, acknowledging the cool air. I lifted my head and, with a small kiss, eased off his lap, missing him even as I felt his slickness between my legs.

"Grab your clothes and come with me," Wyatt said quietly. He led me back through the house, into a modest bedroom. There, he closed the door gently against the little dog (after a pat on the head with a "Good boy, Maverick"), who had followed him with a proprietary curiosity. The bed wasn't made; his luggage and clothes and gear were everywhere; his laptop computer was open on a small desk to a digital contact sheet of row upon row of photos of surfers riding turquoise waves. Wyatt took my clothes out of my hands, dropped them on the floor and yanked down my skirt, leaving me abashed and naked.

"What are you doing?" I asked with a startled laugh.

"Making you comfortable," he said with a boyish grin. He scooped me up and lay me in the messy queen-size bed, sweeping me under the covers with him.

"Are you sure this is OK? I mean, Jen and David — "

"Will not give a damn, even if they come back. And their room is on the other side of the house, anyway." Wrapping his arms around me, he whispered, "I just want to feel you next to me for a while, OK?"

For a while. Forever.

His voice was so intimate, a secret in every sound. Had he really been staring me down only a few minutes ago, monolithic, cold and unmoving?

I'd take this Wyatt, warm and tender. Our mouths met in a drowsy dance, and in the cozy nest of blankets and pillows, skin to skin, we dozed off in a haze of heat, drugged with each other.

MONDAY. The weekend had been a blur. Wyatt and I had parted after our bittersweet, lazy afternoon on Saturday. We both had a lot of photos to edit, him of surfers, me of pinups and friends, and we agreed to have lunch after class on Monday. This parting felt right. I had a feeling we were letting something settle between us, the roiled waters of whatever our relationship was. This time, when he said "See you Monday," it came with a promising kiss.

My students seemed to be suffering the aftereffects of the weekend and took slowly to my lesson on touching up portraits with Photoshop and all the choices that entailed.

"Do you want your subject to look ethereally perfect? Hyper-real and wrinkled? Glowing? Gloomy?" I asked.

Millie raised her hand from behind the school's desktop computer. While some students brought their own, she couldn't afford a laptop yet.

"When you do all this stuff, isn't it basically a lie?" she asked.

"Yes," I said, to surprised chuckles in the room. "Photographers have always done darkroom work. You should see the stuff in the morgue at the newspaper — the archives," I explained after a couple of horrified looks. "Some of the older photos, besides the usual darkroom adjustments, have backgrounds painted out and other features outlined with pen. Now, it's just a lot a easier. It's hard to trust any photo, and journalists have to walk a fine line between enhancement and falsehood.

"But this is a portrait class," I continued, "and I want you to be as creative as you want. Maybe your approach will be strictly documentary; maybe you want to show a woman's every wrinkle. Maybe it's a point of principle for you. But if you want to shoot portraits commercially, consider that sometimes a little enhancement is appreciated by your clients. I kind of look at it this way: When I meet someone, I don't notice all the particulars of their appearance right away.

I notice their energy, the light in their eyes. Living people have a beauty that is very difficult to capture in a photograph. That same person reduced to two dimensions may seem haggard and old and flat. I don't mind enhancing the photo slightly so you notice the light in their eyes and everything the context gives them. I'm telling a story. I'm not just pushing a button."

"What about HDR?" one of the guys asked. "What about erasing stuff from an image?"

"At some point, you cross from documentary into art, and that's totally OK. But if you're documenting something, show restraint. I hate the fakey-fakey look of badly done HDR — high dynamic range," I said to confused expressions, "gray shadows and muted highlights and weird glows and blurs. If you're not sure, walk away from the photo and come back to it later and see how it feels. If a viewer's first reaction is, 'That looks fake,' you haven't done it right."

Wyatt raised his hand.

"Mr. Brooks?" I called, noting a twinkle in his eye.

"What if your subject is so beautiful that she doesn't need any touch-up at all?"

"Then you have a rare subject indeed," I said, warning him with my eyes. "But more likely, you're just trying to get out of using Photoshop."

The class laughed. I let them work, walked around, gave them tips. There were a few prodigies, and by the time the session was done, most of them seemed to have the hang of it.

"You should have your portrait subject by now for your final project," I said as they packed up. "Remember, you want five to eight final photos. So pick someone who has something to work with — an interesting job, a rich setting. Your studio partner will be OK if you both agree. And I have an assignment for you for Wednesday. Remember I was talking with you about photographing nudes? I want you to shoot something that shows off the human body. Your subject doesn't have to be nude or sexual. Maybe you're showing the body of a sick person. Maybe it's a swimmer or a draped model. But your photo should explore the human body. This is not a mug shot. Just keep it tasteful, people. Bring it with you Wednesday."

There were rumbles. I knew the assignment could be challenging, even intimidating, but that was part of the point. I wanted these photographers to be fearless when they left my class.

At the same time, I avoided looking at Wyatt. As a potential subject, I was anything but fearless.

I asked them to bring digital images next time that we would use to create a layered portrait with special effects. I turned off the lights, showed them a few examples on the big screen and sent them on their way.

Wyatt lingered until they were gone and then approached me. I was reminded of that first day, when he came up to me by the light of the screen. A lot had happened since then. He looked around to make sure no one was watching, and then he reached out and touched me behind my ear, trailed a finger down my neck to the depth of the "V" in my soft knit shirt. He bent over and kissed me there, on the curve of my left breast.

"Wyatt!" I hissed.

His head popped up, and he grinned. "Your skin glows in this light. I couldn't help myself. I'm thinking about photographing you nude."

"Not going to happen," I said automatically. "Especially for a class assignment."

"So it might happen if it's not for a class assignment?"

"No," I said. It was one thing to make love under the photo lights; it was quite another to bare myself to the camera. I understood its power. It could strip away any mask, expose any vulnerability. It told its own truth.

He sighed theatrically. "Then I guess I'll have to photograph someone else nude."

I scowled but kept my voice even. "Do what you gotta do. I never said the subject had to be nude, anyway. What about another surfer? I've seen some surfers with beautiful bodies. You know, one of those big, blond guys."

It was his turn to scowl at my oblique reference to Ron Raker and my turn to grin. He nodded and pinned me with his gaze. "I guess you'll just have to wait and see what I get, then."

I swallowed, feeling a twinge of irrational jealousy. Neither of us said anything for a minute, and then Wyatt broke the silence. "So you want to do lunch or what?"

I smiled a small smile of relief at this return to normalcy and packed up my stuff.

We stopped at Picasso's. The bakery-café was packed with students and businesspeople on their lunch hour. A new exhibit of mixed-media work was on the walls, de-saturated macro photos of orchids with their parts annotated with lines and text, not technical terms, but poetic notions and fragments of quotes, a strange and enchanting mixture of beauty and romance framed in the visual language of science. A little part of my brain expanded and took note. Photography was so much more than one person could ever define, so much more than a rectangle clipping of the world captured by a lens.

Wyatt followed my gaze to the pictures after we'd ordered. "Do you like them?"

"I love them. I like my photos to tell a story on their own, but I like the notion of layering ideas."

"I think I'm more interested in catching that moment that will never happen again. That's what surfing's always been like for me. Every day, every wave is different. Now I'm doing it with a camera." He took a sip of his cola. "I had a lot of fun shooting that wedding, too. Did you finish editing the photos?"

"Yeah! The bride was really happy. And your stuff was great."

"Thanks." He smiled.

I studied him and again thought about what a great partner he'd be, not just in bed, but in life, in work.

"There might an opportunity for surf photography at the end of the week," he continued, and my little dream collapsed with the arrival of my tuna sandwich. He seemed to sense the change in my mood. "I mean around here."

"Around here?"

"Yeah. It's early to be sure, but we could be getting a nor'easter that will really whip up the waves here."

"You're going to photograph them?"

"I thought I would surf them," he said. "And maybe you could photograph them. And me."

"Oh." I knew my eyes were wide open.

He showed his dimple. "By the way, this doesn't qualify as my third request."

"What?"

Wyatt leaned close and whispered, " *'I'll do anything.'* "

My face heated, and I leaned back, recovering myself. "Would I have to get in the water?"

"Totally optional. But if you wanted to, you'd be completely safe with me."

His tone was serious and reassuring, and for a moment I pictured myself in the water, shooting beautiful surf photos — and then that shiver ran up my spine.

I tried to sound reasonable. "That water's going to be pretty cold. How about, if the waves happen, I just shoot you from the shore with a long lens?"

He nodded, and I wondered if I saw a trace of disappointment in his expression. "That'll work," he said. "Now just cross your fingers that the waves will come."

"Don't you have some kind of surf god you can make a sacrifice to?"

"Maybe I can throw a burrito into the ocean. But not this one. It's too good." He took another bite of his lunch, and that moment of tension seemed to ease. I quizzed him about surf photography techniques and trends as we ate.

"So," he said, when his burrito and its accompanying nacho chips and guacamole had vanished, "you're going to be my portrait subject, right?"

"Your fully clothed portrait subject? Yes, if you like."

"I like."

My skin tingled at his warm smile. "When do you want to start?"

"How about today?"

"I DID mention being fully clothed, right?" I asked as we put down our bags in the big room at my photo studio.

"Trust me," Wyatt said. "I have an idea. I'm just hoping it will work. Is it OK if I play with the lights?"

"Knock yourself out. Let me know if you need me to do something."

"Can you help me get the black backdrop in place?"

I helped him tear away the pink paper, which was well trodden after the pinup shoot, and we rolled down the heavy black paper.

"Do I need to change?" I asked. "This isn't exactly my best outfit."

"That'll be fine for what I'm planning," he said, scanning me in my clingy black shirt and jeans. But if you want to redo your hair, put it up in that fun spiky way you — "

"My hair is *not* spiky."

He grinned. "You know. You clip it up and it has that sort of exciting electrified look."

I glowered at him. "You mean pieces stick up?"

"Exactly. I love it!" he said, mollifying me with only a hint of good-natured mockery.

I lifted an eyebrow, grabbed a brush out of my bag and sat in one of the big, black chairs, watching him as I brushed my hair and reset it in the clip so the ends fluttered above my head like feathers. Wyatt pulled out the strobes and a few standalone LED light panels with soft boxes, arranging them on stands in a staggered array toward the back of the space. He didn't turn on any front lighting at all. I was starting to get an idea of what he was after.

He set up his camera on a tripod and beckoned me over. "Would you grab your camera and stand in the middle there?"

"In front of the lights?"

"Yes," he said. "I think."

I smiled. "I think it's going to be cool."

"You do?" He smiled back.

"Yes, but it may take some experimentation with the lights."

It took about an hour to get the shot he wanted. Flaring at the back of the image were the strobes and standalone lights, all the veins of their umbrellas and soft boxes visible as they blasted out white light. Together, they silhouetted me, standing still, my features invisible, only my shoulders and torso and cheekbones and "electrified" hair touched with light. I was a black shadow, one hand on my hip, the other elevated, holding a camera.

"I'll make it black and white," Wyatt said. We stood by the tripod and looked at the previews on his camera with the photo lights off and a couple of the room lights on, dim enough so we could really see the pictures.

"I really like it. Though I almost look scary." I glanced up at his face. He seemed startled.

"I didn't think of it that way. You're like a shadow, the invisible force felt in a photo but never seen. Maybe a little intimidating."

"Intimidating?" I burst out laughing.

"I don't know," he said, brushing it off. "It's just an image."

The idea disturbed me. I knew better than anyone that nothing was "just an image."

"Am I really scary?"

"Of course not," he said. "Maybe unattainable."

"Uh, I think you have 'attained' me plenty."

"It's nothing. I'm just telling a story, like you were talking about in class." He didn't sound as if he quite believed it. Good God. If anyone was unattainable, it was Wyatt.

I pushed on his arm, turning him away from the camera and toward me.

"What?" he asked.

"Do you want to know how scary I can be?" I asked in my best I'm-going-to-boil-your-pet-rabbit voice.

He blanched. "Uh — I — I'm pretty sure not."

"Oh, I think you do," I said, more playful this time.

Wyatt seemed to recover, to recognize the game. "Would I like it?" he asked in a low voice.

"Get on your knees," I commanded, wondering how far I could take this semblance of control until I gave in to the wild lust I suddenly felt.

He grinned wickedly before adopting a contrite expression and dropped to his knees in front of me.

"And what is my princess's pleasure?" he purred, placing his hands on my waist and letting them slide down over my hips.

I kicked off my sneakers and unbuttoned and unzipped my jeans as he watched, rapt. "Pull them off," I said.

He pulled them down, and I stepped out of them.

"Now the underwear."

They were rather good underwear today, as I'd hoped I'd see Wyatt — though I hadn't imagined quite this scenario. He "hmmm'd" in appreciation as he dipped a finger through one side of the black lace bikinis and stretched it away from my hip, then did the same to the other side before slowly working them down and off. He boomeranged them across the room with a flick of the wrist, and I tried not to smile.

"Take off your sweatshirt," I told him. "And the shirt."

"And the jeans?" he asked hopefully as he complied.

"Just the shirts." Though I looked down and noticed the bulge straining at his crotch. I bit back my smile as something like anguish crossed his face.

And now he was beautifully shirtless before me, his golden skin shadowed by every contour of his surfer's physique, the muscles of his chest and arms. Threads of dark hair defined the valley that led to his taut belly and into his jeans.

"Taste me," I said softly.

He moved subtly closer to me, still on his knees, and touched me with only his tongue. There. *Oh, God, yes, there.*

He stopped after one tantalizing tease, looking up at me expectantly, eyes wide with faux innocence. He would make me say what I wanted. And in that way, he was in control, too.

"More," I whispered with difficulty. "Until I tell you to stop."

"Yes, my princess." And then his tongue was liquid heat on my clit and I was falling, falling into a pool of fire, struggling to stand as the ecstasy overtook me. I looked down at him, at the rippling of his shoulders, the cryptic shark curling on his back, the movement of his dark head — I had never seen anything so erotic. I was breathlessly drinking in the sight, the sensation, when he looked up at me.

"May I touch you?" he asked, his voice low and throaty.

"*Yes.*"

His hands reached up to cup my buttocks, pressing me toward his mouth as he laved my clit again, as he dipped his tongue into my cleft and teased my bud. His mouth was pure heat in the cool room, his deft tongue bringing me to the edge until I quivered and groaned and bucked against him.

He paused again. "Did you say to stop?" he teased openly this time.

I couldn't stand it anymore. I dropped to my knees in front of him and grabbed at his jeans, struggling to free him. He barely had time to let out a laugh before he helped me get them off, along with his sandals. And then his briefs.

I pushed him to the scarred wooden floor. His head

bumped lightly on the boards, but he didn't seem to mind, smiled even, as I straddled him, grasping his hot erection, sliding my hand up and down until his impishness was gone and he was all gasping desire.

"Now, Cali," he said hoarsely, and I lifted myself, guided his cock to my entrance. I eased onto him and began to move. "Please . . . "

"Yes?" I replied.

"Take your shirt off so I can see you."

I smiled through the pleasure of grinding against him and reached up to my hair clip, freeing it first. My heavy blond locks fell around my shoulders. I reached to the hem of my shirt and pulled it over my head in one motion, then leaned over Wyatt until my hair skimmed his face and my breasts were touching him, spilling over the bra. Black lace. Hard nipples.

"Hmmm," he moaned, cupping the lace-clad globes. "Beautiful."

I still had something on my mind. I felt myself tremble around him as he thrust upward.

"Am I scary?" I whispered.

He rolled me, suddenly, so that I was on my back, and his thrusts went, *oh, God,* so deep. He gripped my wrists and held them to the floor. His brown eyes, with their chocolate-diamond sparks, pinned me, too.

"Terrifying," he finally murmured. He leaned down and took my mouth with his, wide open, as if he would eat me alive. Every part of us was touching: chest to chest, hip to hip, legs entwined, lips, tongues. And the hard floor against my back, his hard, muscled arms confining me, his hard cock in my pussy, made me soft, yielding, mesmerized with the pleasure of his delicious imprisonment. I lifted my hips to meet his thrusts as he slid down and up, teasing, building, until his eyes darkened and lust dictated his speed, the inexorable force of his penetration. I embraced the near pain of it, his thorough taking of me, as he accelerated.

He grunted, and then he released an almost unspoken cry, a sigh of ecstasy as I felt his powerful release possess me. My orgasm blossomed, unfurling petals of pleasure as my body shuddered. I closed my eyes and saw and felt blooms of color and light as I clenched his mass and heat inside me.

Wyatt stayed there, pinning me to the floor, as our breathing slowed. I opened my eyes and gazed up at him, completely under his spell. His face was inscrutable. He raised himself and slipped out of me, and I missed him. I sat up slowly and hugged my knees as he rolled away and got up. He reached out a hand to me, and I took it, allowing him to pull me up, too.

He wrapped his arms tightly around me and pressed his naked body to mine. I buried my head in the crook of his neck and held on.

"Sometimes," he whispered in my ear, "it's good to be a little scared."

I WAS RUNNING. *There was snow everywhere. It was winter. But it was Florida. This was sense and nonsense, but I was committed to it. I had to get there. Where was I going? And why was it snowing?*

And then I was at the beach, and the snow fell hard, filling the air, thick and dense. No, not snow. The whitecaps of the ocean flung wildly around me. Frothing foam from the waves flew high in the air with each crashing collision of water and sand. The foam floated on water and wind and filled the gray sky and covered the ground. I tried to run from it. The sky got darker and darker. The foam got deeper and deeper. It was up to my chin. I could taste the salt in my mouth, and I knew I would die . . .

I woke with a start and a gasp. My throat felt thick and sticky, and I coughed to get a clear breath. I sat up.

I was alone in my bed. It was Wednesday morning. My alarm wouldn't go off for another forty-five minutes. I got up anyway to get ready for the day and for class — and so I wouldn't have to go back to the dream.

I hadn't seen Wyatt at all yesterday, but I knew he had work, not to mention homework. I was anxious to see whom he'd photographed for the body assignment. I was over my jealousy of Jen, but a photo of her might prompt a relapse. There were plenty of other beach bunnies in the sea, if it came to that.

As it turned out, the results from the class were more diverse than I could have imagined — from the expected beautiful female form draped with a sheet to a frail old man getting a sponge bath at a nursing home (the photographer's grandfather) to a luminous, naked pregnant woman tastefully illuminated by natural light in front of a window.

And then there was Wyatt's, which he'd titled "Hang Eleven." The class murmured its appreciation when his slide came up, and it tittered, too. The photo was shot at dawn at the beach, almost certainly from a point in the water. The waves glinted with orange sparkles, and the sky was the color of a sapphire on fire, silhouetting a gorgeous surfer. A gorgeous *male* surfer. He was a dark cutout against the fiery sky, riding a shallow wave, standing straight up on his board like an unflappable David statue, lazily looking toward the shore, his muscles and admirable assets accented perfectly by the rising sun.

"Tantalizing and tasteful," I said, and the women in the class chuckled. "I didn't mean to encourage public nudity for the shoot. Did anyone get arrested?"

"No," Wyatt said from the back, "but we gave a couple of women out for their morning walk a thrill."

"They didn't report you?"

"No, they asked if they could watch."

The classroom erupted in laughter.

"How long did it take you to get this shot?" I asked. "And how did you talk the subject into it?"

"I had to get it at dawn, so I had a pretty narrow window," Wyatt said. "We shot for about twenty minutes, but we were ready to go once the light started getting good, so it was still almost dark when we got to the beach. And this is one of my surfer buddies who knows I like photography, so he said yes right away. At least, after I promised to let him use it for an online dating profile."

I laughed along with the class, partly from relief that Wyatt hadn't had an intimate session with a surfer girl.

"Great photo," was all I said, and I moved on to the next one.

We worked on our Photoshop project. After class, Wyatt met me up front again.

"So you liked it?" he asked, looking pleased.

"Wonderful photography. But I might need your friend's number, just so I can inquire more about your technique."

"Ha ha," Wyatt said, but he was smiling for real. "So . . . it's on."

"What's on?"

"Friday. Big waves. You heard about the storm offshore? There's going to be a good swell. A really good swell. Maybe double overhead."

"Which means what?"

"We could have ten-foot waves here."

"Here?" I felt a twinge of panic, then told myself I was being foolish. "OK. Um, yeah, I'd like to try to shoot some photos of you, then. But you might want to wear something. The Bohemia Beach police aren't really that bohemian, despite the name."

He grinned. "I'll save my nudity for you, darlin.' "

The endearment would have sounded cheesy from anyone else. From Wyatt, it was rakishly charming. "Will I see you tonight?"

"Not tonight," he said. "I'm expecting a call from Corky about some more assignments, and it might take a while."

Corky. California. Right. "OK." I knew I sounded disappointed.

"But tomorrow, I'd like to see you, as long as I get to bed early. I want to be rested up for the waves."

"You know I have no problem with going to bed early," I teased.

He looked around to make sure no one was listening. "I mean, to sleep early," he said. "But maybe we can have a — date beforehand?"

"You and your dates. That's what got me in trouble to begin with."

He touched my lips, traced their outline. "Maybe a little trouble is what you need."

"I've got it in spades," I said, returning his intense gaze, feeling heat and heartache in one beat. After a moment, I broke the spell. "Lunch?"

He lowered his hand and smiled. "Sure. And then maybe a walk? There are some spots around downtown that might be good for portraits of you."

"You don't have to shoot them all at once, you know. It's not due for four more weeks."

"But I want to take photos of you anyway. You know that."

I heard his double meaning. "I'd love to walk with you," I granted. At least I knew those photos would involve clothing. I wasn't about to strip in the middle of Bohemia.

"Perfect," he said, and he kissed my cheek. "Meet you at Picasso's?"

Time seemed compressed as Friday neared. Dread and excitement hurried me along. I would get to play surf photographer. Maybe I wouldn't be frolicking in the waves, but I'd be given an intimate look into Wyatt's life, a chance to feel what he felt when he experienced the ocean. Though I still admired the beauty of the water — even liked getting my feet wet — I couldn't love it the way he did. I wanted to understand.

We spent a pleasant afternoon together Wednesday, taking photos of each other and intriguing sights in Bohemia and talking. Thursday morning, I shot portraits for a realty office, and in the afternoon, I picked up Wyatt so we could get cameras ready in my studio and talk about shooting the surf. I'd take one camera and a spare, as well as one of his in a waterproof case, in case he wanted to do some shooting. Since I didn't plan to go in the water, I packed a couple of towels to wipe off any stray saltwater spray, along with a do-it-yourself version of what pros humorously called a camera condom — a plastic bag with a cutout for the lens to keep moisture out. It wasn't dunk-proof, but it would help. With winds expected to hit twenty or thirty miles per hour by the ocean, conditions would be hell on the gear.

"It was already getting frisky this morning," Wyatt said as we zipped shut the camera bag I'd be lugging to the beach. He had an energy, an eagerness about him that I almost envied.

"Big waves?"

"Getting there," he said. We sat in the big black chairs. "Tomorrow should be classic."

"How early do we have to get up?" I asked with trepidation.

He laughed. "I'll be out there on dawn patrol. Do you think you can handle it?"

"Of course," I said, though I wasn't exactly a morning person.

"I figured I'd sleep at home tonight. Closer to the beach."

"Oh. That's cool."

His eyes twinkled at my disappointed tone. "We both need our sleep. Why don't you come over for dinner, and then we can hang out for a bit?"

"With Jen and David?"

"Dinner with them. Hanging out with me." He grinned.

"I don't want to invite myself over."

"You're not," he said. "Jen suggested it, actually. David's taking tomorrow off so he can surf. She can't miss work, and she's jealous."

Dinner at Jen and David's was a quirky affair. They unapologetically laid out the bounty of the supermarket deli on their kitchen table, from unexpectedly delicious rotisserie chicken to potato salad and Hawaiian rolls.

"You have to catch me on a weekend if you want real cooking, and then I'll dazzle your taste buds," Jen said after the meal as she dug in the freezer for ice cream. "Or David can put ribs in the meat smoker. Hmm. Maybe we should do that Saturday?"

"Sounds good. We'll be hungry after all that surfing," David teased her.

"I hope there are a few waves left by then." Jen glowered comically at him. She scooped ice cream into bowls steaming with fresh blueberry slump, a kind of cobbler that she said was a family recipe. "I did have time for this, though I had to use frozen berries."

Conversation came to a halt momentarily as we savored the mellow, warm dessert with the sweet, cold ice cream. Only the clinking of spoons and rock music on the stereo system marked the time.

"This is why I've gained five pounds since I've been staying here," Wyatt finally said, putting down his spoon and patting his belly, which looked hard enough to me under his long-sleeved surf T-shirt.

"I would've gained twenty," I said.

"Not if you took up surfing," he said matter-of-factly. His smile almost made me believe I could.

"I'm thinking I need a new basecoat on my board," David said as he took our bowls to the sink.

"Good idea. Let's do it. Do you mind?" Wyatt asked me.

"Of course not. I have all these dishes to wash."

Jen chuckled. "Mr. Dishwasher is doing the dishes, but you can keep me company while I load it up."

I smiled awkwardly as the men — boys, at the moment, practically bouncing with excitement — headed out to the garage. I'd had so many images in my mind of what Jen was to Wyatt, and to discover the easy comfort she and her husband had with him — as if he were, if not a son, then a brother — made me embarrassed for my earlier jealousy.

"Do they always wax their boards before they go?"

"Not always," Jen said, putting plates and bowls in the dishwasher. "Often they'll just sit on the beach before they go out and wax and comb. But I know David is serious when he wants to put a new base coat on. It's kind of a ritual before a big day — only happens a few times a year, if that. They're probably out there talking shit about all the big waves they've surfed."

I smiled at this, but I failed to keep a touch of anxiety out of my voice. "It sounds like the waves will be pretty big."

"For here, yeah. But compared with what Wyatt usually chases, it'll be cake."

"And David?"

"For him, too. He's really experienced. And when you can surf, a big wave is always better than a Bohemia Beach mushball."

"So nothing to worry about, then."

"Sharks and rocks and idiots, but waves? Naw. They have it covered." She showed her dimples as she shut the dishwasher. "Wine?"

We retired to the living room with a pleasant pinot noir. Tiny pooch Maverick curled up between us on the couch, and we talked about all kinds of things — how she ended up in Bohemia Beach (her dream of launching rockets at Cape Canaveral), how she started surfing (seeing the "Gidget" movies on late-night TV), how I got into photography (my mom won a good camera in a sweepstakes when I was ten and had no idea how to use it, so she gave it to me).

"You've known Wyatt a long time," I said, hoping to lead her into talking about his teenage years.

"I met him in California," she said, noncommittal. I respected that she respected his privacy.

"He told me how you helped him. How you gave him a home."

She seemed to relax slightly. "I did what I could. What any decent person would do. He just needed a friend, a place. I don't know if he ever thought of it as home."

"He seems to love wandering. Maybe no place is home for him." I tried not to sound wistful.

"He's not really a wanderer."

"Chasing the big waves all over the world? It seems like it."

"He may wander for the waves, but I don't think it's because he loves to wander. He loves the waves. But I also think that since he was young, he's — he's been a little lost."

The words pinched my heart. Wyatt, the lost boy. He exuded so much confidence, but maybe that wasn't the whole story.

We talked about safer subjects then, restaurants and books and wine, as we finished off the bottle. I was feeling loose and comfortable when the guys came back in, carrying beers and a giddy happiness that suggested the bottles weren't their first.

"Ready for tomorrow?" Jen asked.

"More than," David said.

"Soooo ready," echoed Wyatt, his syllables softened by alcohol. "I don't know how I'm going to sleep."

"That's where the beer comes in," David said, emphasizing his sentiment with an impressive burp.

"Right," said Wyatt, trying and failing to release a comparable explosion, making the rest of us laugh. "Cali's going to tuck me in."

"Is that what they call it?" David said.

Jen rolled her eyes. "Don't listen to these goofballs." She got up, leaving the empty wine bottle and glasses on the table. "Take lots of good photos tomorrow. I have to tuck *my* goofball in."

"Thanks for dinner," I said, getting up, too.

"Let's do it again Saturday. Ribs and homemade mac and cheese, and something green so our blood keeps moving. OK?"

"OK," I said with a smile, then switched my gaze to Wyatt. He was looking at me with a funny mix of joy and pride, as if I'd managed to join his private club.

"OK, big fella," I said to him after Jen, David and Maverick had escaped to their end of the house. "Time for you to go to bed."

"Don't you mean us?" he said. "Oh, wait. I'm supposed to sleep for some reason."

"Waves, or did you forget?"

"I never forget a wave," he insisted, and he took me by the arm, leaning against me as we wended our way to his room. He felt warm and mildly unsteady, not the usual stalwart Wyatt.

"Are you going to be in a condition to surf tomorrow?"

He sat hard on the edge of his bed as I closed the door. "Perfect," he said, pulling off his shirt. "I like having a few the night before a big day. I sleep great and dream of waves so big I have to fly up to them to ride them."

I sat next to him and ran a hand down his bare back, my fingers delighting in the hard heat of him. "Where are your wings?"

"You can't see them?" He stood and turned his back toward me, looking over his shoulder as if they were really there. His shark tattoo wriggled as his muscles rolled with the movement. "Damn shark ate them."

I giggled. "You're drunk."

"Only a little," he protested. "We were streaming this old surfing tournament on the iPad, and every time somebody said 'stoked' or 'super' or 'wave,' we took a drink."

"You took a drink every time they said *wave?* No wonder you're drunk."

"Just a little," he insisted, sitting next to me again and leaning his head on my shoulder. After a second, I suspected he'd started to doze.

I shrugged, and he startled. "OK. Pants off."

"That sounds good," he said dreamily, but he didn't make any move to engage me as I slipped off his sandals and jeans and dropped them to the floor. They were right at home there among the other scattered garments.

"I guess you *are* going to get some sleep tonight," I said, more amused than disappointed at his droopy compliance. I pushed him, and he flopped back against his pillows, eyes closed. I pulled the blanket up over him and kissed him softly on the mouth.

"Mmmm," he murmured. "Sweet Calista." He lazily lifted a hand and touched my arm, and then it fell back to the mattress in slow motion. In a moment, his breathing shifted into the gentle rhythm of a sleeper, and I pushed his dark bangs, his wild blond streak, away from his forehead. I kissed him there, too.

"See you at dawn, you rogue," I whispered.

I switched off the lights and left him there to dream about the waves. And I hoped, just maybe, me.

～

I GOT UP AT O'DARK-THIRTY, so long before dawn that I had to turn on a light so I could find the right clothes. Today it was a pair of stretch khakis for mobility, a T-shirt and my blue Gore-Tex rain jacket, with a hood. I donned an old pair of sneakers I didn't mind sacrificing to salt and sand; it was too cool for sandals.

I made tea and poured it into my go-cup. My sleepy brain was stirring, but slowly, swirling with a mix of excitement and dread. I felt as if I were preparing for a duel, only I wouldn't be fighting the angry ocean; I'd be standing on the shore, capturing the daring surfers as they rode the waves.

I remembered what Jen said — these waves were a piece of cake for Wyatt and David. But in my eye, the surf would always look twice as big, twice as dangerous.

I calmed myself by double-checking the contents of my bag, assuring myself that I was prepared. My car grumbled a little, loath to start in the cool, windy morning, and I hit the road for Bohemia Beach.

My anxiety eased as I got out of the car at our appointed rendezvous — the Dolphin Mouth. It was a side street named for a goofy landmark: a cartoonish dolphin whose wide-open mouth held a mailbox for the beach house next door. Surfers knew there was a good break here, and it was a favorite spot for the in-crowd. David's Jeep was already here, and so, I assumed, was Wyatt.

The sky had lightened to a yellow-gray with layers of quickly scudding clouds. The cool air was stimulating, damp with sea mist kicked up by the wind. Even in the tiny parking area, the ocean's roar was tangible. I could feel it in my bones.

I hauled the bag onto my shoulder, along with a couple of beach towels, and headed for the gap in the cabbage palms to the crosswalk that would take me over the dunes. I emerged from the tunnel of palms and sea grapes and stopped for a moment at the top of the uneven wooden steps to take in the expanse of water and sand.

Now, I was awake.

The waves were *huge*.

OK, Bohemia Beach huge, but *still*. And they weren't just big. They had a smooth power behind them. They weren't all topsy-turvy whitewater. They were diamond-bright energy, facets and hard glass faces, flinging foam, and I blinked away the image from my nightmare.

There were a number of surfers here, maybe fifteen, spread up and down the beach. The crowds would probably be a lot more intense at the more public spots, like the board-walk, but these were the serious guys — and one or two women, too. They wore wetsuits, and those who weren't already in the water were waxing their boards with a kind of somber focus.

My eyes lit on a dark, hard form, standing straight, board cradled in one arm, feet slightly spread. His hair blew up and out, a plaything for the wind.

"Wyatt," I breathed, just to myself, marveling at his beauty. He looked so right here.

As if he heard me, he turned slowly and looked toward the steps. His smile was like a flash of lightning, a bright and beckoning light, and I hastened down the steps to meet him out on the sand.

I set down the towels and bag at what I thought was a safe distance from the waves and leaned in to take the kiss he offered, brief and warm in the chill. This close to him, against the backdrop of the wild waves, I could see how well the thick black fabric of the suit snugly advertised his surfer's physique. He looked as if he couldn't belong anywhere else. I looked up into his eyes, golden-brown in the soft light, and saw a sparkle there.

"Are you ready?" Wyatt asked.

I laughed. "I should be asking you that."

"As ready as I can be. The smart thing is to realize that you're never a hundred percent ready. You have to leave about five percent for the unexpected, or for the moment when you really fuck up."

I smiled nervously, hoping he was joking. As if I needed something else to worry about. "Where's David?"

"Already out," he said, waving a hand at the horizon to my south. I thought I saw David's burly form in the surf. "He was too stoked to wait. It's really pumping."

"Anything I need to know?"

"Just follow your instinct. It's stellar."

He knew just what to say. I breathed in the fresh air, drawing on his confidence as the sky behind him seemed to fill with coral light, swirled with pearl as the clouds continued their ominous advance in front of the wind.

"Good luck," I said.

"I've got my gun," he said, patting his board. "I've got great waves. Nothing can get me down."

Wyatt grinned and turned toward the water, wading into the turbulence, pushing his board ahead of him.

I hastily began unpacking the essentials I would need — mainly my camera with the long lens and the plastic bag. It would protect the body from the fine spray that seemed to fill the air, atomized by the crashing waves and wind.

When I looked up again, Wyatt was paddling out, ducking under a wave to go even farther, and I was left breathless again by his grace, his natural ability — the seemingly natural ability that took so much practice and time, so many years of dedication.

Soon he was out far enough from shore that there were moments when I lost him in a trough and took a second to pinpoint his location amid the undulating water and the other surfers.

The moment pulled me in. With a camera in my hand, confronted by the chaotic beauty before me, I fell in love with the ocean again, the way a girl falls in love with a boy who's too old for her, too wild. I loved the smell and sight of the water, gray and green with hints of blue, mountains of glossy reflection and tumultuous whitewater and salty air. But on some level, it still scared me, like that wild boy of girlhood fantasies. I still feared it would pull me under.

A new set was building, and surfers lined up to take on the waves. I walked to the waterline, lifted my camera and started shooting.

I saw the wave Wyatt was going for, a rolling swell that seemed to rise up to meet him as he popped up on the board, and then he was flying across it, cutting into it in cunning maneuvers like a pelican dipping over the crests, until it seemed to reach over his head and embrace him in a sacred hollow of air between its shining surface and his lithe body.

For those few seconds, I understood. I almost wanted to *be* him, to wield that powerful grace through *my* body. Enraptured, I held my breath for a moment, and then I shot as fast as I could, hoping to capture the magic until he gracefully dropped into the whitewater.

I pulled the camera away from my eye and watched anxiously until I saw his head pop up again, and even from where I was, I was almost sure he was grinning. He raised his hand in a shaka salute, lay against his board and paddled back out.

An hour slipped by, then two. The sky grew brighter, a soft pewter mixed with light blue, and the winds seemed to shift slightly to the northwest. More surfers came out, along with a few spectators. Some of the surfers just looked and shook their heads and sat and watched. Others sprinted to the water, fought the swell on their way out and took perilous tumbles that made me wonder how many rocks were hidden under the waves here. It had been a while since I'd hung out at the Dolphin Mouth, but virtually every part of Bohemia Beach had low, sneaky coquina rocks that were rarely seen, except at low tide. And now, the tide was high.

Still, there were quite a few skilled surfers, including a handful who almost approached the grace of Wyatt and David. Wyatt, however, was a breed of his own, and I heard onlookers buzzing about him as he surfed.

My muscles were stiff from standing in the cold, from holding my arms in shooting posture. My eyes watered from the constant wind. But still I shot, switching cards as I filled them up, telling the story of the day, the surfers, the magnificent synergy between Wyatt and the waves.

The waves had not eased. If anything, they seemed bigger as the morning wore on and the tide came in. Some of the exhausted dawn patrol surfers gave up and came out of the water, dripping, to collect themselves and watch. I stopped for a minute and stretched, too, unzipping my jacket, releasing the body heat that had built up as I worked. The sky was brighter now, the sun a watery suggestion behind the clouds, and I shielded my eyes as I looked out, trying to find Wyatt.

He and David were, for the moment, alone in their sliver

of the ocean.

And there, behind them, the ocean rose. And rose.

It was a big wave, part of a set of really big waves, maybe even double what Wyatt had surfed already this morning. I looked around quickly and saw I wasn't the only one who'd noticed. The surfers on the beach sat up, stood up, and a raw, frazzled energy seemed to rush through them all.

My gaze snapped back to the water. David had picked off the first wave and was riding it in, barely maintaining his equilibrium. But it was nothing compared with what followed.

Wyatt, ever patient for the prime kill, was going for a big one. Perhaps the biggest one. Was it as high as twelve feet? No. Higher. Fifteen?

In long, agonizing seconds, he scrambled up onto his board and put himself in its way, riding it with the kind of dogged determination I'd seen in that show on TV. With one eye focused on him through the lens, the other on reality, I shot quickly as he moved. At first, he skimmed along its face with dizzying speed, but after a few seconds, I sensed something wasn't right. His timing seemed off, and the wave seemed more aggressive than the others, angry, grasping at him as it brought him closer to shore. He tried to tame it with a deft slash off the top of the wave, but in what seemed like slow motion, in a violent gush of spray and foam, his feet were sucked back and he tumbled forward, head-first. In a second, he vanished in the whitewater.

With the violent crash of the wave, the dissipation of the froth, I saw where he'd gone down. On the rocks. And precious seconds went by, and he didn't come up. And then I heard David, far up the beach, screaming: "Wyatt! Wyatt!"

His cry confirmed what I thought I'd seen, what I didn't

want to believe — a splash of red in the emerald green. And before I knew it, I'd tossed my camera aside, ripped off my jacket and shoes and rushed into the water.

I gasped at the frigid onslaught as the surf soaked my clothes and tried to drag me down.

Cold. Deep. Deadly.

A million nightmares clutched at my throat, pressed on my chest, screamed at me to go back. Time chilled and slowed to a painful crawl when speed, I knew, was everything.

The rocks weren't in deep water, but the waves were still big and pounding the shore, and every time I tried to jump past one, it gushed over my shoulders, into my face, even over my head, overwhelming me with terror as well as water.

Wyatt. I have to get to Wyatt.

I pushed down the fear and dredged up my swimming-pool skills as I fought my way forward. I crawled and dove through the waves to get to where I'd seen Wyatt, and then I was there, pulling him up so his head was above the water, trying not to lose it when I saw the blood trailing from the gash in his scalp.

I pulled him toward shore, and in another minute, more hands were there to help me — David and another surfer who'd been nearby. We dragged him up to the beach.

"Call 9-1-1," I cried, my voice breaking as we got him onto the sand.

"Already done," the other surfer said, and I glanced at his face, serious and steady. It was the guy Wyatt had shot in a calm, bright dawn for the nude photo for my class, the class that seemed like a hundred years ago.

Other surfers gathered around in a paralyzed circle, and I heard the wail of a siren in the distance.

David pressed two fingers against Wyatt's throat. "I feel his heartbeat. I can't tell if he's breathing."

Shivering, I leaned in. I couldn't feel his breath. First-aid training kicked in. I opened his mouth, looked inside, tilted up his chin and started rescue breathing.

One, two, three, four . . .

A shudder passed through his frame, and a gush of water and vomit came up. We tilted him to the side to let it come out. We laid him back down, and I leaned in again. This time, I felt his warm breath, shallow against my cheek.

"He's breathing," I said hoarsely.

But bright red blood still dripped through his thick, wet hair and onto the sand. I grabbed one of my towels and packed it gently against the wound. I used the other to wipe his mouth.

"Wyatt. *Wyatt,*" I pleaded. "You have to wake up." I kissed his cheek. My tears mixed with the salt water on his skin. I grasped his shoulders — maybe some part of me thought I could shake him awake — and David rested a hand on my arm.

"Just wait for the ambulance. He'll be OK," he said softly, but when I looked into his eyes, I didn't believe him.

HOSPITAL WAITING rooms were the vestibule of hell. They smelled of uncertainty in the face of death. From the under-insured, like the woman with the horrible cough who'd put off going to a doctor, to the severely ill, like the boy brought in with his face swollen and his throat closing after a bee sting, all who passed through here had to acknowledge their mortality.

And if their lives weren't in the balance, it was someone they loved.

I had followed the ambulance to the hospital in Bohemia after grabbing my camera bag and rushing back to my car. David — handed Wyatt's board by another surfer — had stuck it in his Jeep and ridden with me. At the hospital, he told them he and Wyatt were brothers to make sure he stayed in the loop, and we settled in to wait.

We were a sullen, sodden pair; David was still in his wetsuit. I was still in my damp clothes. I shivered in the cool emergency waiting room, and my stomach, thoughtless in the face of the crisis, grumbled loudly. But there was no question of going anywhere until we knew what was going on. David also refused to call Jen before he knew more; he worried enough for both of them, pacing, checking his chunky sports watch.

When the doctor came out to talk to us, tablet computer tucked under her arm, she bore one of those looks of studied patience that made me want to throw up. She was in her thirties, I thought, pale with blue eyes. Her long, russet braid was as neat and calm as she was. David and I stood close to her and politely shook her hand. Inside, I was screaming.

"He was in and out for a bit, but he's awake now," she said. "He sounds OK, but he probably has a concussion. He knew who the president was, but he was fuzzy about how he got here. He's going in for a CT scan now so we can be sure what we're dealing with."

I felt a rush of relief — *he's conscious!* — and worry, too. "Is he going to be OK?" I hated myself for asking the dumb question, but it was *the* question.

"We'll know more after the test, but the fact that he's awake and talking is a very good thing."

"There was so much blood," David said.

"Head wounds bleed a lot," the doctor said. "He's getting stitches. He asked if we could do them in fluorescent green."

A small laugh escaped me, more like a hiccup, and my eyes blurred again.

"Sounds like Wyatt," David said.

The doctor smiled for the first time. "You'll have to wait a little longer, and then I'll know more."

We nodded. She touched my shoulder and gave it a little squeeze before she left. This tiny kindness broke my fragile self-control. I sat on one of the ugly, barely padded vinyl chairs and silently wept.

David watched me helplessly for a moment, and then he pulled out his phone. "I'm going to call Jen."

He whirled to head outside to make the call, and I rested my elbows on my knees and put my face in my hands and hid in the darkness there, slightly relieved, still scared. I'd been having trouble handling the idea of Wyatt leaving, but this — this idea that he might be gone forever — this is what crystallized the answer in all the mental games of Magic 8-Ball I'd played with myself. *What will I do when he leaves?* and *Aren't I better without him anyway?* and *Isn't this all just for fun?* really only came down to one response. And it wasn't *Outlook good* or *Signs point to yes* or *Reply hazy try again.*

I was in love with him.

Once this thought had established itself, my mind cleared. I was still worried, but I knew what I had to do. I would make sure Wyatt was healthy, and then I would make sure he was happy, even if it meant letting him go. Of course, I wanted him to stay, and I was through shielding my heart. But if he needed to go, then — I would help him pack his bags.

I took a tenuous breath and then another, still hiding behind the comforting darkness of my hands, my closed eyes. After several minutes, I lifted my head, wiped away the last of the tears and opened my eyes to see David standing there, staring at me with one of those baffled expressions men get when faced with weepy women and productions of "The Nutcracker." It almost made me laugh.

"Any news?" I asked.

"Not yet."

"How'd Jen take it?"

"She's a rock," he said, sitting down. "She wanted to come, but I told her to wait a little longer until we got an update. She can't do anything here, anyway, and besides, it would take her almost an hour to get here."

It was an hour and a half before we saw the doctor again, and this time she wore an almost imperceptible smile.

"There are no skull fractures, so that's good, and he's more talkative now. It appears to be a concussion. You'll need to observe him closely for the next twenty-four hours, but we're going to send him home. Tylenol if he has pain. No alcohol or caffeine until he feels better. You can let him sleep, but wake him up every few hours and make sure he's responding normally. He may have headaches and nausea for a bit. If it gets worse, bring him back in. Can you take him home?"

"Yes, we can," I answered, and the doctor looked at me and nodded her approval.

"We'll set up an appointment for the stitches to come out and to evaluate his progress. He's a very lucky man."

And then she was smiling again and shaking our hands, and after more anxious waiting, a nurse handed us a bunch of paperwork with the same cautions the doctor had given us, along with instructions on when to take off the bandage. David called Jen with the good news — good, at least, given the situation. Finally, we saw the nurse pushing Wyatt toward us in a wheelchair.

His appearance was shocking. He seemed to have shrunk in his skin, which lacked that healthy glow he normally sported, and he had a bandage wrapped around part of his head. He wore an old Disney T-shirt and sweatpants that the hospital must have given him and carried his wetsuit in a plastic bag.

"He didn't want me to push him," the nurse said as she stopped the chair in front of us.

Wyatt shrugged and gave us a sheepish grin, and then he slowly stood and held out his arms. We both stepped into his wide embrace and hugged him, David and I more tender with him than he was with us. When we let go, he started to sag, and David and I immediately wrapped our arms under his shoulders to support him.

"You ready to go home, pain in the ass?" David asked.

"Sure we can't go back to the beach?" Wyatt queried. One look at him showed he was trying to make a joke. "You're dressed for it."

David wasn't amused. "Hell, no," he said as we moved Wyatt toward the automatic doors. "You are going to rest. And I'm going to put on some real clothes."

"Did you get good pictures, Cali?" Wyatt asked softly as we walked him out into the late afternoon and he got steadier on his feet. The skies had cleared a bit, but the wind was still blustery.

"I think so, especially of you on that wave that took you out."

"Is that what happened? That's embarrassing," Wyatt said. "I — I don't remember the wave. Was it a good one?"

"If that's what you call the wave that tried to kill you." I sounded more grouchy than I meant to be.

"It was epic," David said.

"What did I do?" Wyatt asked.

"You went over the fucking falls, man." David hung on to him, just in case, as I unlocked my car. He helped Wyatt into the front. "You hit the rocks."

"I hope somebody got it," said Wyatt, ever the photographer, seemingly indifferent to the fact that, for a minute, we all thought he might be dead.

"I got it," I said, trying to sound normal and failing miserably.

Something flitted across Wyatt's face, then, a hint of understanding of just how narrow his escape had been.

"I'm sorry, you guys." He leaned back and closed his eyes, and I took us out of the parking lot and toward the causeway to go back to beachside.

"Forget it," David said from the back seat.

"Who's the president of the United States?" I asked, thinking maybe I should make sure his brain was still working.

"Kelly Slater," Wyatt said, and when I looked over at him, he still had his eyes closed, but he was grinning.

"You wish," David said. "Surfer for president."

"You could do worse," Wyatt murmured, and then he seemed to doze off.

At Jen and David's, we found Jen already at home, straightening Wyatt's bedroom and heating up some soup.

"He's got a concussion, not the flu," David said as Jen gave Wyatt a big hug.

"Easy, there, Wonder Woman," Wyatt said with a grimace. It was then I noticed the bruises on his left arm and wondered where else he hurt.

"Sorry!" Jen exclaimed, releasing him. "How do you feel?"

"Like I went through a Bohemia Beach blender," he said. "I'm going to lie down."

"But you can't sleep!" Jen said.

"He can sleep." I took Wyatt by the arm. "I just have to wake him up every few hours."

"That could be fun," Wyatt joked, but his voice carried the thin timbre of exhaustion.

He was too nauseous to eat. When I got him settled in his bed, with his head propped up, Maverick the mutt trotted into the room, jumped onto the bed and curled up next to him. Wyatt lay one hand on the little dog's back and reached out and took my hand with the other.

"I don't want this to stop you from going in the ocean. It's really safe, most of the time. If you're not me," he said wryly.

He really doesn't remember. In truth, things had happened so fast, I wasn't sure how much *I* remembered of my terrifying foray into the water.

"You need to take fewer risks," was all I said.

He shook his head, accentuating the stark white of the wide bandage wrapping around it. "Risks are necessary on the road to happiness."

"Who said that?" I kissed the hand that held mine.

"Wyatt Brooks." His eyes closed again, halfway to sleep. "That guy knows what he's talking about."

JEN GAVE me some old clothes to change into while she

washed and dried mine. Relieved to be warm at last and soothed by Wyatt's presence, I sat in a chair in his room and watched him. I sipped a mug of soup, surprised to find I was starving.

Jen took David to get the Jeep and the boards, but other than that brief absence, she hung around, checking on us. Finally, the couple went to bed, and she encouraged me to do the same.

Instead, I woke up Wyatt again to ensure that he could think clearly and that he could make it to the bathroom. As Wyatt walked gingerly out the door, the dog jumped off the bed and headed for his usual sleeping spot with Jen and David.

Wyatt said little when he came back into the room, but what he did say sounded normal, if subdued. He had a headache. He said his body ached, too, and he felt hot, so I helped him get his shirt off and nearly gasped at the dark, mottled bruising along his ribs and arm and shoulder, all on the left. His body, which I'd thought of as a temple of strength, seemed fragile and vulnerable.

"Here, take this," I said, giving him a glass and a Tylenol as he sat on the edge of the bed, looking groggy.

"What is it?" He popped the tablet and drank.

"Acetaminophen. And ginger ale. That'll do you more good than the pill."

He managed a smile. "How you figure?"

"That's what my mom always brought me when I was sick," I said. "With buttered toast, of course. Ginger ale always makes you feel better."

"Oh, is that what moms do when their kid is sick?" His tone was acerbic.

"Some do," I said, feeling almost guilty that I had a mom

who cared about me.

"Mine told me to stay in my room and not come out until I felt better so I wouldn't make her sick. I had to sneak into the kitchen at night to get water and whatever crappy leftovers were in the fridge."

"How about crackers?"

"Crackers?" He looked confused. "Yeah, sometimes I got crackers."

"Me, too. See, you had an idyllic childhood after all," I teased, trying to get a smile out of him.

"I see," he said. "I've just been misinformed all this time."

"Exactly." I smiled for him, reaching out and then withdrawing my hand, quelling the desire to touch his poor bandaged head. "Don't you want to sleep?"

"Not now. Why don't you lie next to me for a little bit?"

There was nothing sexual in the request, just a hint of loneliness, and it pinched my heart.

"OK." I turned off the lamp so the only light was from the blue glow of the digital clock, then kicked off my shoes. I walked around the other side of the bed and climbed in, snuggling against the pillows next to him.

He laced his fingers through mine and let out a sigh. "I wish I could remember that wave."

"I've never seen anything like it in Bohemia Beach."

"Will you show me the pictures tomorrow?"

"As soon as I can," I said. I hadn't even gone home yet, let alone tried to process any photos.

"I bet they're amazing," he said. "Not because of me. Because of you."

"I always give at least fifty percent credit to the subject," I joked.

He smiled, and his head drifted toward my shoulder. His eyes closed, and he slept.

I drifted off, too. When I awoke, the gray light of dawn had lightened the sky beyond the Venetian blinds, and I looked with panic at the clock. I'd let him sleep too long. We'd both slipped down against the pillows, into a soft nest of blankets. I sat up and leaned over him, touching his face. His breathing was normal, and his eyelids fluttered open.

"Kelly Slater."

"No!" I said with alarm. "It's Cali!"

"Oh, I thought you were going to ask me who's president."

I laughed softly. "Smart ass."

"I'm OK." He sat up slowly. The bruising had crept into the area where the tattooed shark swam against his skin. "I fucking ache like hell, though."

"How's your head?"

"Maybe a little better. I gotta pee."

"Need help?"

"I'm fine," he said, a little less pliant than yesterday. Maybe that was good news. He got up and shuffled out the door to the bathroom. I got up, too, and did the same when he was done. When I checked on him again, he was already asleep.

Instead of going back to bed, I slipped on my shoes and made my way through the dark house and outside to the quiet patio. I stood and listened, crossing my arms against the chill of early morning. A mockingbird began tweeting its round-robin of songs, heralding the dawn. The wind was milder today but fresh on my face. Framed by the backyard jungle around the pool, a handful of drifting clouds lit up pink as the sun crept up in the east. Soon it would be the perfect time for photography, those few minutes when the sun was low and the light was golden. Surfers would be gathering at the beach to try again on lesser waves. The cycle of life, of tide, of light continued, and despite their inevitability, I knew that nothing was certain. The safe path was an illusion.

When I went back into the house, the sky was almost bright, and I heard voices in the kitchen, smelled coffee brewing.

"Did you say you'd get him at the airport?" Jen was saying. I hovered in the dim dining room, wondering who they were talking about.

"He's taking some kind of shuttle from Orlando," David answered. "He should be here by nine or ten. Overnight flight."

"I have to admit, it's more than I expected," Jen said. There was a clanking of pans.

"He's a good guy, deep down. He responded right away to my e-mail yesterday."

"Do you think Calista is OK?" she asked more softly, and I grimaced at my own eavesdropping.

"She is now," David said. "I wasn't so sure yesterday afternoon."

I opened the sliding door to the patio again and shut it hard. The conversation paused, and I headed for the kitchen.

"You all are up early," I said.

They exchanged a glance. "I was worried about our patient," Jen said over a frying pan of bacon that was just starting to sizzle. "I looked in on him. Have you talked to him this morning?"

I nodded. "He still says Kelly Slater is president, but I know he's full of shit."

David's laugh was tinged with relief. "Always."

"He'll be OK," I said, and this time, I believed it.

"Of course he will." Jen got a carton of eggs out of the fridge. "Breakfast?"

I shook my head, though the bacon's aroma made my stomach rumble. "Since he's sleeping, I'm going to run home and take a shower and change. I still feel like I'm covered with salt. But I'll come back in a couple of hours, OK?"

"Sounds good," David said, and I saw them exchange another glance. So they weren't telling me who the mystery guest was, and I couldn't ask because I wasn't supposed to have heard them. But I had a notion of who it might be, and I wondered what he would mean to Wyatt's future, and to mine.

AT HOME, I unpacked the gear to make sure everything damp got dry. I dumped memory cards into my computer while I took a shower and made myself some scrambled eggs. I'd shot several hundred photos, and even though I didn't take the time to peruse them thoroughly, I could tell there was strong imagery. The dark energy of the day suffused the work, the stormy skies, the mighty sea. The surfers seemed to be delicate dancers atop the waves, sketching graceful, muscular lines. I picked just a few of the photos of Wyatt, a couple of the waves and one or two of David, gave them a hasty edit and transferred them to my phone.

I was back in dry, clean, loose jeans and my nubby sweater, the soft one with rough stripes of blues, grays and greens, with the small, sparkly earrings to match. I'd dried my hair and let it hang long, hoping it might cheer up Wyatt. He always loved my hair down. A wall of longing hit me as I brushed out the thick, blond waves. I wanted him whole again. I wanted to hold him tight.

It took about twenty minutes to get over to Wyatt's street in Bohemia Beach — the street where I grew up. My dad was outside my childhood home, digging around the mailbox. Or the dirt that used to hold the mailbox. A new box lay on the ground. I slowed and pulled up next to him, rolled down my window and waved.

He squinted at me, pushed up the brim of the floppy hat that hid his mostly bald pate and wiped a hand on his plaid flannel shirt. "Cali? What are you doing here?"

"Visiting a friend down the street."

His eyes lit up. "I think I've heard about this friend. A couple of the ladies on the block told your mother their kids saw you making out with some guy."

This was not a conversation I wanted to be having with my dad.

"It might have been a kiss," I said, refusing to confess to anything, "but I was definitely not making out."

"You can make out all you want to. You're an adult."

"Thanks, Dad," I said, returning his light sarcasm.

"If only all those catty gossips saw who stole our mailbox. Then I might listen to them."

I laughed. "Seriously?"

"Yeah. Usually the hooligans just beat it with a bat." He leaned on the shovel and cocked his head. "Is everything good then?" he asked, a question that said nothing and everything.

"I think so. I'll talk to you later, OK? Love you."

"Love you, too, Cali. Be careful."

Parents — my parents — always said, "Be careful." I almost always had been, until I met Wyatt.

I parked next to the Jeep in Jen and David's driveway and paused at the front door, wondering if I should knock. Wondering who was inside.

I opted for stealth. The door was unlocked and noiseless as I slipped into the foyer and living room. Maverick ran up to me, his nails clicking on the hard floor, gave me a sniff and trotted off again. I dimly heard raised voices. I looked through the back sliders, first; Jen and David were out on the patio reading the newspaper and drinking coffee. Staying out of the way, I thought. So somebody else was talking, and I was sure they were in Wyatt's room. I left my purse in the kitchen and walked toward the sound.

The words resolved as I moved to the hallway and paused. This eavesdropping was getting to be a bad habit.

"You're going to be better in no time," came the booming voice.

Ron Raker.

"Probably," Wyatt said.

"So when are you coming out to surf again? We're headed for Hawaii."

"I'm not doing that again," came Wyatt's strained voice. "Not full-time. I told you. I have other plans."

"What, here? I grew up here, Wyatt. Everybody's plan is to get the fuck out of Bohemia Beach."

"I like it here."

"You like that girl." Ron's voice held a trace of bitterness. I realized I was holding my breath, trying to hear, waiting for a response. None was imminent. "She was my date, you know."

"Your photo op, you mean?" retorted Wyatt.

"You stayed for her, didn't you?"

There was silence again. I tried to picture Wyatt. Was he

shaking his head? Shrugging? Finally, he said: "It was a lot more than that."

"Try to tell yourself that," Ron said. "This is the longest you've ever stayed anywhere."

"I was in California last week."

"On a job. And you came back *here.*" Ron's tone was incredulous.

"Lay off, man. I feel shitty enough."

"And you were tossed by a Bo Beach wave. That's what really kills me." Ron's laugh was not altogether pleasant.

"Biggest anyone's ever seen here, or so I'm told."

"That may be." Ron's voice was gentler now. "I might see if there's anything left this afternoon."

"It should still be decent. Your public will love it."

"Shut the fuck up," Ron said, but now he sounded more like a guy teasing his buddy. "What about *your* public? I saw surfers posting about your wipeout about two minutes before David e-mailed me. They know you as well as they know me."

"Not quite."

Funny. I had never really thought about Wyatt being famous. I guessed, as one of the surfers in Ron's entourage, as a big-wave chaser who traveled the world, he had a following, too. Why would he stay in Bohemia?

"They will know you just as well if you — when you come back out," Ron said.

"I don't want to live out there."

I felt almost gleeful at this response, though I quickly wondered if Wyatt was just trying to get rid of Ron.

"You've changed, man."

Wyatt's response was more faint. "Maybe I have." There was a pause. "My head is killing me."

Oh, shit. Poor Wyatt. I walked up to the bedroom door and knocked softly. Ron opened it. He looked surprised to see me.

"Hi, sweetheart," he said, opening the door wide. He was a hale and hearty mountain in jeans and a thick, navy-blue sweater, white T-shirt peeking out at the collar. He sported no tropical glamour today, though his tan glowed under his shock of bright blond hair.

"Hi, Ron." I turned to Wyatt. He was sitting up against the pillows on the bed, and lines of worry creased his forehead. "You OK?"

"Just saying goodbye to Ron. How long have you been here?"

"Just arrived." It was a little white lie, I told myself. He didn't need to know how much I'd heard. I went over to him and planted a quick kiss on his lips. The tiny electrical current that shot through me reassured me. His smile suggested he felt it, too.

"You were supposed to be *my* date," Ron said, almost petulant.

"The line was too long," I quipped, and amusement eased some of the tension in Wyatt's face.

Ron just shook his head with a rueful smile and spoke to Wyatt. "I'm going to check into the hotel, and then I'll get settled, maybe check out the surf and come back later. David invited me to dinner. He says I can borrow the Jeep. I'll see you then, OK? Get some rest."

"That's all I've been doing. I thought I might surf this afternoon."

My eyes snapped from Ron back to Wyatt. *"What?"*

"He's kidding, sweetheart," Ron said. He reached out to shake Wyatt's hand, shifted his grip and held it for a second, squeezing, bro style, almost as if he were starting an arm-wrestling match. Then he let go of Wyatt's hand, if not his gaze. His voice got lower as he uttered a warning that wasn't quite funny enough to be a joke. "Stay off my beach till I say so."

"I thought you abandoned Bohemia Beach," Wyatt said.

"Never. It's all mine," Ron teased, and his eyes shifted to me. "You look pretty in that sweater. You wore that last time I saw you. Let me know if you'd like to get a coffee or something." *Last time when you scared me to death, you mean.* When I didn't respond to his carefully wrought boyish charm, his smile faltered, and he turned back to Wyatt. "Later, bro."

The door closed behind him, and I heard his heavy steps in the hall, and then his voice in the kitchen, mixed with those of Jen and David.

"Prick." The word just slipped out, and I covered my mouth after my slip in front of Ron's best friend.

Wyatt laughed. "No boundaries," he said. "He's never needed them. He's a good guy, really. I was pretty shocked to see him."

"Are you OK?"

"I do have a headache. Want to pamper me with ginger ale and crackers again?"

"And acetaminophen? Sure." I was relieved to be doing something, instead of contemplating what I'd heard. I got Wyatt's ginger ale and crackers from the kitchen — Ron had left — and Jen put bread in the toaster for him. I brought him the pill, crackers and soda, and he seemed more relaxed as I sat in the bed next to him, as I'd done the night before.

Wyatt closed his eyes. "This is going to get better, right?" he asked, and I could hear the pain in his voice.

"Of course it will," I said softly, brushing his cheek. "We'll take off that bandage a little later and see how things look."

"You're not going to like it."

"What are you talking about? Go to sleep, oh god of the surf. That's how I see you, you know."

Wyatt shook his head, but his voice was getting groggy. "Minor deity at best," he said. "Just ask Ron."

I ENDED up eating the toast Jen had made, because Wyatt fell asleep again. I worried that he was sleeping too much, given the concussion, but he'd been lucid every time I'd talked with him, and he seemed much better.

An hour later — it was afternoon by now — I heard the sound of running water and looked at Jen, who was making potato salad for dinner. We'd been talking in the kitchen while David was outside playing with the meat smoker and tinkering in the garage. The aroma of pork ribs was just starting to invade the house.

"Wyatt must be in the shower," she said, looking toward the sound. "That's a good sign."

Several minutes later, he appeared like a ghost in the doorway of the kitchen, wearing a fresh T-shirt and long, soft, baggy shorts.

"It felt good to get all that grit off," he said. "And that meat smells incredible. I think I could eat something now."

"Of course," Jen said as I guided him to a chair at the table. "Antelope? Water buffalo?"

"Just toast with some peanut butter, I think. I hear toast is all the rage."

He sent me a tiny smile that made me want to slather *him* with peanut butter and lick it off.

Wyatt seemed brighter after his shower and snack, and

we decided it might be time to take off the head bandage. I unwrapped it slowly as he sat rigidly at the kitchen table — the long strip of gauze would have been a fine first step to mummification — and fought to control my expression as the end of the ribbon and the bandage under it fell away.

"Your hair!"

Wyatt reached up and gingerly touched the stitches. They were the railroad tracks down a canyon on the left side of his head, a path of close-cropped hair through his once gorgeous mop.

"Forget the hair," he said. "How do the stitches look?"

"Like Frankenstein," Jen teased, but I could hear the shock in her tone, too.

"Are they disgusting?" he asked.

"Pretty neat, actually," I said. "I don't think you'll have to bandage it again. Just try not to butt heads."

"But Ron is coming over," Wyatt teased in return. He felt around again on his head. "I guess I'm going to have to go punk for a bit."

"I'll cut it for you," Jen volunteered. "I always used to when you were in high school, anyway."

"I'm not in high school anymore."

"Exactly. You can't play the whiny teenager anymore."

"I never," Wyatt said.

I was busy staring at his hair.

"Don't take it all!" I exclaimed. "There are already enough bald surfers."

Wyatt and Jen both laughed.

"Hair fetish," Wyatt explained to Jen.

"Trust me, Cali," she said. "I won't cut all of it. And it can always grow back."

"I guess it could be worse. They could have shaved it," I said. "How did they cut it?"

"One of those electric hair trimmers." Wyatt gingerly touched the remaining fuzz. "They said there's less infection that way."

In sympathy, I sat silently as Jen took her hair kit out of a drawer, withdrew sharp scissors and snapped them in the air. For the first time, Wyatt looked worried.

"Just a little," he said, scooting the chair away from the table. "Be careful of my melon. There's no growing the whole head back."

Jen went to get a towel as I frowned at him.

"What?" he asked, almost laughing.

"I love your hair."

"You're cute when you pout." He leaned forward and squeezed my knee. His hand traveled up my thigh.

I smiled and resisted jumping into his lap. "You *are* getting better, aren't you?"

He sat up when Jen returned. She wrapped the old beach towel around his shoulders to catch the hair and set to work.

She used the electric trimmer to crop the sides first, leaving decent fuzz but skimming close enough that the buzzed hair seemed to ease almost naturally to the strip of stitches. Then she trimmed the top with scissors, giving him a spiky strip of thick black hair that resembled a Mohawk. The blond streak was prominent in the front.

"What do you think?" Wyatt asked as she finished. "Got a mirror?"

"Punky," I observed. I didn't love it, but it suddenly looked better when he greeted his image in a handheld mirror with a wide grin.

"Jen, you're a genius," he said.

"I *am* a rocket scientist," she replied.

I laughed. "At least you left something for me to run my fingers through."

Jen took away the towel, and I vacuumed up the hair on the floor while Maverick barked at the droning machine.

"He's always had a love-hate relationship with the vacuum," Jen noted.

Wyatt scooped up the dog and petted him, and we sat together in the kitchen, chatting and watching Jen make her famous mac and cheese. David came in for a beer, and I remembered the pictures.

"Hey, you guys might want to see these." I dug my phone out of my purse while the guys sat on either side of me. I opened the photo gallery and swiped slowly through the photos I'd grabbed earlier.

When I got to the big wave, with Wyatt teetering on its face, they both said, "Whoa!"

"Let me see that!" Jen stood behind me to get a look.

"That looks even bigger in the photo than it did in real life," David said.

"Well, you were in the water already," I replied.

Wyatt gazed at the photo with the scrutiny of Sherlock Holmes. "I remember a big set was coming in," he finally said.

"Yes!" David said. "Anything else?"

Wyatt shook his head in frustration. "Nothing else. But I'm glad you got the photos. It's a pretty good wave for these parts."

Jen laughed. "Pretty good? Incredible, more like. Was anybody shooting video?"

"Maybe," I said. "I was pretty wrapped up in photos, but

spectators came and went through the day. Let's look on YouTube."

"Here," Jen said, grabbing her iPad off the counter and handing it to me. We searched for "Bohemia Beach" and "surf" and found a bunch of videos. Halfway down the first page was one titled, "Big wave surfer Wyatt Brooks wipes out in Bohemia Beach."

"Great," Wyatt said darkly.

"We don't have to look at it," I said, almost afraid to look myself.

"Fuck, yeah, we do," he said. "Fire it up."

The video was shot by an amateur, and it started wide and shaky. Soon, the shooter seemed to grasp that there was an unusual wave in the works. He — you could tell it was a guy from the inane running commentary, punctuated by exclamations of "dude" — zoomed in as Wyatt popped up on the board, darting down the gleaming face of the wave. From this angle, his ride looked beautifully smooth and fast, at least at first. And then it was clear that he was struggling for control. The moment when he went down made all of us, except Wyatt, gasp anew.

"That would have been just another day at the beach if you hadn't hit the rocks," David said.

"I've been hurt before," Wyatt said dismissively as I set the tablet down on the table. The video was still playing, and Jen and David weren't paying much attention, but Wyatt leaned in close, transfixed.

"Cali!" he exclaimed.

"What?" I looked at the screen — and at the shaky image of me, with my clothes on, splashing into the rough surf. The video ended when I was just knee-deep. I looked up at him, weirdly embarrassed.

"What were you *doing?*"

"Hey, Wyatt, you look like a freakin' porcupine!" Ron was back, booming in the kitchen, and the moment was gone.

The energy in the room shifted at once, finding a new focus in Ron as he talked about surfing one of his old Bohemia Beach haunts. He deprecated the waves as middling at best. Still, David made him look at the photos on my phone of a few of the big moments from yesterday, including the wave that had taken Wyatt down.

Ron nodded in appreciation. "You should shoot some real surf sometime. You're really good."

"Yes, she is," Wyatt echoed.

"Thanks," I replied, shocked at the compliment. Wyatt was the surf photographer. But the idea was, for the first time, strangely appealing. I'd really liked connecting with nature the way I had when I shot those photos, at least before it all went wrong.

During dinner, I could tell Wyatt was getting tired, but he gamely listened to Ron's stories, smiling at times, interjecting a few details of his own. By the end of the meal, Wyatt was smiling often, and I felt more charitable toward Ron. These were guys who had spent a lot of time together, much of it facing down the wild power of the ocean, and they had a bond I was only just beginning to understand. They had a private word in the hall before Ron left, and Wyatt came back to the kitchen to announce he was going to bed.

Before he went, he kissed me lightly. "Go home and get some rest, Cali. That's all I'm going to do tomorrow. I don't want you to see me grumpy and tired."

"I don't care if you're grumpy. You've been a model patient so far."

"I'll be grumpy tomorrow," he said, "because I'll feel well enough to do something and Jen won't let me."

"That's right," she said, putting the last of the dishes in the dishwasher, and David laughed.

I didn't want to leave, but I didn't want to be clingy, either.

I kissed Wyatt on the cheek. "I'll call you, OK? And I'll work on the surf photos. It'll probably take me a while, but when I'm done, I'll post them in a gallery where you can see them."

"Awesome. I'll see you at class on Monday." He gave me a tight, preoccupied smile and went to his room, Maverick at his heels.

I was bemused and, I had to admit, exhausted.

"I guess I'll go home, then," I said to no one in particular.

Jen came over to me and gave me a hug, a hug I found I really needed.

"He's a guy." She held my shoulders and looked me in the eye. "When guys don't feel well, they're like wounded bears. They retreat to their caves and growl at intruders until they feel better."

"You think that's it?" I asked.

"He's not used to all this attention," David said. "Don't worry, Cali. You did good."

I nodded, more unsure than ever, and headed out to my car. Switching radio stations, I lost myself in a late-night New Age broadcast. Its contemplative music carried me on star-stuff through the darkness all the way back to Bohemia, helping me forget my worries, my questions. When I crawled into bed, I fell asleep to an inner soundtrack, the imagined sounds of the ocean.

~

WYATT WAS PREOCCUPIED AGAIN during class on Monday, but I put his mood down to his discomfort, which was still obvious. He took some ribbing about his hair, and after class, he showed a couple of the guys the YouTube video. He joined them for lunch after quietly telling me he'd call me later. We had a brief chat; he still didn't feel all that well, he said. I didn't see him Tuesday, and Wednesday, he barely talked to me, coming and going like the other students. I left him a voicemail that he didn't return. And then I started to get a sick feeling of deja vu. Was he going to be like all the other guys I'd dated, fading away and out of my life?

The stupid thing was, he hadn't been anything like them. And had we ever really dated in any kind of formal way? It was more like we'd collided and caught fire.

The irony was too much. For the first time, I was absolutely clear about the way I felt about him, and he wasn't there.

When I got home from riding bicycles with Sloane along the river Saturday afternoon, I checked my phone and found a text message.

"Sorry I missed your call. Getting better but not there yet. Don't want to inflict myself on you."

I texted back: "I would love to see you anyway."

"Let me work through this," he answered. "See you in class."

Work through what? I wondered. It didn't sound as if he were talking about a headache.

I flopped onto my couch and called Jen's cell.

"Wyatt's not with you, is he?" was the first thing I asked after her hello.

"No. Are you trying to reach him?"

"Sort of. I finally heard from him, but he's acting kind of

weird, and I — I'm worried. I thought maybe you could tell me what's going on. Is he doing OK?"

"He's in more pain than he's letting on. At his follow-up, the doctor told him he'd bruised his ribs, too."

"How bad is that?" I asked.

"Not too bad in this case, but it'll likely be a couple more weeks until he's feeling himself again."

"But why won't he talk to me?"

"Ah," Jen said. "We went over the bear in the cave analogy, right? That's probably it."

I heard something in her voice. "You think there's more to it."

There was silence on the other end for a few seconds. "I think Wyatt is going through something right now, some kind of struggle. He won't talk to me about it. David is trying, too."

"What is it? Is he sick?"

"It's not that, other than his injuries, of course." I heard a noise and then the soft rush of wind in the background, as if she'd gone outside. "I think he's facing a big change in his life, and he's not sure how to handle it. Which way to go."

"And I'm in the way," I said miserably.

"No," Jen said thoughtfully. "I think you are part of his decision. Maybe he can't face you while he thinks about it. He tends to hide from his emotions. For so many years, he locked them away so he wouldn't have to deal with the pain. But he talks about you all the time, Cali."

This time I was silent for a minute. The Bohemia street noise outside seemed to mingle with the white noise from the line, the faint chirps of a bird in Jen's tropical backyard.

"I don't know what to do," I finally said.

"Don't stop calling him. He needs to know you're there for him, even if he doesn't realize it. I want him to realize it," she said, earnest now. "I can see it — you really care for him, don't you?"

"Yes," I said, barely above a whisper.

"I'm on your side. He needs you, even if he doesn't completely know it yet. Be patient."

"Will you tell me when it's time to stop being patient?"

She laughed. "I'll try. The dripping of water wears down the stone."

"Nice," I said. "You're a rocket scientist *and* a philosopher."

"Hang in there, Cali. It'll be OK."

I felt a little better after I hung up the phone. I saw how Wyatt must have relied on her strength, on her and David during his toughest years. Still, patience wasn't my strong suit.

Instead of pleading to see him, I sent Wyatt a text with one of the photos I'd shot of him the previous weekend, during one of those rare moments when the sun had shone through the thin clouds and made the sea glimmer. He was airborne, flying off the lip of a wave in a gorgeous trick that he'd landed perfectly.

"Wow, you make me look good," he texted back. I wished I could see his face, his smile.

"The subject gets 50 percent of the credit," I responded, repeating my joke from the other day.

"I think you deserve at least 75," he typed back, and I laughed. And then, with agonizing self-discipline, I put down the phone.

I needed him to come to me.

Over the next several days — when I wasn't seeing him in class — I dropped photos his way, visual teases by text. I ached when I saw him, when I felt the artificial distance between us, but it wasn't a cold distance. It was warm, like a breathless summer evening, when the lightning bugs floated through the soft air, hinting at magic. There was still a sparkle in his eyes, but it was shielded from me, light hidden behind the shutter on a lantern.

The suspense was killing me.

It didn't help that on Thursday, after I'd shot a dreadful chamber of commerce ribbon-cutting at a pizza shop downtown, my walk home was bombarded with pink and red messages in every store window about Saturday — the bane of all single people, Valentine's Day.

The truth was, I'd rarely been single for this unabashedly commercial holiday, and I'd had my tame boyfriends well-trained. I'd told them what I wanted and where to get it if we were at the gift stage, or hinted broadly about my favorite kind of flowers (roses in varying shades of pink, preferably in a rose bowl). I saw now how insufferable I'd been, but I was pretty sure those guys had been happy to be told what to do. There were no surprises and no disappointments.

And now? Now, roses be damned, I was waiting to find out if Wyatt would ever want to see me again. Touch me again.

When I got back to my studio, I texted him another photo, another dreamy moment of him on the board, this one a wide shot I'd taken with my second camera that showed the wild seas around him.

An hour later, as I worked at the desk downstairs, my lobby empty as usual, my phone rang. I felt almost giddy when I saw it was him and pressed the button.

"How you doing?" I asked softly.

"I feel a lot better," Wyatt said. "That was a really cool photo."

"Thanks."

"It's nice to hear your voice."

"Ditto," I said casually. *Yay!* my heart yelled.

"So, I'd like to take one more photo of you for class."

"OK." So this was business? "I'm available." Understatement of the year.

"How about Saturday at your studio? We could do dinner first."

Saturday? The most irritatingly romantic day of the year? Did he even realize what Saturday was? I really didn't care. "Why don't I order takeout? Restaurants are going to be crazy."

"Oh, yeah, I guess. Saturdays are busy."

God, men are clueless. "Sushi OK?"

"Excellent," he said. "Six o'clock?"

"Perfect. You, uh, need me to pick you up?"

"No, I'll borrow the Jeep."

"See you then."

"Later, Cali."

I gingerly pressed the button to end the call and laid the phone down on the desk. I didn't know whether to dance or scream or cry. Another portrait sounded like homework. But dinner sounded like a date. Either way, I decided, this was a good thing.

I was going to see Wyatt on Saturday, and I would have him all to myself.

EVEN ORDERING takeout was a hassle on Valentine's Day. The sushi restaurant was packed. It was a ten-minute walk from my place, and at 5:45, despite calling an hour earlier, I was still standing next to the crowded sushi bar with three other takeout-ees. Their world-weary expressions and sloppy clothes suggested they had anything but a date on their minds. I was dressed a little better, in soft gauze black pants and a cowl-neck, light blue sweater that glinted with subtle silver threads and drooped just enough to show a hint of my modest cleavage. My hair was pulled up on one side with a sparkly comb. I was keeping my look simple, but no one could say I hadn't gone to a little effort.

At 5:55, I was finally handed a big paper bag packed nearly to the brim with boxes, and I texted Wyatt that I would be there shortly.

"Waiting out back," he typed in response.

I walked quickly through throngs of Saturday night revelers dressed up for their big night downtown. I went through my front door, set the food on a table I'd put in the studio and ran for the back.

He was in the lot, leaning against the Jeep, aglow in the pink and orange sunset coloring the sky above him. He wore a black leather jacket over a black button-up shirt, jeans and his familiar, thick sandals. He smiled at me, a mysterious smile, and picked up the camera bag that sat on the cracked pavement.

My heart swelled at the sight of him.

"We're fools!" I said.

He paused, his brow furrowed.

"Because it's golden hour, and we're not shooting," I explained. "Look at that light. It just transforms everything."

He looked around, but his eyes came back to mine with that intensity I'd missed so much. "You're already beautiful."

I was afraid to grin, to reveal just how happy I was to see him, so I offered only a shy smile and held open the door.

"Dinner upstairs?" he asked.

"No, the studio, since we're working. Come on in."

I'd left only a couple of the studio lights on at half-brightness, a more civilized light for dining. While Wyatt shrugged off his jacket and unpacked his camera bag, I opened the boxes of sushi — rolls and sashimi and nigiri, miso soup and sesame-sprinkled seaweed salad — and arranged them on the square table, atop a shiny gray tablecloth. I'd put out a couple of pretty blue-green, rectangular ceramic plates Sloane had made, along with two pairs of nice chopsticks, and as Wyatt sat in one of the folding chairs, I pulled the beers from the cooler and popped them open.

"Kirin Ichiban," he noted with approval.

"That's my sushi beer." I sat, too, and wondered why I felt so nervous.

"A toast, then," he said, lifting the bottle. I did the same, thinking Wyatt wasn't the kind of guy who did toasts. "Happy Valentine's Day."

"Oh, you rat, you knew all along!" I exclaimed.

He leaned in and kissed me, a short, sweet kiss, and took a swig of the beer. "Of course I knew."

"It was nice of you to think of me."

"I've thought about you a lot," he said quietly.

"And I've been thinking about you."

"I know you have. The pictures — you sent so many. And I loved them all. When do I get to see the whole gallery?" He sounded almost plaintive, and I laughed.

"I'll stop teasing you. I can show you tonight, if you want. I have them all edited now."

"Excellent."

We dug into the delicious sushi, but beneath our light chatter — about class, about how much better he was feeling — there was an intangible weight to the conversation, heavy words still unsaid. All in good time, I thought, enjoying being with Wyatt again, even though our vibe seemed different. Maybe it was because I was different, because I knew now how I felt.

Wyatt looked good; his hair — though not restored to its former, thick glory — had grown in enough to look almost respectable. The stitches were gone. But beyond his physical presence, which I always appreciated, I knew now that something more bound me to him. I relished his ready laugh, his sense of humor, the sparkle in his eyes. His belief in me. His sense of adventure. His energy. His soul.

I just had no idea what the hell he was thinking.

"So," I said lightly, "you ready for the Japanese whiskey?"

"Ah, so it's a themed dinner. What you got?"

I got the chilled rocks glasses out of the cooler, put a homemade ice sphere in each one and grabbed the bottle from where I'd stowed it in the shadows.

"That's not bad," Wyatt said when he sipped his, "but I thought we were working?"

"You're working. I'm modeling. And I need a little whiskey if you want me to be cooperative."

"Oh, really?" He sounded more flirtatious now, and his gaze was a magnet I could not resist. "You'll do anything?"

I took a slow breath, and then another sip of whiskey.

"I'll do anything," I said.

His dark eyebrows lifted, and he regarded me with a hint of lust and something much more serious.

"I wouldn't ask you to, you know. You've already done more for me than I can ever repay, more than I would have even thought to ask for."

A jolt of nervous anticipation shot through me. "I don't know what you mean."

"David and I had a chat earlier this week. Well, we've been having a lot of chats, but mostly it's been me talking. Working some stuff out." He looked into his glass, swirled the whiskey around the glistening ball of ice, then looked back at me. "This time, he was talking about that day I went down at Bohemia Beach. He told me how you went into the water. *All the way* into the water. He said you got me out before anyone else. And he didn't even know what I knew. That you were terrified of the ocean."

I flashed on the memory and tried to shrug it off. "I didn't even think. By the time I realized I was chest-deep, I was more afraid for you than I was of the water. All I could think about was you."

He reached across the table and grasped my hand. A thrill ignited my hopes, a current that was much more than physical.

"You did something extraordinary for me," he said softly. "Maybe it doesn't seem like much to you, but I know what it meant for you to go into the water. I'm not used to people fighting for me. Seems like, for a long time, they were almost always fighting against me." A shadow passed over his features. "And then Jen and David befriended me, and then Ron. But I was drifting, following nothing more than instinct, content to orbit around the big personality, fine with following the surf even though I knew it was getting harder and harder. Don't get me wrong. I loved it. I still love it. Sometimes it was all I thought I ever wanted. But the injuries piled up, more than you know about, and then there was the feeling that I was always going to be in someone else's shadow, running in a race that got more crowded every day. I wanted to do things in a new way. And then I met you, and every inkling of a plan I had went right out the window. To tell you the truth, you scared me."

His words were too much to digest at once. My defenses kicked in.

"So I really am terrifying," I joked.

Wyatt didn't laugh. "Let me clarify. I scared *myself* with what I felt when I met you."

The silence between us was fraught, and the silly thought flitted through my brain that I should have put on some music.

"Are you still scared?" I finally asked.

"Yes. Because I know now what I want. I want to be with you. And I'm scared you won't want to be with me."

I felt the tears well up and did nothing to wipe one away as it rolled down my cheek. I squeezed his hand. "Being with you is all I want, Wyatt. I was so afraid you would leave and never come back."

His eyes shone at my words.

"Sometimes I'll leave," Wyatt said. "Sometimes, I hope, you'll go with me. Either way" — he stood and moved toward me — "I will always come back."

I rose and looped my arms around his neck, my heart hammering. He searched my eyes, his own filled with light and promise, and he bent his head over mine. I met his kiss with a purity of passion I had never known until now. He squeezed my body against his, devoured my mouth. Our kiss tasted of whiskey and desire, and of something far greater.

"I love you," I whispered into his ear, and hugged him harder.

"Ouch," he said, wriggling a little.

"Sorry. I forgot. Are you OK?"

"Much better than OK." He kissed me again, this time more thoroughly. My body trembled in his arms.

He took a breath and held my face with both hands. His features were etched with something I hadn't seen there before: joy.

"I love you, too," he said. "It feels so good to say it. *I love you.*"

He started to pull me toward the back — toward the stairs and my apartment and my bed — but we kept stopping to kiss, new emotion fueling our fire now. Halfway up the stairs, he pressed me against the wall and kissed me again, and I worked on unbuttoning his shirt as he slipped his hands under my sweater, caressing my back. We left the sweater and the shirt on the dark stairs and moved up to the landing, where we stopped again. I ran my fingers lightly over his skin, relieved to see the bruising was almost gone. I kissed his chest, then laved each nipple, sucking briefly as he groaned.

He lifted me to meet my lips again.

"Nice," he whispered, running a finger along the lace-covered ice-blue satin of my bra. He lifted one breast out of its cup and suckled tenderly before turning to the other rosy peak, licking and drawing on my nipple with sweet, focused desire, shooting heat through my body. I brushed a hand through his hair and pulled him close as he sucked, sensing the need that ran through him.

And then he took my hand and led me into my apartment.

In the dark bedroom, I turned on the fairy lights. They glowed in their twisting path around the metal cross-pieces of the headboard and gleamed in Wyatt's eyes. He pushed me down against the mattress and enthralled me with a posses-sive, smoky stare as he slipped off my pants and reached for my panties. He nudged them off slowly, taking in every inch of me with his eyes, then reverently tongued the bud at the center of my sex. My sigh was long and fragmented, a sigh of bliss, of relief, of love.

He moved up, kissed my mouth, salty and hot. I took off my bra, reveling not just in the exposure of my skin, but of my heart. I was opening it completely to this man. I knew he would take it, the part of myself I had never truly risked, and keep it safe.

He pulled the comb out of my hair and tossed it aside — I chuckled, as he could never resist liberating my hair — then stood before me, gazing into my eyes. He exuded power as he removed his jeans and set his stiff erection free. The sight was gratifying after the past two weeks of deprivation. I couldn't believe this boy — this beautiful man, every hard line of him — was mine. He must have seen my delight, my grateful wonder. He responded with a smoldering smile.

I spread my legs and Wyatt lowered himself, nudging with his cock. His eyes were locked on mine, and with his seriousness now was a softness, a vulnerability that I wanted to protect.

In one smooth motion, he slid inside me. My wet, eager passage clenched around him, an aching, exultant feeling as I arched to meet his measured thrusts. He held his chest just above mine, the muscles in his arms standing out as he artfully built a cadence. He was all heat and strength and intensity, driving deep inside me. I met each hard push as we climbed the sweet mountain of pleasure together, higher, harder, faster. I grasped his hips as I neared the summit, finally crying out with my quaking climax. A moment later, I felt his release inside me, that most intimate of conquests. He groaned, and I pulled him to me as he finished, pulsing, hot and solid and mine.

He breathed hard against me for a minute, and then he eased out. We lay on our sides, facing each other, and kissed.

"God, I missed that," Wyatt said.

"I'm glad to know I wasn't the only one."

He laughed softly. "There are two of us now, for everything."

"Even frustrated lust," I replied.

"Only if we're apart, and when we have to be, it won't be for long."

We kissed again, and again.

"Let me ask you something," he said. "Would you get in the water again? I mean, now that you know you can?"

I took a moment to imagine myself in the ocean, and I was surprised to find I wasn't choked by fear.

"I'll think about it," I said. "I'd like to think I can do it if I don't have to worry about something terrible happening to you. Do you think you can arrange that for me?"

He smiled wryly. "I'll do my best not to split my head open again, if that's what you mean."

"That's all I can ask."

We kissed again.

"You know," he said, "I got you something for Valentine's Day."

"Now I feel like a heel. I didn't get you anything."

"You got me sushi and whiskey and you. And maybe something else."

"What?" I found delight in the way the lights danced in his eyes; I brushed his bangs away from his forehead so I could see them better.

"You're going to pose for me, aren't you?"

"Yes," I said without hesitation. "Though if you could keep it tasteful — for class, you know."

"I'll keep it tasteful. Artistic, actually. But this one isn't for class. Their heads would explode."

I giggled.

Wyatt rolled out of bed and held out his hand. I took it, feeling strange and sexy and exposed. He tossed me the short robe that was draped on the chair in the corner, and I donned it and followed him downstairs.

He slipped on his clothes, leaving his shirt distractingly open, then dug around in his bag and pulled out a bundle of light blue fabric, just my color, that he set aside. Then he pulled out a small box, opened it and took out the pendant inside. He held it up for my inspection.

Hanging from a short, black leather cord was a spiral made of an iridescent, blue-green material.

"Is that a shell?" I asked.

"A paua shell, or you might call it abalone. The spiral is a Koru, a Maori symbol of new life and strength, like the unfurling of a fern frond."

He fastened it around my neck, then looked me over with frank admiration.

"You are full of wonderful surprises," I said, touching it.

"I had to get it for you. It matches your eyes." His own eyes said even more. "Now are you ready to do my bidding?"

He grinned that grin that made me swoon. He was going to be hard to refuse, ever.

I shrugged the robe off my shoulders and let it puddle at my feet.

Wyatt let out a low whistle. "Let's see if I can do this without stopping to ravish you."

I gave him a slow smile. "As long as you ravish me afterward."

My GALLERY WAS full and noisy. That's how I liked it. From a spot near the reception desk in the lobby, I observed the kaleidoscope of friends and artists and visitors milling around the space, checking out the art. Through the open door to the studio, where the real party was going on, I could hear Ez and her band playing a rollicking, angsty tune, and patrons drifted in and out with glasses of champagne, bottles of beer and plates of hors d'oeuvres.

It was Friday night, the first day of spring, and we were well into short-sleeve weather in Bohemia. Storms were in the forecast, but the weather had held off long enough to bring in a great crowd.

I had a new class to teach; my first-session students had celebrated the opening of their "best of" show just a week ago at the school.

But this show was different. "Female Forms" featured my work and other talent, other friends. I hoped it would be the first of many such events here. Tonight was an opening-night party for not just the show, but for the gallery and the studio.

At the very least, the exhibit had already prompted three groups to book portrait parties, and more were signing up for my e-mail list.

I caught sight of a tall figure moving toward me in blue jeans and a silky, light blue, button-up shirt, rolled up at the sleeves. His hair was back to its wild self. He lifted the camera that hung around his neck and took my picture as people swirled around me.

I met him halfway across the room and kissed him, lost myself in his arms in a few sweet heartbeats, then opened my eyes.

"I love that you wore blue tonight," I said.

"I knew *you* would wear blue." He paused. "Besides, I saw your dress hanging in the closet next to my Hawaiian shirts." Wyatt's eyes drank in my long, sleeveless, loose-fitting dress of romantic sky-blue floral lace over white. "There are enough people wearing black around here, anyway."

He nodded toward Damien, who was drinking beer and talking animatedly with a new, handsome friend and a few other artists I recognized.

"I don't think Damien owns any other colors," I said, "except for maybe that crazy suit."

"So what does he think of The Picture?"

"You might ask what my parents think of The Picture." We both looked toward the other end of the gallery, where a very large photo of me took up the middle third of the wall.

"The corollary question being," Wyatt said, "what do they think of me, who lured their daughter into depravity?"

I laughed. "Honestly — my mom is in total denial, as she is of most things. She asked me how I could let you take photos of a naked model if you're my boyfriend."

"She did not!" Wyatt exclaimed.

"You don't know my mom."

"What did you say?"

"I said that I knew the model very well and was totally comfortable with it."

"Good," Wyatt said softly in my ear, "because I'd like to do that again sometime." I buzzed from his touch as he caressed my back and guided me toward the photo, and my body remembered that night, the feeling of putting myself in his hands as he draped the sheer, light blue fabric over me. I'd sat on the floor against the black backdrop, bent to the side, my legs folded, my long hair cascading over my face. My hands stretched up and out, lifting the fabric, suggesting I struggled to escape a web or, perhaps, to give birth to myself. One high, strategic light revealed the sensual outlines of my body but cast much of it in shadow. The photo was everything I'd hoped — daring but tasteful, exquisite and artistic, and not immediately identifiable as me — though if one looked closely, one might see the blue swirl of a pendant, the same one I wore tonight. Wyatt had called the photo "Emergent."

"Damien just laughed when he saw it. Not because of the image," I assured Wyatt, "but because he said that when our parents figured it out, they were going to disown me. I pointed out that they had not yet disowned him, despite ample cause. We're still negotiating what it will take to buy his silence. Of course, he's been impossible since he got a commission out of his exposure at the regional show."

"You shouldn't be shy about it," Wyatt said, smoothing back hair that had escaped from my messy up-do. "You're beautiful, and if I do say so myself, it's art."

"Yes, it is." I regarded the photo's thick shadows, the barely saturated colors, the blue like a mist against the black. "So I'm just a big chicken, I guess."

"You're careful, but that's who you are," Wyatt mused.

He was right, but I wanted to shed my fears. I was still working on it.

"OK, I'll tell them," I said. "But please, let's wait until Thanksgiving. We thrive on incredibly overwrought Thanksgivings."

He laughed. "I like your sense of timing."

"Speaking of grueling Thanksgivings, there are Sloane and Alex. Don't ask," I said to Wyatt's lifted eyebrows.

"She's OK with the photo of her?"

The couple were looking at the tall vertical of Sloane leaning against the turquoise Vespa, slyly lifting her dress to show off the lacy top of her stockings, her garters, a hint of suggestive shadow where her underwear hid, and the shapely length of her legs.

"I asked her first." I grinned at Wyatt. "She seems fine with it, doesn't she?"

Alex whispered intently in Sloane's ear. His hand caressed her back where her low-cut, draped dress revealed her skin. His fingers slipped lower, beneath the fabric, and she leaned into him. From their body language, I thought they might burst into flames on the spot. Now, I could say I knew the feeling.

I tore my eyes away from them and surveyed the walls. There were other images: Wyatt's photo of me as the backlit photographer in front of the studio lights; Millie's portrait of the well-dressed old woman she'd taken for our class; and more of my shots of Thea, Penelope, Ez and the pinup models. All of them were here, and the pinups were turning heads every time they walked through the space. I really needn't worry that anyone would notice me, in or out of a photo.

We followed a pair of them through the double doors and into the studio. Lively chatter mingled with the music. The band filled the room with energy. Our potter friend Gary hovered near Ez and her keyboard, a silly grin on his face, drinking a beer. A cluster of tipsy souls danced nearby. My old friends from the paper were here, including Joan and Bart and Jordan, who'd landed a job at the space center. Jen, her arm linked with David's, aimed a happy smile in my direction. My parents stood in a corner, looking uncomfortable, before sneaking out the door we'd just come in.

Wyatt snapped several photos of the action while I got him a beer and me a glass of champagne.

"I think I'm going to like working for you," he said when he returned to me.

"You're not working for me!" I handed him the cold bottle. "We're partners."

"OK." He took a sip. "Tonight, I work for you. And when we go to Tahiti next month, you'll work for me."

In his broad smile I saw the adventure ahead, the sun and the sea and the light that we would see together.

I took a deep sip of the champagne and leaned against him. He wrapped an arm around my shoulders and squeezed.

"Well, if you're working for me tonight," I said, "I hope you like party cleanup."

Wyatt chuckled.

He spoke softly in my ear, creating an intimate bubble in the crowded room that exhilarated me.

"You should know by now," he said, "for you, I'll do anything."

～

AFTERWORD

Thanks for reading! I hope you'll sign up for my newsletter to hear about my latest releases and for occasional news, amusements and giveaways. I also have a fun Facebook group where readers can hang out and chat about books and life — please join us in Lucy's Lounge.

MORE ONLINE:
LucyLakestone.com
Facebook.com/LucyLakestone
Twitter.com/LucyLakestone
Bookbub.com/authors/lucy-lakestone
Pinterest.com/lucylakestone/
Amazon
Goodreads
YouTube

ACKNOWLEDGMENTS

Thanks to my writing friends who have been generous with feedback, kindness and wine. Also, many thanks to the members of Spacecoast Authors of Romance for their support and inspiration. Thank you to the staff at Sky Diary Productions and Velvet Petal Press and, especially, to editor and friend Holly Martin for her sharp observations. And final thanks go to the wonderful readers who take the time to read and review books. You give the stories life.

ABOUT THE AUTHOR

Lucy Lakestone is an award-winning author who lives on Florida's east central coast, among the towns that serve as an inspiration for the hot romances of her Bohemia Beach Series, including *Bohemia Beach, Bohemia Light, Bohemia Blues* (winner of the Golden Quill), *Bohemia Heat, Bohemia Nights* and *Bohemia Bells*. She's been a journalist, photographer, editor and video producer but prefers living in her imagination, where the moon is full and the cocktails are divine. She is also the author of a novel of romantic suspense, *Desire on Deadline.*

BOOKS BY LUCY LAKESTONE

The BOHEMIA BEACH Series

Award-winning romance by Lucy Lakestone

In a beautiful small city on Florida's east coast, artists struggle to make their way. Where creative minds meet and restless hearts yearn, where emotion and ambition vie with lust and dark secrets, romance is impossible to resist. Welcome to the seductive tropical escape they call home – Bohemia Beach.

These steamy contemporary romances are the perfect escape for anyone who loves a love story with lots of heat and a shot of laughter. Though the books have a common setting and characters, each can be read as a standalone novel.

BOHEMIA BEACH

BOHEMIA LIGHT

BOHEMIA BLUES

BOHEMIA HEAT

BOHEMIA NIGHTS

BOHEMIA BELLS

and don't miss

DESIRE ON DEADLINE

BOHEMIA BLUES

The third BOHEMIA BEACH novel

WINNER OF THE GOLDEN QUILL FOR BEST HOT ROMANCE
AND A NATIONAL READERS' CHOICE AWARD FINALIST

good guy, meet bad reputation ...

Ez Falcon, a talented singer-songwriter for an up-and-coming band in Bohemia Beach, keeps her love life simple by dallying with guys she's only too happy to toss aside. When her latest boy toy goes ballistic in a very public breakup, she turns to steadfast groupie Gary Gorski for escape. Expecting little from the gawky artist who adored her in high school, she's shocked by their scorching chemistry. But their would-be connection is frustrated by his sense of honor, her agonizing past, drama with the band and, it seems, all the forces of nature. Can Ez find a way to shed her armor and embrace love as fearlessly as she makes music?

LEARN MORE AT
LucyLakestone.com